Worlds Apart

Worlds Apart

Apart

Joe Haldeman

The Viking Press   New York

First published in 1983 by The Viking Press
40 West 23rd Street, New York, N.Y. 10010

Published simultaneously in Canada by
Penguin Books Canada Limited

Library of Congress Cataloging in Publication Data

Haldeman, Joe.
  Worlds apart.
  Sequel to: Worlds.
  I. Title.
PS3553.A353W65 1983   813'.54   83-47875
ISBN 0-670-78987-9

Grateful acknowledgment is made to Harcourt Brace Jovanovich,
Inc., for permission to reprint a selection from *Complete Poems
1913–1962*, by E. E. Cummings. Copyright 1944 by E. E. Cummings,
renewed 1972 by Nancy T. Andrews.

Printed in the United States of America
Set in Melior

This book is for Rhysling and Joe-Jim,
Harriman and Harshaw, Lorenzo and Lazarus,
the Menace from Earth and our gal Friday
—and all you other zombies who so
delightfully live on.

pity this busy monster,manunkind,

not. Progress is a comfortable disease:
your victim(death and life safely beyond)

plays with the bigness of his littleness
—electrons deify one razorblade
into a mountainrange;lenses extend

unwish through curving wherewhen till unwish
returns on its unself.
                              A world of made
is not a world of born—pity poor flesh

and trees,poor stars and stones,but never this
fine specimen of hypermagical

ultraomnipotence. We doctors know

a hopeless case if—listen:there's a hell
of a good universe next door;let's go

                         —e e cummings

Worlds Apart

Prologue

✦

It had been the third world war or the fourth, depending on who did the counting, but nobody was counting anymore. It was simply "the war": March 16, 2085, when a third of the world's population had died in less than a day.

Most of the survivors had no idea why the war had been fought. A breakdown of antiquated systems. A series of misunderstandings. A run of bad luck that culminated in one side's systems being under the total control of a man who had lost his mind.

The automatic defenses worked quite well; fewer than one in twenty warheads found their marks. So there were still many billions of people left to wonder what to do next, as the radioactive ash settled down, as the biological agents silently spread. There were some who suspected that the worst was yet to come, and they were right.

It was very nearly the end of the world, but it wasn't the end of civilization. There were still the Worlds, what was left of them: a collection of more-or-less large Earth satellites, a quarter of a million people who didn't have to worry about fallout or biological warfare. Most of the Worlds had been destroyed during the war, but the largest one had survived, and that's where most of the people lived: New New York.

Year One

1 ✦

Marianne O'Hara was in the last group of shuttles to lift off from Earth, just before a direct hit turned the Cape into a radioactive inlet. Born in New New York, she'd been given a trip to Earth by the Education Council, for a year of postdoctoral work.

The six months she did spend on Earth were rather eventful. Her interest in Earth politics led her to join a political action group that turned out to be the cover organization for a cabal of violent revolutionaries. Her only friend in the group, who had also joined out of curiosity, was murdered. She herself was stabbed by a would-be rapist. She had a trip around the world and a small nervous breakdown. Finally, the man she loved managed to save her life by getting her to the Cape in time to leave Earth, but the shuttle had a strict quota system—no groundhogs—and she had to leave him behind. They comforted each other with the lie that he would join her when the trouble was over. But the warheads were already falling.

She knew that she was one of the lucky ones, but when they docked at New New she was still numb with shock and grief. Two men who loved her were waiting. She could hardly remember their names.

✦ ✦ ✦

For some weeks after the war, life in New New was too desperately busy for much reflection. Survivors from a couple of dozen other Worlds had to be crowded in, and everybody somehow be fed, though more than half of New New's agricultural modules had been damaged or destroyed. (The "shotgun" missiles couldn't penetrate New New's solid rock, but they devastated the structures outside.) They got by on short rations and stored food, but it wasn't going to last. Modules had to be repaired and rebuilt, new crops sown, animals bred—and quickly. Every able-bodied person was pressed into service.

O'Hara was young and hyper-educated (had her first Ph.D. at age twenty), but none of her formal training was applicable. Like every other young person in New New, she had spent two days a week since the age of twelve doing agricultural and construction chores, but since her destiny clearly lay in other directions, she had only done dog work—slopping hogs and slopping paint—leaving more sophisticated chores to those who needed the training. Nevertheless, her first assignment was animal husbandry: collecting sperm from goats.

They could force estrus in the nannies and didn't want to leave the rest of it up to nature. So O'Hara stalked through the goat pens with a suction apparatus, checking ID numbers until she found the one billy the computer had selected for a given nanny. Predictably, the billies were not enthusiastic about having sexual relations with a female of another species, so O'Hara got thoroughly butted and trampled and sprayed. It did keep her mind off her troubles, but after a week of low sperm count they decided to give the job to someone with more mass.

She asked for a job in construction and was mildly surprised when she got it. She'd spent many hours playing in zero gravity, but always indoors, and had never even worn a spacesuit, let alone worked in one. She looked forward to the experience but was a little apprehensive about working in a vacuum.

She was even more apprehensive after her training: one day inside and one day out. Virtually all of the training concerned what to do in case of emergency. If you hear this chime, it's a solar flare warning. Don't panic. You have eight minutes to get to a radiation locker. If you hear *this* chime, your air pressure is falling. Don't panic. You have two minutes at least, to get to the nearest first-aid bubble. Unless you're also getting cold, which means your suit's breached. Above all don't panic. Have your buddy find the breach and put a sticky patch on it. Never be too far from your buddy. Presumably your buddy will not panic. She and thirty others practiced patching and not panicking, and then were given work rosters and unceremoniously dumped out the airlock.

With no special construction skills, O'Hara's work was mostly fetch-and-carry. This required a certain amount of delicacy and intelligence.

You get around in a spacesuit with the aid of an "oxy gun," oxygen being the only gas of which the Worlds always had a surplus. It's just an aimable nozzle connected to a supply of compressed oxygen: you point it in one direction and hold down the trigger, and you go in approximately the opposite direction. Only approximately.

O'Hara and her buddy would get an order, say, for a girder of such-and-so specifications. They would locate the proper stack on their map and cautiously, very cautiously the first few days, jet their way over to it. The stacks were loose bundles of material that got less orderly as time went on. Once they found the right girder, the fun began.

Those girders weighed exactly nothing, being in free fall, but moving one was not just a matter of putting it on your shoulder and hi-ho, away we go. A tonne of girder still had a tonne's worth of inertia, even in free fall. Hard to get it started. Hard to point it in the right direction—and hard to tell which direction is right. Because when something's in orbit, you can't change its velocity without changing its orbit, however slightly. So you have to aim high or low or sideways, depending on which direction you're aiming.

O'Hara and her partner would wrestle the girder into what they guessed was the proper orientation, then hang on to either end of it (strong electromagnets on their gloves and boots) and jet away. As the girder crawled its way toward the target, they would use their oxy guns to correct its flight path and slow it down, with luck bringing it to a halt right where the user wanted it. Sometimes they crashed gently, and sometimes they overshot and had to maneuver the damned thing back into position. The work was physically and mentally exhausting, which was just what she needed.

2 ✦

O'Hara clumped into the room she shared with Daniel Anderson and sat down hard on the bed. For a minute she just stared at the floor, sagging with fatigue, maybe depression. Then she arranged both pillows and turned on the wall cube, planning to punch up the novel she was reading. But the cube was showing a pleasant modern dance performance that she'd never seen, so she eased back onto the pillows and let herself be entertained.

In a few minutes Anderson came in. "Home early?" she said.

"Going back later." He set his bag down on the dresser and stretched. "We started some tests, color chromatography, and can't do anything until they're ready. Couple of hours. Eat yet?"

"Not hungry." She turned off the dance program.

"You ought to eat something."

"I guess." She slid down to a horizontal position and put her hands behind her head, staring at the ceiling.

"Bad day out there?"

"The usual." She laughed suddenly. "You know what I've got?"

"Is it catching?"

"Penis envy. I've got a delayed case of penis envy."

"What the hell are you talking about?"

"You never studied psychology."

Daniel shrugged. "The psychology of oil shale is pretty well established. It just sits there. You can say anything about it and it doesn't mind."

"Freud thought little girls had penis envy. They saw little boys pee in any direction they wanted, and they knew they'd never be able to do that, and felt uncompleted."

"Are you serious?"

"Part way, I really am. Not in the Freudian way." She ran her fingers through her short red hair. "Did you ever try to do anything difficult while wearing a wet diaper?"

He sat on the bed and put his hand, neutrally, on her hip. "I guess learning to walk is pretty challenging. Don't remember that far back."

"I tried the catheter-style suit but just couldn't work in it. It was like...it was awful."

Daniel nodded. "Most women can't use them." He was from Earth but had spent a lot of time in spacesuits.

"So I get a diaper. A wet diaper, if we're out long enough."

"Nothing to be embarrassed about."

"Who's embarrassed? It's just distracting, uncomfortable. I'm getting a rash. I want a penis and a hose, just during working hours."

Daniel laughed. "Those hoses aren't all they might be.

You get cold enough, or startled, and you'll retract out of it, but it feels like you still have it on. Nasty surprise when you start filling your boot."

"Really?" She looked thoughtful. "What about erections?"

"Anybody who can get an erection in a spacesuit is in the wrong line of work." They laughed together and he cautiously moved his hand; she stopped him.

"Not quite yet," she said quietly.

"It's all right." They had been lovers when she went to Earth, and had planned to marry when she came back.

He stood up quickly and went to the dresser—two steps; the bed took up most of the cubicle—and pulled a comb through his hair.

"Do you want me to sleep someplace else until it gets better?" she asked.

"Of course not. I haven't had such interesting dreams in twenty years."

"Seriously. I feel like...such a—"

His reflection stared at her. "I can live with your grief easier than you can. And I want to be the one around when you do recover."

"I didn't mean I'd move in with somebody else. I could get a hot berth in the labor dormitory."

"Sure you could. And when they found out I was living here alone, they'd assign me a dormitory space too. Crowded as things are, it might take years to get a room again."

O'Hara turned to face the wall. "Nice to feel useful."

He opened his mouth and closed it, and set the comb down quietly. "Anyhow, I'm meeting John for chop. Want to come along?"

"Oh." She sat up and rubbed her face vigorously with both hands. "Might as well. See what they did to the rice this time." She went to Daniel and hugged him, or leaned on him, from behind. "I'm sorry."

He turned around inside her arms, gave her a solid

kiss, and eased away. "Let's get on up there. Running a little late."

✦ ✦ ✦

New New, like all of the Worlds, derived its gravity artificially, by spinning. Along the axis of spin, there was no gravity; the farther "out" you went, the greater the force. Most people lived and worked close to the one-gee level, where all the parks and shops were.

There were laboratories, small factories, and some living quarters at the low-gee levels, which is what brought John Ogelby to New New. Born a hunchback with a debilitating curvature of the spine, he had lived most of his life alternating between pain pills and agony. He developed expertise in a particular corner of strength-of-materials engineering, so that he could emigrate to the Worlds and find work in a low-gravity lab, where his back would stop hurting.

He was a close friend of O'Hara's—she had met Dan Anderson through him—and she and Dan often went up to the quarter-gee area where he lived and worked, to visit the Light Head tavern (now being used for emergency housing), or to take advantage of the short cafeteria lines there. Not many people ate in low gravity often enough to be comfortable with it. A cup of hot coffee can do amazing and painful things.

The quarter-gee cafeteria was the only room in New New that had wooden paneling on the walls. Some philanthropist had shipped it up from Earth after the low-gee hospital saved his life. A few cases of Scotch would have been more appreciated: to people who grew up surrounded by steel, the Philippine mahogany felt sinister and unnatural. (It didn't look all that homey to people born on Earth, for that matter, since it was secured to the real walls with conspicuous bolts.)

Ogelby was already seated at a table when they came

in. He greeted them with a listless wave.

Dinner was rice covered with a gray substance, with a few molecules of cheese and a spoonful of well-aged lima beans. And a generous serving of wine; they were rationing protein but had vats of alcohol.

"Have you heard about Earth?" he said when they sat down.

"Nothing good, I suppose," Daniel said.

"Plague. If it's not a hoax, or a misunderstanding." He speared one lima bean and ate it with reluctance. "Eastern Europe first, then Russia. The SSU accused America of having used a widely dispersed biological agent. But America's got it too, it turns out."

"What sort of plague?" O'Hara asked.

"Hard to say. The news broadcast was in very colloquial Polish, hysterical, and they've only been able to get a word here and there. It affects the brain, it's fatal, and it appears to be very widespread. They've been trying to contact someone in the States, or at least intercept something. Not much in the way of communication going on nowadays."

Dan checked the time. "Well, let's eat up. Ten minutes to Jules Hammond."

They went to the low-gee library, which was so crowded they had to stand in the rear. Dan helped John up onto a table so he could see the cube. The screen was blank except for the time. At precisely 2100, the cube filled with the avuncular and soberly dramatic features of Jules Hammond.

"This is May 5, 2085. All of you must know by now that there is a rumor of plague on Earth." He paused. "The rumor is true. How widespread the epidemic is, we aren't yet sure. It may be all over the planet.

"We haven't yet gotten through to the United States, but we did intercept a broadcast in Nevada." Nevada was an independent, rather lawless country in the middle of America.

Hammond's face faded and was replaced by that of a young female. The picture had a bad Z-axis flicker: the image twitched between three dimensions and two, solid and flat.

The sound was clear. Her voice cracked with hysteria. "Everyone who has been to the States, or anywhere outside of Nevada, since the war started must *clear out*! Don't stop to pack, just get out. Whatever this shit is, we don't want it. The Assassins' Guild is cooperating fully with the Public Health Syndicate...anyone who might have had contact with the plague has until midnight to *be missing*.

"If you know anybody who's been outside, report his name to any assassin. They're gonna be busy, so don't use this to settle old business, all right? It might be life or death for all of us—it looks like this shit spreads fast and gets everybody.

"Likewise, if you see anybody with symptoms, go get an assassin. Or do the job yourself—but only if you have a flamer. Then report it to Public Health.

"Symptoms are fever and sweats, and talking nonsense. Whatever it is, it hits the brain first. But they can walk around for days before they die. Don't take any chances."

Jules Hammond returned in all his comforting solidity. "I have with me Coordinators Markus and Berrigan."

The camera rolled back to show that Hammond was seated between the two Coordinators. Weislaw Markus, the Policy Coordinator, had glossy black hair but showed his age in his eyes and the deep creases that worried his face. Sandra Berrigan, Engineering Coordinator, was new to her office and young for it, forties, but her face was also a portrait of stress, slack bruises under sad eyes.

Markus shifted in his chair. "It's virtually certain that this plague is the result of biological warfare, one side or the other. Our main concern is that it not spread to New New, of course. Anyone who was on Earth when the war started is a potential carrier."

Dan put his arm around O'Hara, but it was a stiff, self-conscious gesture.

"We certainly don't have sympathy for the Draconian approach Nevada is taking. But our reaction must be equally absolute, equally swift. Your department, Sandra."

"It may not be our problem at all," she said. "Even if some of us were exposed to the microorganism on Earth, it's not likely the bug would live through the prophylaxis series everyone has to complete before they come through the airlock." O'Hara agreed; the shots were a combat assault on your body. It seemed as if everyone on the slowboat spent half their waking hours in the john.

"However. We do have to consider the remote possibility that some of you are carrying the plague. We're in the process of converting Module 9B into living quarters, to quarantine and examine you. If you were on Earth within the past year—because the agent could have been released long before the nuclear exchange—you must go immediately to Module 9B. Don't pack. Don't even pick up your toothbrush. We don't know at what stage of incubation this disease becomes communicable."

O'Hara squeezed John's hand and kissed Daniel antiseptically on the cheek. As she made her way to the door, people gave her a lot of room.

They had all the tomatoes and cucumbers they could ever want; that was the crop in Module 9B. Seconds after O'Hara floated through the module airlock, she knew she'd grow to hate the tomatoes' vinous smell.

The agricultural modules, the farms, were glassed-in bubbles that contained rigidly controlled environments, floating around New New York. They provided most of the vegetables and some of the meat for a quarter of a million people. (Only fish and chickens grew well in zero gravity; the rabbits and goats had to live inside with everybody else.)

The module was big, since it had been built with expansion in mind, but it wasn't big enough for 1,230 people. Besides the potential carriers, there were several dozen technicians, mostly medical, with a few engineering and agricultural workers to make sure that the people, tomatoes, and cukes all survived their period of close communion. The technicians wore spacesuits, in case somebody sneezed.

At least it wasn't like being cooped up with a bunch of strangers. People began to form in clusters of friends, swapping stories and speculations about Earth. O'Hara found her bunch, a group of students who used to meet every Tuesday at the River Liffey in Manhattan. Seven hadn't made it.

They were asked all to assemble at one end of the module, where a gruff medico told them they'd have to be quarantined for at least five days. There was a lot of predictable harrumphing about that. Only about one person in three hundred got a trip to Earth in his lifetime; these were some of New New's most important people.

Someone asked about solar flares—and got the answer, "Just hope we don't get a bad one." A Class 3 would kill them all in minutes, without shielding, but they were rare.

The first order of business was a thorough medical examination. Being in the middle of the alphabet, O'Hara handed in her samples and then loafed around for a couple of days. She couldn't read, since there were only a dozen cubes in the place, each being watched by twenty or thirty people at once. She got tired of movies and plays, and wound up with a group that was laboriously filling in "the world's largest crossword puzzle."

Finally she spent some hours being scanned and poked and thumped and swabbed. The doctors were fast, bored, and tired; O'Hara felt like a product on an assembly line. There was one moment that made her laugh, though, floating naked in midair behind a rack of tomato vines (for privacy), upside-down, holding on to a gynecologist's boots so he could keep his bearings while taking smears, both of them slowly rotating in a posture that was a parody of *soixante-neuf*. She remembered her last conversation with Daniel and wondered what it would take to give an erection to a gynecologist, in a spacesuit or otherwise.

The examination turned up nothing beyond an allergy to cow's milk, which was no surprise (and no problem, since the nearest cow was 36,500 kilometers away). Neither she nor anyone else had the plague. They were kept under observation for ten days, then returned to New New.

Very tired of the bland emergency rations they'd been fed in the module, O'Hara went straight to the cafeteria. The day's lunch was centered around gazpacho, cold tomato and cucumber soup.

Charlie's Will ✦

Most of the weapons that roared into the sky, 16 March 2085, were antiques, fifty to a hundred years old, but one type was quite new. Experimental; inadequately tested.

The Koralatov virus was a humane sort of weapon. It was meant to induce a lengthy period of mental confusion in the enemy population, some months of being unable to think effectively. Better dumb than dead, if it had worked, but it hadn't worked well at all.

Eighteen missiles were loaded with Koralatov-31. All but two were destroyed by America's defensive laser net. One accidentally aborted somewhere over Eastern Europe. Another had been targeted for Chicago and almost made it. A near miss from a geriatric anti-missile missile cracked it open and spilled K-31 into the jet stream. The result was the same as in Europe: over the ensuing weeks and months the virus drifted down and found its human hosts quite hospitable. By the end of the year it was as ubiquitous as the common cold. But it didn't have the effect Koralatov had planned; in fact, it was some time before any symptoms appeared anywhere. When the first victim lapsed into idiocy and died, the only humans left uninfected were a handful of desert nomads, some scientists stranded in Antarctica, and the people who lived in space.

The ones in Antarctica could hang on for a few years, while their supplies lasted, and the nomads would survive so long as they remained out of contact with the infected population. For the rest of the Earth, the plague was swift and complete.

Almost everyone over the age of twenty died in the first few weeks. Younger people didn't seem to be affected. In the chaos of a world suddenly leaderless, parentless, ten times decimated, it took a while for the morbid truth to become clear: no one would live for very long. Sometime between the ages of eighteen and twenty-one, everyone got sick and died.

A couple of billion doomed children couldn't keep the twenty-first century running. Everything didn't grind to a halt at once, since much of the world was automated, and the systems kept working for a while. You could go into an autobar and get a drink, or punch up a public-service number and have a dead woman pray for you. But sooner or later a crucial part would decay, or there would be vandalism, and no one left who knew how to fix things up, no one in the world.

There was at least one group that the war did not take by surprise, neither in its timing nor its ferociousness. The Mansonites were an underground and quite illegal religion, claiming tens of thousands of members in the southern United States. They had been predicting for some years that there would be a period of "helter-skelter," followed by the end of the world, and they figured it would

happen in 2085, the hundredth anniversary of their savior's deliverance.

The Mansonites based their creed on the writings of
Charles Manson, a charismatic loony who in the previous
century had led his followers in a small orgy of mass
murder. To the Family, death was a blessing and murder
a sacrament. They were the only church whose member-
ship increased dramatically after the war.

Year Two

1 ✦

There had been some hope that Australia, New Zealand, and Pacifica might in their isolation be spared. But the virus drifted down everywhere. On every tiniest speck of land, if there were people, all but the very young sickened and died.

As life on Earth sloughed into desperation and savagery, life in New New became more safe, more comfortable, at least for a while. The farms were repaired—O'Hara gratefully traded in her spacesuit and diapers for a desk—and people stopped worrying so much about their next meal and, in grim pursuit of normality, resumed worrying about which fork to use. They also worried quite a bit about who was sleeping with whom, and what went on when they weren't sleeping, and why they didn't at least get a document to legitimize it.

Marriage was a pretty complicated affair in New New York. Not the civil part of it; that could be done in a couple of minutes, by computer. The problem was deciding whether to marry one person, or two, or six, or several thousand.

There were dozens of "line families" in New New. The term was an archaic one that was now applied very loosely to any more-or-less permanent connection involving love, sometimes reproduction, cohabitation (if the group was small enough and the room was big enough), and so forth.

As an example, Marianne O'Hara's various families. When she was born, her mother belonged to the Nabors line. This was a conventional old-fashioned line family, several hundred people who were all husband and wife. Careful genealogical tables were kept to prevent inbreeding, but there were no inhibitions on nonreproductive sex. A pretty young girl like O'Hara's mother spent a lot of time being nice to relatives, and even more time saying "no." She wanted out, and she picked the quickest way: soon after menarche she got herself impregnated by an outsider. The Nabors line took care of her until the baby was born, and then kicked both of them out.

By that time she had a Nabors lover, who quit the line to be with her. Along with Marianne's father, they joined the Scanlan line, which was actually a loose association of three-way marriages, rather than a true line. It was a fairly cold-blooded decision on her mother's part. Marianne's father was a groundhog, and (as had been prearranged) a week after the marriage he returned to his Earthside wife. So mother and lover became a simple married couple, but with the housing and schooling advantages of the Scanlan line. Marianne was the only child of a broken triune, which made her an outsider to the other children, and they were vicious in their clannishness. Growing up, the only thing she knew for sure about her future was that she would never join a triune marriage.

She was wrong. She'd been living with Daniel—as lovers again, finally—for over a year when a law was passed that forbade single people from occupying multiple dwellings. (A lot of families from other Worlds had been split up, living in dormitories, and once they had coordinated their interests, they made a substantial voting bloc.)

For the past year, O'Hara had been resisting social pressure to get married. Girls and boys from most lines in

New New were encouraged to "butterfly," to seek a variety of sexual contacts. But as one grew older—certainly by O'Hara's advanced age of twenty-three—one was ˊexpected to settle down. (In joining the Devon line, for instance, "settling down" meant restricting yourself to a few thousand potential sexual partners.) She knew her family and coworkers thought her relationship with Daniel was immature and even a little indecent. This annoyed her and might have delayed their marriage indefinitely, if the practical matter of housing hadn't interfered.

There was no line she wanted to join, which was a relief to Daniel, so she suggested they start their own, and he nervously agreed. They filed the necessary documents, patterning the line after the old-fashioned Nabors one: new members accepted only on unanimous approval; old members divorced by majority vote. She drew the long straw, and the line was named O'Hara.

Before they'd filed, O'Hara brought up the possibility of their asking John Ogelby to join them, as a symbol of their mutual affection. Daniel thought it over for some weeks. He and John were closer than brothers, but, damn it, you can't *marry* another man! Daniel's parents had had a conventional pair-bond marriage, until-death-or-boredom-do-you-part, and nothing else really seemed right to him.

Marianne kidded and argued with him until he finally agreed. One thing that had never entered the discussion was sex. Daniel knew that she and John had tried on one occasion, and it hadn't worked, and the presumption that he wouldn't be gaining a rival in that arena probably influenced his decision. It's likely that Marianne suspected otherwise. Daniel was nine years older, but she had literally worlds more experience in sex.

At any rate, the predictable transformation occurred. John Ogelby, forty-two years old, physically deformed, Irish Catholic upbringing: besides the unsuccessful event with Marianne, and two equally frustrating youthful encounters with Dublin prostitutes, his only sexual partner in thirty years had been his own imagination. One simple ceremony and he was a different man.

Daniel suddenly found himself with a lot of time to reflect, alone, on the ways of a maid with a man. Marianne spent the first week of their expanded marriage up in John's quarter-gee cubicle, with occasional forays to the zerogee gymnasium, where there were small rooms with locks.

There was no possibility of the three of them living together, since John couldn't tolerate normal gravity for long. Eventually they settled down into an informal migratory pattern. Marianne would spend a few days upstairs, a few days downstairs, free to change at her whim or either man's desire. She got into the habit of carrying a toothbrush in her bag. The three of them took most of their meals together. Daniel was surprised to find himself not jealous.

✦ ✦ ✦

O'Hara's advanced training had been in the areas of American Studies and administration; she'd been aiming for a liaison position between the Worlds and the U.S. That didn't look like much of a career now.

She had a temporary, or tentative, position as a minor administrator in Resources Allocation. Administrative trainee, actually, which turned out to be assistant to anybody junior enough not to have his own assistant. Being in Resources, though, gave her a realistic view of New New's current situation. It was a fool's paradise.

She and John and Daniel were taking their slow Friday walk through the park. Ogelby had to spend a few hours a week in normal gravity, or progressive myasthenia would trap him forever in the upper levels.

"I'm getting used to it again," O'Hara said, "not having a horizon." They sat down to rest on a bench beside the lake. The lake rose in front of them, a sheet of still water that curved gently away to be lost in mist. If you looked straight overhead, squinting against the brilliance of the artificial suns, you might just make out the opposite shore.

"I never will," Anderson said. A duck swam toward them, slightly downhill. Ogelby snapped his fingers at it.

O'Hara frowned. "Don't tease the poor thing."

"Tease?" He opened a pocket and took out a piece of rice cake. The duck waddled over and snatched it. "We must share with the less fortunate." His speech was slightly slurred, and his eyes bright, from the pain pills.

"Time will come when you'll wish you'd saved it," she said. "When we're up to our ears in Devonites."

"They'll come to their senses," Ogelby said. "The whole line's still in a state of shock." Two years before, the Devonites had over fifteen thousand souls in their lines. Most of them lived in Devon's World, a toroidal settlement in the same orbit as New New, about three thousand kilometers downstream. Devon's World had suffered a direct hit during the war, and all but a few hundred perished. They were rescued and joined the several thousand who lived in New New.

Even in normal times, a Devonite woman was expected to have many children; their religion was a celebration of fertility. Now they were pregnant constantly, and taking drugs to guarantee multiple births. This put them at odds with public policy; for conservation of food and water, the administration of New New had asked for a five-year period of strict birth control.

Most women in New New were in the same situation as O'Hara. She'd had a half-dozen ova frozen and filed when she was a girl, and then had herself sterilized. If she wanted a child she could either choose a father and have the fertilized ovum implanted in her womb, or opt for parthenogenesis—have her cell quickened by microsurgery, then bear a daughter who would be a genetic duplicate of herself. Since neither of these procedures could be done outside of a hospital, New New's administration had de facto control over population growth, if they wanted to exercise it. Many people, O'Hara included, did want them to shut down the conception labs for a few years, and they could do it as a simple administrative procedure (though there would be noise), since the right to bear and keep children was not guaranteed by the Declaration of Rights.

That was the demographic rub, though. Freedom of religious expression *was* guaranteed, and women being baby machines was fundamental to the Devonite religion. (Sterilization, of course, was an unforgivable sin; their ova were quickened the old-fashioned sloppy way.) In five years a lucky woman might have six or seven multiple pregnancies.

"It was different when they had a whole World to themselves," Anderson said slowly. "They could feed themselves or starve."

Ogelby came to their defense. "But they will be feeding themselves. They have a thousand people out there building extra farms, all volunteers."

"It won't work," O'Hara said. "I've seen the projections. You know how long it takes to make soil from scratch. More time than it takes to make babies."

"I thought they were mining Devon's World."

"What's left of it. We'll be lucky if they reclaim ten percent of the topsoil, and that's been sitting exposed to space for two years. Sterilized and desiccated. We have to supply water, worms, microorganisms."

"And nitrogen," Anderson cut in, "and carbon—that's it, ultimately. The same old story." It was a problem as old as the Worlds themselves. Metals they had in plenty, and oxygen, from the lunar surface and the interior of New New, which was a hollowed-out mountain of steel. But you can't grow food without carbon, nitrogen, and water, and although every molecule of these precious substances was meticulously recycled, no such process is perfect. Because of inevitable steady losses, closed-cycle agriculture can't even sustain a stable population, let alone a growing one. Before the war there had been active commerce between the Earth and the Worlds, Earth trading hydrogen (which the Worlds burned to make water), carbon, and nitrogen for energy and exotic manufacturing materials and pharmaceuticals that could only be produced in zero gravity. So the Worlds' population could steadily grow.

"No more," Ogelby said to the duck, who was pacing nervously in front of him. "I guess we lose perspective in the lab. As if Deucalion were coming in tomorrow." Deucalion was the name of a CC ("carbonaceous chondritic") asteroid that was being slowly moved toward New New. They would be able to mine it for nitrogen, carbon, hydrogen, and other useful things, but it was still five years away. Ogelby was involved in designing and setting up the factories that would eventually take the asteroid apart. Right now, though, they just had a pilot plant, working on small amounts of CC material sent up from the Moon. It didn't manufacture enough to offset any population growth.

"If they could only wait a few years," Anderson said. "We'll be rebuilding Devon's World. Right now Deucalion has to take precedence." Originally, the towing job had been a very long-term project, twenty-eight years from Deucalion's original orbit to New New. After the war they knew they had to speed it up. This was why so much amateur talent had been pressed into repairing the farms: most of the regular construction crews were frantically building mass-driver engines and solar-powered tugs to haul them out to intercept Deucalion. If things went according to schedule, they would cut down the remaining transit time for the asteroid from nineteen years to five.

"It's just happening too fast," O'Hara said. "If two

thousand women have two-point-eight babies a year for five years, that's twenty-eight thousand new mouths to feed. With six or seven hundred deaths per year, overall, that's a population increase of about ten percent.

"And if they all grow up to be Devonites, we have a regular yeast culture on our hands. In a couple of generations, every other person is going to be bald and holy and fucking anything that moves." O'Hara skimmed a flat pebble out over the lake; it skipped twice, curving to the right. "I wouldn't like to be Coordinator."

"Change of heart?" Ogelby said. That was her ambition.

"I don't know anymore. I may just sit and watch."

2 ✦

When O'Hara returned to work there was a message at her console telling her to go to Level 6, Room 6000, and talk to Saul Kramer. The woman she was working for didn't know anything about it, but a quick directory check showed that Kramer was in charge of personnel at the Department of Emergency Planning. That was pretty exciting, as was the unusual request for a face-to-face meeting—you expect a Ranking Bureaucrat to talk to you through memos, or at most on the cube.

Her excitement took an anxious twist as she approached Room 6000. A man about her age, vaguely familiar, came out the door and walked swiftly by without greeting her, his face pale and grim.

A white-haired woman in the stark anteroom glanced at a console and asked whether she was Marianne O'Hara, and said that Mr. Kramer would see her. As O'Hara pushed open his door she remembered where she had seen the young man. Module 9B, the quarantine—a surge of adrenaline shocked her and she stopped halfway through the door, took a breath, and realized it couldn't be. She didn't have the plague; if that were it she wouldn't be walking around free.

Kramer's desk was littered with paper, a rare sight. He even had a recycler in the corner, with a stack of new paper beside it. A dramatic-looking man, completely bald, large and muscular, with pale gray eyes. He looked up at her with concern. "O'Hara? Are you all right?"

She laughed nervously. "I just frightened myself with a thought—that man who just left..."

"Lewis Franconia." He gestured. "Have a seat."

"We were together in the quarantine."

He nodded vigorously. "No coincidence."

She sat down and clasped her hands together, to stop the shaking. "Something showed up?"

"What—no, nothing like that, nothing medical. It's just no coincidence that you were both on Earth recently. That's true of almost everybody who's come in here today."

When O'Hara didn't say anything, he continued. "We have a favor to ask of you. A very big favor."

"For Emergency Planning?"

"We're implementing it. But the request comes straight from the Coordinators."

"I'll do what I can."

"We need a group of people to go back to Earth."

"Earth?" She leaned forward. "Now? What about the plague?"

"You'll be isolated in spacesuits. Sterilized by vacuum before you get out of them." He shuffled some papers. "This is absolutely secret. Whether you say yes or no, you can't tell anybody about it. Not even your husbands."

"All right."

"You know why New New survived the war."

"Sure. You can't hurt a mountain with a shotgun."

He nodded. "The missiles that got the Worlds were

designed, built, and put to bed more than eighty years ago. They were set afloat by the Americans to use against Socialist military satellites, but they weren't deactivated after the Treaty of 2021. Just retargeted, in case the Worlds did something the States didn't like. Fortunately for us, they were designed for use against relatively small, fragile targets. To destroy New New would take a direct hit from a large hydrogen bomb."

"I understand."

"Well, that's just what we're faced with. They have a hydrogen bomb and they plan to use it on us." He waved at the cube on the wall, which was showing a map of Africa. "From Zaire."

She stared at him. "*Who* has a hydrogen bomb? How could they get it here?"

He sorted through papers and handed her two sheets. "Read this. It's utterly fantastic."

It was no secret that many of the survivors on Earth thought the Worlds were responsible for the war. An energy boycott against the United States had precipitated the revolution that within hours escalated into nuclear war.

So here was a group that had decided to do something about it: revenge. *Die Schwerter Gott*, the Swords of God, a group of young Germans who had managed to remove the warhead from a missile that hadn't fired. They were moving it to the spaceport in Zaire, one of two launch facilities that had survived the war. There was a shuttle on the pad; they planned to load the bomb into the cargo hold and launch a suicide mission.

"But that's not possible, is it? There aren't any engineers left, no pilots."

"It is barely possible. That shuttle is one of the luxury designs from Mercedes. Very fast, very wasteful of fuel, but it can take twenty or so people from Earth to high orbit in one go, two days' flight. It's automated to a fare-thee-well; anyone who can read the manual and punch a computer could get it here. They couldn't dock safely, not without a skilled pilot, but that's immaterial to them."

She handed back the papers. "You want us to go to Earth and stop them?"

"Actually, what we hope is that you'll get to Zaire before they do. They're having trouble transporting the bomb; there's no air transport left in Europe. They're moving it overland to Spain, where they'll get a boat to Magreb. That's how we found out about them, intercepting radio messages while they were arranging for the boat."

"What if we get there too late?"

"You're stuck. Our shuttle will get you there, but you have to take theirs to get back."

"Is there anybody there, at the spaceport?"

"The telescope shows a few people wandering around. No organized activity; no communications we've been able to monitor."

"But they aren't likely to let us just walk in and hijack their shuttle."

"Who can say? You might scare them all off when you land."

"I suppose." She shook her head. "I have to make a decision right away, can't talk to anybody?"

"Just to me. You have to decide before you leave this room."

"When would we be taking off?"

He looked at his watch. "About seven hours from now. You go from here straight to the hub."

O'Hara stood up and crossed the room. She stared at the cube for a minute. "I just don't understand. Why me? Just because I've been to the Zaire spaceport?"

"Partly because you've been there. Partly because...there may be violence. Not many people in New New have any experience with that."

"You seem to know an awful lot about me," she said evenly. "Who gave you that bit of information? One of my husbands?"

"Says here...it's from a transcript, um, of the therapy sessions you had last year."

"How the hell could you get your hands on that?"

"I couldn't. But if the Coordinators want something, they can generally get it."

"You want me to believe that one of the Coordinators sat down and went through confidential medical records, just in case something useful might show up?"

"Of course not; it was done by someone in my office. But under the Coordinators' authority. It was a simple computer search, semantic association—and we didn't single you out. Everybody's records were searched."

"That's nice to know. Nobody has civil rights."

"It's temporary. You have to admit that the situation—"

"I guess we don't have time to argue about it. But if you want me because I can supposedly handle violence, you didn't read that record very thoroughly. That's why I was in therapy."

"All I personally know is what's on this piece of paper. That you've carried guns and fired them—"

"No plural. **Once.** I carried a gun once, in my lap, trying to get to the Cape when the war started. I also fired it only once."

"That's one more time than the rest of us."

She looked back at the cube. "You mainly want people who've been on Earth."

"That's right; the more recently, the better. There won't be any time to get accustomed to it." He paused and leaned forward.

"You fit other criteria: we need people who are young and physically strong, who have experience working in spacesuits. And people without children."

"That's encouraging." She returned to the chair and slumped into it. "I suppose you also want people who are relatively useless, who won't be missed."

He shook his head. "That's not a factor at all. In fact,

the expedition's leader is the Engineering Coordinator."

"That's not very smart."

"It was her decision." He crumpled up the piece of paper with O'Hara's data on it and tossed it into the recycler. "What's yours?"

"Oh...I suppose I have to do it."

"No one's forcing you."

"That's not exactly what I mean."

3 ✦

She wasn't even allowed to say good-bye. They taped a message for her to leave for Daniel and John, that she and several others were going back into isolation, but not to worry, it wasn't the plague.

The lift to the hub was empty. O'Hara put on her sticky slippers and pushed the middle button, marked "0."

The sensation of weight decreased as the lift rose, or fell, toward the hub. When it stopped she was weightless, which of course was no novelty. The doors slid open and a man walked in upside-down and stood on the ceiling, also with Velcro slippers. They nodded and O'Hara walked down the short corridor, making a little ripping sound each time she lifted a foot. A sign said PLEASE WALK ONLY; it would be more natural to use handholds and float through the corridor, but you were liable to collide with somebody coming around a corner or through a door.

She went into the locker room and checked out the spacesuit she'd been assigned last year, and a bundle of those damned diapers, and floated into the Operations Room.

There were four men there, her age or younger, and one woman, Coordinator Sandra Berrigan. Their spacesuits were hanging in midair by the opposite wall; O'Hara pushed hers gently in that direction.

O'Hara swam over and introduced herself. She already knew one of them, Ahmed Ten, but hadn't recognized him at first. A short black man, back on Earth he'd worn his gray hair long, in a huge frizzy cloud; now he was shaven bald. It made him look younger.

"Two more to come," Berrigan told her. "We'll hold off the actual briefing until we're aboard the shuttle. Goodman, you want to show O'Hara how the guns work?" She'd wondered about that; by statute, there were no weapons in New New.

Goodman was a beefy youngster with a quick grin. He beckoned for O'Hara to follow him through the airlock door.

The shuttle floated huge in the pressurized bay. There was a strange smell in the air, burnt metal, like the smell around a welder.

"What they done," Goodman said, "was take an oxy gun and put a fuel feed on her, then put a sparker at the nozzle. Fuel's a mixture of vegetable oil and powdered aluminum." He brought her an oxy gun with an extra tank and a ceramic extension on the nozzle. "Point her down there and give the trigger a quick one."

She aimed down the long dimension of the bay and pinched the trigger. A squirt of bright flame roared out twenty or thirty meters, orange shot through with blinding blue-white. The noise of it echoed around the chamber. Recoil from the blast pushed O'Hara gently back against the airlock door.

"We all have these?"

"You and me and two others. They wasn't time to make more."

"Let's hope we don't have to use them. That's terrible."

"Yeah, awful," Goodman said, without too much conviction. "Remember, it won't go in a straight line on Earth. You got to aim high, for the gravity."

"Right." O'Hara wondered what virtue the computer had divined in Goodman.

The airlock opened and Berrigan peered in. "Everybody's here. O'Hara, come give us a hand. Goodman, you have two more customers."

All that was left to be loaded were the spacesuits and some paper crates of food. They put them in nets and hooked the nets one at a time to a centrifuge device, to weigh them. Berrigan entered their masses into a console inside the shuttle.

There was nothing dramatic about taking off. Pumps hammered, fading away as they drew air from the chamber. Then the outer lock irised open, there was a tiny push of acceleration, and they drifted, slower than a walk, out into space.

"Change orbit in an hour and twenty minutes," Berrigan said. "Let's go over our plan, such as it is."

She switched on a cube and tapped in some instructions. A flat map of the Zaire spaceport came up. "All we really have to do is leave this ship here," she said, pointing to the end of the runway, "disabling it so that it can't be refueled and used against us. Then we just walk down this track to where the shuttle's waiting.

"That's where it gets a little complicated. If it looks like there'll be any trouble, we get aboard in a hurry and leave. Assuming the ship does work.

"If we have free run of the place, though, there are some interesting things we might do. First, Goodman and O'Hara run up to the operations center, here, and burn anything that looks important. We don't want to leave them with any launch capability at all."

"What about us?" Ahmed Ten asked. "Can this Mercedes take off without any launch support?"

She laughed. "With a trained monkey at the controls. Everybody'll get a chance to study the manual for it, but basically all you have to do is ask the computer for a catalog, punch in your destination and launch time, and strap yourself in.

"While you two are having fun, the rest will be down

in this building here. That's a cryogenic storage area, and it appears to be intact. Cryogenics means nitrogen; we'll take as much as we can. Goodman and O'Hara will keep their eyes open for a vehicle. But even if we have to hand-carry it, we should be able to move a few tonnes, to bring back to the farms.

"I'll go straight to the shuttle and do a systems check on it. It should only take a few minutes to find out whether it's still working."

"If it isn't, we're all dead?" O'Hara said.

"There's a chance not. This isn't a suicide mission.

"We have enough air, tank switching, to stay in our suits for forty hours. And we can probably find compatible air tanks at the spaceport, though that's not certain. Standard German ones won't fit.

"Still, we could probably make time, perhaps indefinitely. Find or make a hyperbaric chamber, keep the inside of it sterile. If the shuttle is down but repairable, Michaels and Washington and I might be able to fix it.

"If that doesn't work, we still have a slim chance. Antarctica." New New was in regular contact with the scientists trapped there. "The Mercedes can land on its tail, though it takes a level surface and a steady hand. Even if we can't get into orbit, we might be able to fly it like a floater. Or actually find a floater that could get us there."

"I thought there weren't any working floaters in Europe or Africa," Ten said.

"There aren't, but that's because the power net's been destroyed. With three good engineers we should be able to jury-rig a portable power source."

"What happens when we get down there?" Goodman asked. "Take the place over from the scientists?"

"No; we've made a deal with them. They'll share their supplies with us until a rescue mission can be staged. That probably wouldn't be until Deucalion comes in. But we could make it. Then they'd come back with us."

"Five years," O'Hara said.

"They say the penguins are fascinating," Berrigan said. "Never get tired of watching them." She turned off the cube. "That's it. Any questions?"

"This is all happening so fast," O'Hara said. "Nobody's explained why we have to go down there in the first place. I'm no engineer, but it seems to me there must be a dozen ways we could stop them from up here—I mean, that bomb has to be in actual contact with New New, doesn't it?"

"That's right. If we could make it detonate even a kilometer or two away, it would just be so much extra sunshine."

Goodman scratched his head. "So why don't we just shoot the goddamn thing with a laser?"

"That would work if they came in slowly enough. A mining laser would at least scramble their electronics, maybe detonate the bomb prematurely, or defuse it. But they'll be coming in at as much as thirty kilometers per second; we can't get enough energy flux on target. That'll be tried, of course, if we fail in Africa. We can also put a wall of dust and rock in their way, using a mass driver, which would be even more effective, if they're stupid enough not to make evasive maneuvers. But even if we fill the ship with holes, kill them all, the bomb might still make it through. And it's not just the bomb; when it goes off it'll ignite all the deuterium and tritium in the ship's fuel tanks. That's enough to blow New New into gravel. And melt the gravel."

✦ ✦ ✦

Nothing eventful happened during the five days it took them to spiral in to low Earth orbit. They did a lot of calisthenics, enjoyed unusually good food, read the

Mercedes manual with some interest. Twice they took jolts of amphetamine, so they would be ready for the drug's effects when they landed.

O'Hara got fairly close to Coordinator Berrigan, not just because they were the only women. Berrigan had also been given a year on Earth, to study, twenty years before, and like O'Hara she had chosen NYU in New York City. They hadn't had any academic work in common, since O'Hara was in American Studies and Berrigan pursued systems analysis. But they'd both had the City—fabulous, sinister, challenging.

They got into their spacesuits just before the ship started biting air, to brake for its final approach. O'Hara was vaguely annoyed to see that Berrigan's spacesuit was the catheter type.

4 ✦

It was a bumpy ride, screaming in over the African jungle, and there was a bad moment when they came down onto the concrete strip, perhaps a shade too fast, the strip still wet from the morning rain. The shuttle started to fishtail, and Berrigan slapped a button that released an emergency parachute. It probably saved them from slithering off the runway, but they were all slammed painfully forward into their restraining straps. Michaels hit the inside of his helmet hard enough to knock himself out for a few moments; O'Hara felt like one blue bruise from shoulders to hips.

Then they were rolling calmly along, engines throbbing a high-pitched whine. About a kilometer from the end of the runway, the Mercedes shimmered in the hot damp air.

"Well, it hasn't left yet," Berrigan said, over the helmet intercom. Before they entered the atmosphere, New New had told them that it was still on the pad. They didn't know how close the Germans were, though; the telescope had lost track of them soon after they got to North Africa.

"Might as well unbuckle. You four with guns get ready to jump out as soon as we stop." The engines quit and they rolled silently to a halt. "Go!"

The inner door of the airlock was open. Goodman spun the wheel on the outer one and a crack of bright sunlight appeared; then a solid hard square of it. The exit ladder slid out and unfolded with agonizing slowness.

Goodman was the first out, scrambling down the ladder, pointing his gun this way and that. "Nobody here," he said when he got to the ground.

O'Hara followed close behind him. The area did look deserted, and the jungle was reclaiming it. Thick undergrowth lapped over the edges of the runway, and here and there the concrete had cracked, grass muscling up through it.

She had never used a spacesuit in gravity before. It felt like being wrapped up in stiff heavy bindings. She hoped they wouldn't have to move fast.

It took twenty minutes to get to the Mercedes shuttle. By that time O'Hara was breathing hard, cold with evaporated sweat. The air conditioner was working unevenly, with cold spots on her chest and under her chin, but her back was warm and clammy.

"Trouble," Berrigan said, pointing into the jungle beyond the Mercedes. "People in there." Her amplified voice boomed out. "We mean you no harm. Just stay away from us."

A single arrow arced toward them, falling far short. Goodman raised his gun but Berrigan pushed the nozzle down. "No. Not yet—Ten, you repeat what I said."

Ten shouted a loud string of Swahili. A high-pitched voice answered him. "He says they know we're from the Worlds; they know we're the ones who killed their parents. If we don't leave they'll kill us."

"Tell them we'll leave when we're ready to. Then all four of you fire into the air."

While Ten was talking, two more arrows sailed in, falling only a few meters short. One skidded along the concrete and came to rest almost at Ten's feet. When he stopped talking he picked up the arrow and broke it. Then the guns roared and he spoke again.

"I told them to throw their weapons on the ground and leave. That if they hinder us we'll burn down the jungle with them in it."

"Good. I hope they believe it." After a minute seven or eight children, one of them conspicuously tall, stepped out of the bush and threw down a collection of bows, arrows, and spears. The little ones ducked immediately back into shelter, but the tall one shook a spear at them, shouting, and then buried the spear in the ground. He stood with his back to them for a minute and walked slowly into the bush.

"Some sort of a curse?" Berrigan asked.

"I imagine. Some dialect I don't know."

"Well...everybody keep a lookout while I do the systems check."

At the entrance to the lift there was a human skull and crossed femurs. She kicked them away and slapped a red button. The lift hummed and the doors began to slide open. "Well, at least...my God. Look at this."

A black cloud of flies swarmed out. Inside the lift were dozens of clean-picked skeletons and three fresher bodies, busy with insect life. Spacesuits have a provision for vomiting, an emergency aspirator, and several of them were put to use. O'Hara was surprised the sight didn't make her sick, and decided that was because it was too Grand Guignol—so revolting she couldn't really accept its reality. But she didn't look twice.

"Somebody help me clear this out. But keep watching."

O'Hara scanned the edge of the jungle intently for a few minutes, but there was no motion. "Ahmed...this was one of the most civilized places on Earth, when I was here. How could they revert to savagery so quickly?"

"Oh, I don't think you can say they've reverted. Not in the sense that they've forgotten civilization. I think what we see here is partly a game—they are children, after all—and partly an attempt at social organization." In normal times, Ahmed taught anthropology. "Before the war, most of them got some tribal lore at home and studied precolonial history in school. The popular folk heroes dated back to tribal times, and so did a lot of mass entertainment. They're just acting out a pattern that's reassuringly familiar."

"Living in the jungle, hunting wild game?" O'Hara said.

"I don't know. More likely, they're living in the city and stalking supermarkets. There's probably not much game around here, and it takes years to become a good hunter. It would be fascinating to study them."

A sudden thought chilled O'Hara. "What if they have guns?"

"I was thinking about that. Private ownership of firearms was strictly forbidden in the Pan-African Union; I think even the police were only armed with tanglers."

"We're lucky it's not America."

"We are...they're acting out their own tribal rituals over there."

O'Hara suddenly tensed. "Did you see that?"

"No," Ahmed said.

"I did," Goodman said. "The big one's still in there. We oughta start a fire."

"Better check with Berrigan," O'Hara said.

"Go ahead," she said over their intercom. "But use Ten's weapon, or Jackson's. Goodman and O'Hara should save fuel."

"He was over by that big tree with the pink flowers," Goodman said.

"All right," Ten said, and fired a burst into a thicket about fifty meters to the left of the tree. "We just want to scare them away." He let the thicket smolder for a minute and then gave it a sustained blast. It burst into bright flame and the flame began to spread.

"I wonder," Marianne said. "When I was here we visited a game preserve about a hundred kilometers south. The man who showed us around did have a gun, an air rifle that shot tranquilizer darts. I guess something that could pierce a rhino's hide would punch through a spacesuit pretty easily."

"And if it could put a rhino to sleep, it'd probably kill a human being," Ten said. "But there can't be too many of those guns."

"Besides," Jackson put in, "if they had anything like a rifle we'd sure know about it by now."

"Or they mighta gone to get it," Goodman said. "How far can one of those things shoot, I wonder."

"Probably farther than we can," Jackson said.

"Why don't you stop making each other nervous," Berrigan suggested. "We're going up now." The doors squealed shut and the lift rose smoothly, up a hundred meters to the control-room hatch.

Nobody talked while they eavesdropped on Berrigan and the other two engineers, muttering numbers and arcane jargon. Over the buzz of the feeding flies they could hear clicks and whirs from inside the gleaming machine.

"Seems to check out," Berrigan said finally. "Marianne, Jimmy, you go mess up the op center. Then meet the others at the cryogenics area. I'm going to stay here, just in case."

They started down the crumbling sidewalk as fast as the suits allowed. Goodman switched to a private channel. "I don't like that much. She can take off without us."

"She wouldn't. She just wants to make sure the children don't come aboard."

"They ain't gonna come aboard. They had two years to go inside there and they didn't." Berrigan had had to break an inspection seal to get into the control room.

"It might have been taboo, with all the dead people in the lift. Everything's different now."

"I still don't like it."

"Let's just get this job done as quickly as possible." They passed by a long black window and mounted marble steps that were slick with green growth. The sliding doors of the entrance were frozen shut, the shatterproof glass crazed from a hundred impacts. A sustained blast melted one of the doors and set off a yammering alarm.

Inside, there was another hindrance. It was a once-comfortable reception foyer, now gone to dust and mildew. There were prominent signs directing you to various places, but they were all in German and Swahili. Two years before, O'Hara had been rushed through the building on a tour, but she couldn't remember which direction they'd gone.

"Maybe we should call Ahmed," O'Hara said.

"Nah...we couldn't pronounce that Swahili, or spell it. Let's just you go one way and I go the other, and we burn anything that looks important."

"We ought to go together. We don't want to get trapped if the building catches on fire."

"Okay, that makes sense. This way?"

"Good as any." They went down a corridor marked ZEITUNGSWESEN BEREICH. They encountered another stuck door, and Goodman kicked it open.

"Well, I'll be God damned. Would you look at that."

O'Hara's glove slapped against her helmet as she instinctively tried to cover her mouth. Instead of screaming, she squeaked.

They were in an observation area over a large room full of muted sunshine. There were forty or fifty consoles in neat rows, and forty or fifty bodies slumped over the consoles or sprawled on the floor. They wore identical white uniforms, stained, and their faces and hands were mummified, shrunken around bone, skin dark gray with a white dusting of mold.

"What the hell happened to them, I wonder."

O'Hara leaned against a rail for support. "They—they've been sealed in here since they died. And they must all have died at the same time. Probably poison gas in the air conditioning. Or radiation, like a neutron bomb. I wonder who did it."

"Well, it must be the place we're looking for. Let's burn it up."

"Sort of hate to."

"Yeah." They clumped down the stairs together. "Break the window first," Goodman said. There was a bay window of polarized plastic, overlooking the landing strip and launch pads. He melted a hole in it and the Sun glared through.

"Careful," O'Hara warned. "We don't want to be standing too close to those consoles when the picture tubes blow out."

"Don't think they're cubes. Look like flatscreens to me." But he aimed carefully and sent a squirt of flame all the way across the room, enveloping the two farthest consoles. He was right; the screens just melted down. The bodies burned passively at first, and then their limbs started to stir.

"Christ that's ugly. Let's get this shit over with." He fanned the flame in a sustained roar over half the room, and O'Hara added hers to the inferno. They backed up the stairs together, spraying fire. The tile floor caught, burning bright orange with greasy black smoke.

Something pinged against O'Hara's tanks, and she saw a shiny needle spin off into the fire. She whirled around. "Jimmy!"

It all happened in less than a second. At the top of the stairs were four boys, tall boys in their teens, naked except for body paint. Three of them held spears, and one had a large rifle with a wooden stock. He was working the bolt of it.

O'Hara shot high and to the right, flame splashing

against the wall behind the boys. The one with the rifle fired; his dart and the fire from Goodman's gun crossed in midflight. All four boys were suddenly covered with burning oil. Two fell and two ran screaming.

Goodman's firestream tilted up, spraying the ceiling. O'Hara turned and saw him topple backwards down the stairs, a metal spike in his chest.

He lay on his back on the burning floor. O'Hara started down to help him, saw the flames licking around the tanks of oxygen and fuel, hesitated, called herself a coward, grabbed his foot, and pulled with all her strength. Halfway up the stairs, she heard a terrible rattling groan. She looked at him through the helmet and he was dead, his face dark purple with eyes bulging, swollen tongue forcing his jaws apart. She let go with a cry and his body bumped down the stairs as she backed away. She almost tripped over one of the bodies at the top of the stairs, then turned and ran. She passed two more smoldering bodies in the hall. As she stepped outside there was a tremendous explosion, Goodman's tanks, and the black window popped out in one piece, sailing through the air with ponderous grace in a rain of smoking human fragments.

She stopped dead and sat down and tried to put her head between her knees. Then she remembered the drug pack on her wrist, tore it open, and pressed the tranquilizer button.

Her teeth ached when her jaws unclenched. The pulse stopped hammering in her ears. The muscles in her arms and legs deliciously relaxed. A spear clattered on the steps next to her.

She looked up and a small boy was running away. Languidly she aimed in his direction, thought about it, and fired deliberately high. His hair caught on fire and he ran on even faster, beating at it.

"Poor child," she said. "I ought to do you a favor." She stood up and resisted the impulse to brush herself off. Someone was shouting at her.

"Goodman! O'Hara! What happened down there?"

"Goodman's dead now. I'm coming back." She switched off the intercom for a while and started walking back up the runway. Every now and then she fired a random burst into the brush. That seemed prudent.

Funny how the jungle had taken over. Two years before, these grounds were all carefully landscaped. She remembered the fat funny woman who had shown them around the place, stream of wisecracks in her lovely lilting accent. They'd each been given a flower, a lily red as blood. You come back some time now.

From the cryogenic warehouse to the Mercedes, the jungle was a solid sheet of flame. The paint on one side of the warehouse was starting to blister and smoke. Jackson and Ahmed were standing guard. She turned on her intercom and went inside.

They had found a forklift and were loading it with long gray cylinders. There was a large vault door beside the racked cylinders. O'Hara didn't care to think about what was behind the door. Heads.

This was a storage area for Immortality Unlimited, the only one in Africa. Dying people would have their heads separated from their bodies, the blood replaced with some more lasting fluid, and then have the head quickly frozen to the temperature of liquid nitrogen and sent here for storage. The idea was that a new body could eventually be cloned from a cell, and the brain recharged with some memories intact. No one knew how much. When they did it with dogs the dogs would remember some tricks. O'Hara thought it was ghoulish—and so much like groundhogs, to stockpile millions of new mouths to feed someday, when half the world was starving already.

She remembered the fat lady talking about it, talking seriously for a change. The storage area was here because some of the heads were bound for orbit. The initial cost was higher but there was no maintenance fee. It was easier to keep things cold in orbit, and you wouldn't have to worry about earthquakes or anything. She didn't say war. O'Hara wondered whether anybody had bothered to waste a missile on the vault satellite. It was possible. There were a lot of politicians up there whom some people would like to have stay dead.

Another forklift came rumbling through the door, and Berrigan told her to help with the loading. They should be able to empty the rack in two more trips.

The cylinders were heavy. Two people could barely handle them. O'Hara worked with Berrigan and another engineer, alternating, two wrestling the cylinder into place while the third held the stack together on the fork. She was glad for the strain of the work but noticed it was getting rather smoky.

"You're sure he was dead?" Berrigan asked.

"Oh, he was dead all right. They shot him with a dart from a rifle, it must have been a poison dart. His face got all puffed up. And then his tanks exploded. He's really dead." She set the cylinder into place but didn't move to get another one.

"Are you all right, Marianne? You could go trade places with Ten or Jackson."

"No, I'd rather do this. I've really had enough of guns." She went to another cylinder and knocked the supporting flange away, and stood holding the cylinder in place.

"You took something." Berrigan did the same on her side, and they rolled the cylinder out.

"A trank. I was starting to really lose it."

"Don't blame you. We should never have taken those damned 'phets. Plenty of excitement to keep us awake." They dropped it on the stack, and the forklift man leaned up against it. "Two more and we'll secure this load."

They tied a cable around the load and sat while the other rolled away to stow it. Marianne told her about the mummified technicians in the operations center.

"I wonder," Berrigan said. "It's not important anymore, but I wonder whether it might have been the Americans or the Socialists. It is strange that neither side bombed here."

"Leave a spaceport intact for whoever wins," O'Hara said.

When the forklift came back they loaded it up again, but while they were waiting for it to return, the metal wall facing the fire started to creak ominously. The wall thermometer was stuck at fifty degrees Centigrade. There were enough cylinders for one more load, but Berrigan decided not to risk it. Everybody went up in the lift and helped secure the nitrogen for takeoff, then took seats in the passenger area. It was cramped, since the acceleration couches hadn't been designed for use with space suits.

"Anybody here who can't take seven gees?" Berrigan asked. Jackson and Ten said they'd never been in a high-gee vehicle. "Well, we'll keep it down to five. The more gees down here, though, the less fuel we use overall. The less fuel, the more water for the daisies."

The ship's electrical activity made loud crackles of static. O'Hara could hardly hear what Berrigan was saying, the tranquilizer humming a lullaby in her veins, her body sagging with fatigue. With her chin she turned down the volume and stared through the porthole, out over the jungle canopy. Her last view of Earth, but she didn't feel any real emotion.

Berrigan's voice droned quietly through the countdown. It was only a couple of minutes, but O'Hara started to doze and didn't hear the warning: look straight ahead.

A clear chime sang out, then an impossibly loud grinding roar. O'Hara's head was suddenly clamped sideways, staring out the porthole as the ship swiftly rose. In seconds, the horizon bent to a curve. Something popped in her neck; the cartilage in her nose crackled, and her nose began to bleed. The aspirator started hammering; she wondered idly whether it would work in five gees, or seven, and then she got her answer. The ship tilted sideways suddenly and rivulets of blood splashed over the inside of her faceplate. They evened out to a thin red film that was barely transparent. To the suit's little brain, it felt like condensation: the faceplate heated up and baked it to a black crust. She tried to curse but couldn't move her lips or jaw.

After what seemed like a very long time, the acceleration stopped abruptly and they were in free fall. She turned her head cautiously and her neck felt fine. She could see a little bit through the cracks in the blood crust.

A figure in a spacesuit floated in front of her. It was Berrigan. "Marianne—what's wrong? Did you—"

"I'b jusd fide. Bud I god a broggen fugged nodes. You wadda helb be ged dis fugged helbed off?"

"You got a *nose*bleed?"

"Ndo, id's all a big agt. You wadda ged duh latch odd duh bag so I cad geh duh helbed off?"

Berrigan laughed with silly relief. "You can't take your helmet off, not until we've disinfected. That'll be a few hours. Better get used to it."

"*Used* do id!"

The first step was to set off the spray bombs of biocide, everybody swimming around through the fog for an hour. Then they evacuated all the air out of the control room and the passenger area, and went over every square centimeter of the ship and each other with powerful ultraviolet lamps. Then they filled it with air again and heated the air to two hundred degrees Centigrade, their suits' limit. That combination would kill any virus or bacterium, but it was hell on the leather upholstery.

They got out of their spacesuits and everybody drifted up to the control room to listen while Berrigan made her report to New New. Ahmed, who'd had paramedical training, peeked and poked at O'Hara's nose, and pronounced that it probably wasn't broken; at any rate, there wasn't much he could do if it were. He helped her clean the dried blood off her face and gave her a cold pack to hold against the back of her neck.

Berrigan talked with the Policy Coordinator, Weislaw Markus. He had released all the details of the plan once they'd left—hard to keep a shuttle to Earth secret—and some people, predictably, were incensed that it hadn't been put to referendum. Paranoia about the plague was running high. Their reward for a job well done would be twenty days of quarantine.

She signed off. "Good thing they don't know we have enough fuel to get to Mars. They might suggest we go start a new settlement." She tapped out an order on the console. "Guess I'll evacuate the cargo bay. Won't sterilize it completely, but—"

"Overridden," the console said, with a thick German accent. She cleared the board and retyped. "Overridden," it said again.

Ahmed looked up from packing his medical bag. "What's going on?"

"Oh, I'm doing something wrong." She thought for a minute and typed a short command.

"Diagnostic." It clicked. "Overridden because bleed areas were currently are currently occupied."

"Occupied?" She typed out a sequence and the cube lit up with a view of the cargo bay. Floating in the middle of it were two children, a boy and a girl, both six or seven years old. The girl was wailing, and the boy was either unconscious or dead.

They all stared at it. "She has a broken arm," Ahmed said.

"Here." Berrigan handed a throat mike to Ahmed. He stuck the disk next to his Adam's apple and said something stern, in Swahili.

The girl stopped crying and mumbled something, then started to sob again. Ahmed touched the disk to silence it.

"Damn. She doesn't speak much Swahili. Just Bantu."

"They must have followed one of the forklifts in, and hidden," Berrigan said. "Those storage lockers."

"We can't take them back," O'Hara said.

Ahmed nodded. "No matter what you mean by 'back.'" He sighed heavily. "They have to die."

"Maybe not," Berrigan said. "When we were roughing out the mission plan, two people were in favor of abducting someone, for medical experimentation. It's pretty certain that this plague is spread by a virus. If we could isolate it we could make an antigen."

Ahmed stared into the cube. "The risk..."

"I don't think it's too great. Harkness, Robert Harkness, claimed that we could keep a subject in the old isolation module, handle him completely by remote control. Knock him out to take samples and run tests, if that were necessary."

"Damned complicated."

"Yeah. And no way really to keep it secret. Guess I'd better call Markus again."

Ahmed headed toward the spacesuit locker. "I'll go set the girl's arm. See whether the boy's alive."

"We can't disinfect you again."

"I can live in the suit for two days." He looked at the cube. "But probably the kindest thing we could do for them is open the bay doors right now...if that's the decision, let me know. I'll give them something so they won't feel it."

"Okay." Some of them went to help Ahmed get into his suit. Berrigan cleared the board and the control room was suddenly silent, without the little girl's crying. She sat for a minute without typing anything, peering into the glowing cube, her lips moving slightly. O'Hara was quietly scrubbing the inside of her helmet.

"Marianne—you want to be in my shoes someday, on the Policy side?" O'Hara nodded. "Well, here's a cute problem for you to think about.

"What Coordinators can or can't do on their own is a vaguely defined mixture of statute, precedent, and common sense. There's no precedent for something like this, but since it so obviously involves the general welfare, it has to be put to referendum.

"I know we can isolate them adequately. The quarantine procedures we used on you people would be enough." She tapped out a sequence and the cube showed the storage bay again. Ahmed was holding the girl's hand, talking quietly.

"So what do you do if your people vote to make you a murderer?"

Charlie's Will ✦

Some of the grownups didn't die.

Perhaps one in a hundred thousand suffered a peculiar dysfunction of the pituitary gland, which made the body manufacture an abnormal amount of GH, growth hormone. This prevented the normal aging process from triggering the virus. The side effects of the hormonal imbalance, though, could be severe. One was acromegaly, gigantism: people grew very tall, with large hands, feet, and heads. They were often mentally retarded.

The ones who raided pharmacies and hospitals to keep up their supply of the compensating hormone, NGH—these prudent ones died, as all adults did. The others lived, if the environment allowed it.

In many parts of the world the children killed them, or at least refused to care for them. In Charlie's Country, which used to be Florida and Georgia, they were venerated. The more batty, the more respected, for madness was truth's disguise.

5 ✦

Two percent of the population saved Coordinator Berrigan from having to commit murder. The vote, after twenty-four hours of debate, came to 51 percent in favor of trying to find the cure, 49 percent in favor of not taking any chances. (The juvenile vote, which was not binding, showed 82 percent of citizens under sixteen in favor of exterminating the children, or protecting New New, or spacing the groundhogs, depending on whose rhetoric you favored.)

O'Hara and the six others moved back into the tomato-and-cucumber paradise of Module 9B for a few weeks of appeasing their neighbors' paranoia. O'Hara was bitter about it. Like every other sensible person, she knew that there was no slightest chance that any of them was carrying the plague. Berrigan claimed to enjoy the vacation. She did most of the work on the cube anyhow, and this way she didn't have to go to lunch with people who were trying to sell her something.

The African boy never regained consciousness. Evidently his body had cushioned the girl during the fierce acceleration; his neck and back were broken. He died while they were setting up the isolation module, and they froze him for eventual autopsy.

The isolation module was a small sphere that had never been intended for use by human beings. It was a holding area for cuttings, seedlings, and livestock imported from Earth. If any sign of disease appeared, the stock would be consumed by fire and the ashes blown into space (once there was enough evidence for the insurance people). It was a tiny cage, and the little girl cried and babbled and refused to eat the strange food that robot arms offered her.

Nobody in New New spoke Bantu; Ahmed set about learning it. Within a week he was able to explain to the girl approximately what had happened, and soon after, she reciprocated: she and her brother often went up there to play, not being afraid of high places or bones; it was especially fun since the older ones forbade it. She only dimly understood the rules of the game the older children were playing. They kept talking about a "brain devil" that would kill her if she didn't behave, and she vaguely remembered that a cousin had died and they said that was why. But they said a lot of things that made no sense.

Her name was Insila. She and her brother had climbed up the emergency stairs to the cargo bay level, and had gone inside the spaceship while the door was open. When one of the forklifts came back, they hid in an empty locker. They came out when everything was quiet and dark, and tried to get the bay door open. Then there were noises again, and they ran back to the locker to hide. Then something knocked her out. When she woke up they were floating and her brother was hurt bad, and her arm wouldn't work, and then Ahmed came in and helped her.

She wondered what would become of her. Ahmed tried to explain what the brain devil actually was, and what doctors were, and how they would try to cure her. He suspected that she didn't believe a word of it. He didn't tell her that in all likelihood she would spend the next ten years floating in that cage, with occasional forays into unconsciousness, until whatever it was did whatever it did, and she would go insane and die. And be sliced up, analyzed, and incinerated, like her brother. She knew he was dead but never once asked what had happened to him.

Year Four

1 ✦

Before the war, the economy of New New had been a carefully controlled form of socialism, perhaps logical for a quarter of a million people living in a 99.9 percent closed ecology. People earned dollar income only for overtime work and as bonuses, and there was a limit to the number of dollars you could accumulate. But since there were few possessions not held in common by everyone, there just wasn't much to spend money on. There were credit exchanges for gambling and prostitution, neither of which was illegal, but the luckiest gambler or the most skillful whore could not possess more than $999.99 at one time (along with an arbitrarily large stack of IOUs), since all credit transfers were handled electronically, and anything over a thousand dollars went straight back into the bank. Most people spent their money on luxury foods imported from Earth or trips to other Worlds.

But now there was no imported food, no other Worlds. A few people managed to spend their money becoming alcoholics, but that took some concerted effort, since wine and beer were rationed like any other food, and it was difficult to slip carbohydrates out of the food chain to ferment and distill.

That was one real advantage to having two husbands who worked in the CC laboratories. Every now and then

John or Daniel would come home with a flask of what they euphemistically called "gin." It was 180-proof industrial alcohol with a few aromatic impurities, and only an internal-combustion engine could drink it straight. But it made a beer last a long time.

The Light Head tavern, which had been temporary housing for two years, was finally open again, and O'Hara spent quite a bit of time there with John and Daniel, as they had in the old days. There was amateur entertainment, musicians and sometimes a girl who was clever at undressing, but the main attraction was that it provided a link with everyone's more pleasant past. It was a place to reminisce, and sometimes to talk about the future.

"It's about the most hare-brained thing I've ever heard," John was saying. "Shows how wonky people have gotten about Earth. Pure and simple paranoia."

"It *would* get us out of range. Some of us," Daniel said. People were talking about building a starship.

O'Hara splashed some gin in her glass and decanted a measure of beer over it. "You engineers. No sense of romance."

"How can you say that to an Irishman who plies you with liquor? But I have a sense of priorities, too. We have to rebuild the Worlds first. Get some redundancy in the goddamned system."

Daniel nodded. "If something happened to New New," he explained carefully to O'Hara, "we wouldn't have anyplace to go."

"Really." She watched the girl on the other side of the room doing tricks with her navel. She could rotate it clockwise, wink with it, and then rotate it the other way, all in time to a badly tuned mandolin. The room was palpable with male speculation as to her other talents. "Maybe it is irrational, John, but it's not simple and it's not purely paranoia. You didn't grow up here. The starship has been a dream since before my mother was born."

"I'm not arguing against dreams. I just think it ought

to be postponed for twenty years or so. Hell, I'd like to work on it myself. But not until we have things... straightened out."

"Seems to me we could do both, once Deucalion comes in. Give people more of a sense of purpose, less bitterness. Everything else is just cleaning up after the groundhogs' damned war."

"You know, they wouldn't even have to H-bomb us." Daniel had had an hour's head start on the gin, and it was beginning to show. "Just walk in the fuckin' airlock and sneeze. All be dead in a week."

She patted his hand. "Watch the girl, Dan. She's winking at you."

The basic idea behind the starship was even older than the Worlds. A generation ship: hundreds or even thousands of people aboard a vessel that would crawl out to the stars on a voyage of centuries. Their n-times-great-grandchildren would land on another world.

By the twenty-first century it was not such a preposterous idea. People who lived in the Worlds might as well be aboard such a ship; an incurious person, or one who didn't care for the zerogee at New New's only observation dome, could live his entire life without seeing Earth, Sun, or stars. If you have to live in a hollow rock anyhow, it might as well be going somewhere.

Furthermore—as had not been true in the previous century—the generation ship would have a definite target. A lunar observatory had discovered several earthlike planets orbiting "nearby" stars; one was only eleven light years away.

The main problem was energy. Not just the enormous push it would take to move a World-sized spaceship, but also the energy necessary to maintain life. The Worlds had been possible in the first place only because of the abundant free energy from the Sun. The generation ship would have to carry its own sunlike power source, with fuel enough for centuries.

In theory, the power could be supplied by conventional fusion. The deuterium could be mined either from Jupiter's upper atmosphere or the frozen surface of Callisto. But the scale involved was vast.

A more elegant, but necessarily untested, power source was the mutual destruction of matter and antimatter. Antimatter could be contained in a magnetic bottle and fed out a few particles at a time, and the result was pure $E = mc$ squared. It had never been done on a large scale because antimatter was tremendously expensive, in terms of energy, to produce: like burning down a forest to warm your hands. To manufacture enough antimatter to fuel the ship would require a solar collector the size of a planet; a synchrotron the size of the Moon.

Fortunately, the antimatter didn't have to be manufactured. It could just possibly be mined. In A.D. 2012 astronomers had discovered the tiny double star Janus, tagging along with the Sun a mere tenth of a light year away. The stars were both black dwarfs, barely hot enough to be considered stars. But one of them, Alfvén, was made of antimatter.

O'Hara belonged to a discussion group, where bright young people met one evening each week to talk over current issues with one or both Coordinators. For the past couple of weeks they had been talking about the administrative and engineering problems associated with a possible starship project. O'Hara was not fascinated by engineering, but she was intelligent enough to understand and be awed by the scope of the undertaking.

The outline was simple enough: two overlapping stages. With raw materials supplied both from Deucalion and the salvage from various wrecked Worlds, they would build two starships. S-1 was just a fuel-gathering vessel, hardly a proper starship at all. It would take a small crew out to Alfvén, to collect antimatter sufficient for the actual long voyage.

Meanwhile, S-2 would be a-building—a smaller version of New New York, large enough to support ten thousand people. It should be finished by the time S-1 came back. They'd gas up and head for Epsilon Eridani, a ninety-eight-year voyage.

The projected expense in dollars was staggering, more than ten times what it had cost to build New New. But money was only a bookkeeping convenience in New New's closed economy. The main counterargument was that the same sort of effort applied at home could rebuild the Worlds and do it right—not only a choice of utopias, dozens of different social and physical settings, but a guarantee of a safe future. The new Worlds, built without groundhog money or interference, could be built with unbreakable defenses against aggression from Earth.

This was the nagging worry partly motivating both the starship project and plans for reconstruction. Earth was a shambles now, but its industrial establishment was still there, dormant, orders of magnitude larger than New New's. If the plague ran its course, or if a cure were found, they might rebuild within a generation or so—and then what would become of the Worlds? Groundhogs were a little crazy under the best of circumstances. What would happen if they were crazy for revenge?

The Coordinators told O'Hara's group something that wasn't yet generally known: New New was having its own epidemic, one of suicide. Suicides were the leading cause of death in all adult age groups, and there were enough of them almost to counterbalance the Devonite population increase.

There were other indications of an alarming sag in New New's morale. Productivity lower than ever before; absenteeism at a record high. Drug addiction and alcoholism were growing, in spite of the difficulties involved in feeding the habits.

During her conversation with John, Daniel had quietly fallen asleep, slumped in his chair. Did one blowout a week make him an alcoholic? He was putting in twelve-

and fourteen-hour days at the lab, with Deucalion less than a year away. He was the only specialist in oil shale chemistry in New New—the only one anywhere—and was group leader for the entire applied chemistry section, always on call. Maybe he needed getting away. But she worried about him.

"Guess I'd better be taking the hero home," she said. "Okay if I sleep with him tonight?"

"Somebody's got to look out for him." John peered into the gin bottle and shook it. "Better take this along. Breakfast of champions."

"Champions?"

"Used to mean something."

2 ✦

While she was getting ready for work the next morning, O'Hara's cube beeped. She pulled a brush through her hair a couple of times and answered it.

It was the newscaster, Jules Hammond. "Marianne O'Hara?"

She just stared at his image and nodded. She had talked with him two years before, after the Zaire raid, but had never expected to see him again, outside of the nightly broadcast.

"Can you come down to the studio, Bellcom Studio One, this morning?"

"Wh—whatever for? Something about Zaire?"

He leaned forward, peering into his own cube. "That's right, you were on that." He shook his head. "Interesting. But this is something else, what we call a reaction story. Can you come down?"

"Sure...I'll, uh, call in late." Hammond nodded and rang off. She called the office and left a message for her assistant, asking him to cover a meeting for her if she didn't get away in time. Reaction story? She almost woke up Daniel, who was snoring open-mouthed, but decided not to complicate his hangover.

At the studio, an effeminate young man greeted her like an old friend, took her by the arm, and steered her into a side room. He sat her in one of two overstuffed swivel chairs facing a bank of six cubes and some complicated electronic equipment.

"Now, dear, we do want you to look pretty." He unfolded a case and took out two combs; whistled through his teeth while he worked on her hair. He stood back and surveyed his work critically, head cocked, then applied a little powder to her face and neck. "We don't want to shine." Finger under her chin. "Tilt up just a wee...that's it. Hold it. Sammy, you can calibrate now."

She felt a warm laser spot on her cheek. "I feel like I'm having an X-ray taken," she said with her mouth closed.

"Oh, we see through a lot of people here. That's fine; you can move now. Mr. *Hammond*."

The man left, slightly flouncing, and Jules Hammond came through the same door. He gave O'Hara a strange look and sat down next to her.

"We want you to listen to something." He sat and pushed a button under the arm of his chair. "Ready on Four."

One of the cubes lit up, but it was just a white block, no picture. Then there was a faint voice, metallic, crackling with static. She didn't recognize it:

"This probably can't work but it's worth a try. I checked and the antenna is pointed at New New. Found a fuel cell with a little juice and plugged it into the 'DC Emergency In' slot. It moves the power needle a little bit."

That night a quarter of a million people would see her gasp and burst into sudden tears. "This is Jeffrey Hawkings calling New New York, specifically calling Marianne O'Hara, root line Scanlan. Marianne? I hope you got home all right. For some reason I'm alive. The plague didn't touch me.

"I'm pretty sure it's my acromegaly. You know I had to take NGH every day. After the war I couldn't find any; it's a pretty rare disease.

"Well, I've met two other adults who survived the plague, and they were both acromegalic. One's an idiot who runs a tribe north of here, in Disney World. The other I just met on the road. He was mentally retarded, too; I guess neither of them got proper treatment when they were young.

"If anybody up there is interested in finding a cure for this thing, then there's your main clue. Something to do with the pituitary gland. That's what's wrong with acromegalics, they put out too much growth hormone. My own physical profile should be in your records somewhere, since I applied for immigration just before the war.

"Things are pretty grim here, Marianne, as you can imagine. I understand it's even worse up north. Not too bad for me personally—I'm in a place called Plant City, at the St. Theresa Pediatrics Hospital. I found the key to a civil defense vault here, full of medicine. I fill my saddlebags with it and pedal from town to town, playing doctor. They treat me as sort of a demigod...there's a lot of violence, a lot of ritual killing from this damned Family business, but nobody lays a finger on me. My long white beard protects me. I'm glad it grew in white."

There was a long crash of static. "—sure there isn't enough power for me to receive. But I'll keep looking for fuel cells, maybe figure out how to make one.

"I don't have any way of keeping track of the date. But I'll be back here, St. Theresa's Pediatrics Hospital in Plant City, Florida, at every full moon, about midnight, to broadcast and try to receive an answer.

"Things must be tough up there, too...if you're there at all. If the plague got carried up I guess I'm wasting my time. But I hope, Marianne, you made it okay and got to marry Daniel. It seems like another life, a lifetime ago, when you were—" Static took over and when it quieted there was no more transmission.

Charlie's Will ✦

He turned off the radio transmitter and stared at his large hands. Maybe he shouldn't have said midnight. That meant either traveling at night or holing up in this hospital for hours. The place was a boneyard. But he remembered his police radio used to receive best at night. He picked up his full saddlebags and his scattergun and followed a large cockroach down the hospital corridor to the fire stairs. Funny how you changed. One time, he would have chased the cockroach down and crushed it. Today he was obscurely glad that something else in the hospital was alive. Maybe it was affecting his brain, the growth hormone. It was affecting his hands and feet and other joints, aching like arthritis. He would treat himself to more aspirin, first stop.

On the ground floor he retrieved his wagon from its closet hiding place and put the saddlebags on top of the canvas bag that held his various possessions. He rolled the wagon out and wired it to the back fender of his bicycle, unlocked the bicycle and pedaled away, in search of customers.

The town was pretty well deserted, as all towns were once the shelves had been emptied. There was usually someone to trade with, some group of scavengers willing to dig deeper than the last group. But the house he'd stopped at a month earlier was deserted now. He pedaled on for an hour, quartering the downtown area, and had just about decided to break into his emergency rations when he finally heard voices. He turned down an alley and saw a group of little girls playing a complicated hopping game. They were singing badly:

Mary was a virgin but she had a baby boy.
Jesus died upon the cross to give us peace and joy.
Charlie had a vision but they put him out of sight.
Helter-Skelter saved us from a hundred years of night.
Death is the Redeemer; only death can make you
    well—

They stopped singing when they heard him rattling up the alleyway. One ran away but the other four stood and stared at him.

"I need food and water. Where is your family?" One girl, then all of them, pointed in the direction the other was running. He walked his bike slowly after her, scattergun pointed forward. The girls resumed their game, finished the rhyme:

Life on Earth is nothing more than twenty years of
    hell.

She ran through an open door, yelling for her daddy. He leaned on his bike and waited, gun casually aimed at the door.

A rifle barrel pointed at him from a dark window. "Whaddayawant?"

"I'm Healer."

"We heard about you."

"So I want to trade. Is there anybody in your family needs healing?"

"A woman. What you need?"

"A fully charged fuel cell."

"No got."

"Food and water, then."

"We got some of that. You come in but leave the gun outside."

"Piss on that. She goes where I go." And the two concealed pistols and the boot knife and the spraystick.

There was some muted conversation inside. "All right. But you know we got you covered all the time."

"Yeah, yeah." He locked the bike and gathered the saddlebags and the canvas bag in his left arm. On the way to the door he passed a garbage pile. On top of the pile was a teen-aged girl only a few hours dead, head crushed and body covered with purple bruises. He thought she had been disemboweled but saw that it was a placenta, partially expelled, and what was left of an infant.

"Monster birth?" he said, passing through the door.

"No eyes," said the man with the rifle.

"Should have let the woman live."

"It was her second. Family rules. The first was twins with just one head between them."

He stood just inside, getting used to the dim light. "How long have you had this rule?"

"It's a rule. It's sign-tific."

"Sure it is. What about the father?"

He shrugged. "That's all of us. We just take turns."

"Sounds scientific. Where's the sick woman?"

They led him into a dark bedroom. It stank. He could barely make out a small form on the double bed, twitching and moaning incoherently. He went to the window and slid the knob to unpolarize it, flooding the room with sunlight. The girl cried out.

"The light hurts her eyes," the leader said. The girl was twelve or thirteen, breasts juvenile. She was about six months pregnant. All she wore was a pair of filthy bandages wrapped around her upper thighs.

"Boil some water."

"You want some coffee?"

"For washing. Boil a big pot." The girl was flushed, her skin hot and dry. She had four degrees of fever. He gave her some children's aspirin dissolved in water. The leader came back, with most of the others crowding around the door.

They had to hold her down while he cut away the bandages. She was a mess. "How long has she been sick?"

"She got a rash last week. It's only been bad for couple of days." He'd never seen anything quite like it. On the inside of both thighs, from the crotch down about fifteen centimeters, was a growth of gray fungus. The flesh under the fungus was angry red and discharging pus. There were three prominent syphilis chancres on the lips of her vagina, which was probably associated, since the fungus was spreading up over the pubic mound.

"She gonna die?"

"Charlie knows when," Healer said with only a little sarcasm.

"Charlie's will," the others muttered in ragged chorus.

He poured hydrogen peroxide on the infected areas and they foamed impressively. He rinsed with water from his canteen and applied the peroxide again, then rinsed again and patted the mess dry with a clean gauze pad. He turned her over and shot her full of wide-spectrum antibiotics.

"Here is what you do. Take this filthy sheet and burn it. Keep something clean under her. Don't bandage it; let it breathe. Make her drink a lot of water. Anybody who touches her wash up afterwards with hot water and soap. Can you remember that?"

The leader nodded. "If she *does* die, you bury her. Or at least take the body far away. Don't just chuck it out the door like that other one—and bury it too. You can get real sick, having dead people around."

"We was going to. Two guys're still out hunting, they gotta get their throws in. For luck."

"Yeah, luck. I suppose all of you have syphilis, don't you?" They looked at him blankly. He pointed to the chancres. "Sores like this."

"'Course we get them, all the grownups," the leader said.

"Except for Jimmy," a girl said, and giggled. "He's got hair but all he does is pull himself."

"Jimmy's scared to fight me," the leader said proudly. "You don't fight, you don't fuck. That's sign-tific. Natural selection."

"Where did you get all this 'scientific' shit?"

"Old Tony taught us. He lived to be twenty-one, he could read really good."

He tugged on his white beard. "You listen to me. I'm older than Tony ever was, and I've been reading since before any of you were born. Now, you've had children born blind, haven't you."

"Two or three," the leader admitted.

"How do you suppose I knew that?"

"You're pretty old."

"That's what happens when people have syphilis. They have babies born blind and stupid. It's a *disease*. You don't have to get it."

"Sure," the giggling girl said, "like you don't have to get babies. Just don't fuck." The others giggled along with her.

"This is serious business. If you don't get this syphilis cured, you'll all go crazy before your time." He looked at the leader. "You won't be able to get it up any more. It'll hurt too much."

He was pale under the grime. "What do we have to do?"

"I'll give you each a shot. Then I'll leave a bottle of pills. Everybody takes one each morning; you watch and make sure they do. And no fucking for ten days."

"Ten *days*! You can't go ten days."

"You can and will. Absolutely no sexual contact; not even boy-boy girl-girl. I want you to swear on Christ and Charlie."

They all looked at the leader. He hesitated, then made

the sign of the cross and muttered "Charlie's will." The others did the same.

"Okay, call in the children. Then everybody line up in the living room and drop your pants." He screwed a bottle of omnimycin into the hypodermic gun.

"We don't do it to the children," the leader said.

"Glad to hear it. But they can pick it up other ways, living with you." He wasn't sure that was true, but then neither could he be sure they actually did leave the younger children alone. That would make them an unusual family.

Waiting for the two hunters to come home, he treated various minor complaints. For most of them, he gave aspirin or an innocuous salve. His police training, many years before, had included a few days of emergency first aid—mostly what to do if you or your partner were shot. He did know how to assist childbirth, which often came in handy now. But everything else he'd had to learn from medical texts and the little brochures that came packed with medicine.

Medical books were rare. Before the war, a doctor could sit at a cube and punch up any text in existence, usually with three-dimensional illustrations of typical cases and techniques. Most of the books he'd found were heirlooms, their medicine a century or more out of date. The drugs prescribed no longer existed under the same brand names, since the books were written before all the manufacturers had merged into a single Pharmaceuticals Lobby.

He had no idea, for instance, what the girl's fungus was. Would it start cropping up everywhere? Was it actually dangerous, or had it been just the dirty bandages that caused the infection and fever? Maybe he'd find a dermatology text.

The hunters came home triumphant, with a full case of freeze-dried beef stew. Healer took two boxes of it, a gallon of rainwater, and a bottle of old wine. He gave the hunters their shots and left. As he pedaled away he could hear wild laughter and the dull smack of rocks hitting dead flesh.

Nothing could shock him any more, he thought; nothing could be revolting enough to get through the shell that contained his sanity. If you could call it sanity. In the country of the blind, the one-eyed man is weird. The people now dying of the plague had barely been teen-agers when the war came. Their memories of the old days are distorted and vague. In another ten years there will be nothing but rumor and speculation. The old order changeth, he remembered from a poem; making place for new; and God fulfills himself in many ways.

Year Five

1 ✦

At first Deucalion was a star, and then a bright star, moving slowly through the heavens. Soon it was definitely a shape, not a point, growing daily, and the observation dome in the hub of New New was often crowded.

It came to rest about twenty kilometers away. From that distance it looked like a small elongated potato, but with craters. The factories had been waiting in place for months, tiny bright toys attached to outsized solar collectors.

Now it was John Ogelby's turn for overwork. He spent two months out at the factories, helping to supervise the interfacing of machine with rock. There was no way a spacesuit could fit his twisted body, so he worked from inside a modified emergency bubble, floating here and there, and using other people for hands. He loved zero-gee work—the mobility and freedom from pain. But he did miss Marianne, and they spent many hours chatting, sometimes about inconsequential things, often about the suddenly complicated futures in store for them.

It seemed as if everything had happened at once. Scientists working with Insila had isolated the plague virus and synthesized a cure. After much argument, a very close referendum approved the manufacture of large quantities of the antibiotic, which would be sent to Earth by robot drones.

The starship question was finally resolved by a series of carefully worded referenda. The available work force (only a third of the population was really needed to run New New) would be split into two roughly equal groups. The stay-at-homes would work on refurbishing Devon's World and Tsiolkovski, which together would eventually provide enough room for another 150,000 people.

The rest of them would be working on the starship, which would bear the name *Newhome*. Salvage teams were at work on the remains of Mazeltov and B'is'ma'masha'la, mining them for useful parts. The army of engineers no longer needed for Deucalion dove into the "Janus Project" with enthusiasm.

Daniel wanted to go, and so did John. O'Hara was not sure. The idea did excite her, as an abstraction, but the actual details of it boiled down to sitting in a spaceship playing gin rummy and waiting to die of old age. She would also probably have to raise a child. Her experience with her baby sister, now five, seemed to indicate that she had no great talent in that direction.

If she stayed in New New she would doubtless continue to advance. Having attained Grade 15 in only five years of service made her something of a prodigy, and although she was realistic about the influence of her continuing friendship with Sandra Berrigan, she didn't doubt that she would have advanced on her own. She had access to her own psych profile and the analysis of it made by the Executive Evaluation Board.

The people who had set up New New's charter, more than a century before, had done their best to ensure that the World's administrative structure stay free of the taint of politics. Nobody got "on the track"—advancing beyond Grade 12—without minute investigation of his or her past and exhaustive psychological testing. They looked for a balance of altruism with practicality; leadership ability without emotional dependence on having power over others; patience and deliberation. Nobody could insert himself into the power structure by dint of personal charisma, bribery, or influence. So New New's history was rather dull, its leaders a succession of careful, phlegmatic people who usually retired with a great sense of relief. The Executive Evaluation Board was anonymous, but it was no secret that it consisted of a staff of professional psychologists overseen by past Coordinators and retired Justices. They had looked at Marianne and given their tentative blessing; now that she had reached Grade 15 she was subject to annual review, because power corrupts in subtle ways. A negative evaluation could mean anything from a temporary freeze in grade to demotion back to Grade 12, with no chance of appeal.

One reason this system had worked in the old days was the safety valve of emigration. There had been forty other Worlds then, with many different political setups, and a mutual pact required any World to accept an emigrant from any other World, so long as they had room. (They might put him in sewage maintenance and make sure he stayed there, but they did have to accept him.) Without that safety valve, and with guaranteed freedom of speech, New New was getting to be a rather noisy place. People who liked the old days were anxious to get a few new Worlds open for business. Many of them were also in favor of the Janus project, figuring that it would absorb a lot of the rowdier element.

Daniel and John, perhaps independently, both presented O'Hara with a "big fish in a small pond" argument. The social structure of Janus would parallel New New's, with Engineering and Policy Coordinators at the top of two separate tracks, but with less than a tenth of New New's population to draw from. So she would be much more likely to make it to the top.

She didn't doubt this was true, but was not sure that

it was an attractive proposition. The motivation that drove her ambition was to her complicated and obscure. The Board's analysis was that it stemmed from a need to be admired, rooted in the rejection she had received from her Scanlan playmates and the lack of appreciation her mother and stepfather had shown for her academic achievement. To O'Hara that explanation sounded facile and incomplete. It ignored the abstract pleasure she took in problem-solving, which she thought was the main driving force behind her desire to advance: the higher you got, the more important and complex the problems were, and the more satisfaction in their solution. That also made her hesitate to accept her husbands' argument. Janus would be a World, but it was primarily a spaceship. The Engineering Coordinator would be the captain; the highest she could aspire to would be chief stewardess.

And there was Earth, too. Once the plague was under control, there would be a need for administrators who had experience with Earth—though how relevant her experience would be in dealing with the strange world Jeff described, she couldn't say.

Every month she went down to the Bellcom studios and listened to him, hoping that he would have found a new power source, so they could have a two-way conversation. (Intact fuel cells were rare because the most common variety contained a small silver bar inside; for a while after the war those bars were used as currency.) But his signal grew progressively weaker, and during the past two full moons there had been no transmission at all. The technicians said it was likely that was because the power he could generate had fallen below their antenna's threshold of sensitivity. She hoped they were right.

In the course of seven communications Jeff had given them a vivid picture of the brutal world that was Charlie's

Country. Heavily armed bands of children and teen-agers, "families," either settled on farms or roamed from city to ruined city, looting. They sometimes traded with one another and sometimes fought desperate battles for each other's supplies. Girls were impregnated soon after menarche, and would keep on having babies until they died, usually around eighteen or nineteen. Many of the babies were born dead or were grotesque mutations. Most of the families destroyed the mutations, but some kept them around as pets.

They had two holy books, the Christian bible and a booklet called *Charlie's Will*. Jeff thought that *Charlie's Will* must originally have been a heavy-handed satire against religion; now it was taken literally. A version printed about a year after the war contained an explanation for the plague—it was God's reaction to the sin of contraception. Living a sensible twenty years or less, people had to make a lot of babies. It explained the war itself as punishment for mankind's assault of the heavens. Thus the Worlds were responsible for all misery, both in historical "fact" and by theological fiat. Jeff had stopped trying to convince people otherwise; heresy could be very dangerous.

The insanity of daily life was compounded by reliance on oracles. For a week or two before a person died of the plague, his brain was infected and he raved, rambling nonsense. They thought it was disguised advice from God or His avatar, Charlie.

Jeff knew about Deucalion; he had watched it move across the sky and merge with the bright star that was New New. He said he hoped that was proof they had survived, since he was under the impression that the asteroid wasn't due for another twenty years or so, and he assumed they had done something to speed it up. Other people had seen it too—some families used a simpleminded kind of astrology, watching the sky for omens—and their interpretations of it were interesting. God had finally destroyed the World, or Charlie's spirit had moved into it, or aliens from outer space had taken it over and were going to invade Earth.

2 ✦

John was weaker than ever, coming back from two months of zerogee. When their schedules matched, O'Hara walked with him in the low-gravity sections, trying not to lope as he shuffled painfully along.

"So how's the promotion working out?" Ogelby looked up at her sideways.

"Too early to tell." She took two long steps, then caught herself and waited. "Actually, it's a pain. I wish they'd let me stay in Resources Allocation. Everybody under me knows my job better than I do."

"Take it from an old hand. It's time to be very careful." Ogelby was Grade 20, the highest.

"Oh, I know that. They're testing me... my profile said 'the subject's main weakness is an unwillingness to delegate authority.' So they put me in a position where I can't do anything *else*." She'd been shuffled up and sideways to become Director of Statistics in the Public Health Division. "I hadn't even thought about statistics since I was sixteen. And that was just a basic, you know—'if you have six black balls and four white balls—'"

"You're a male basketball team. Mixed—"

"Spare me." They stopped at a picture window that overlooked the curved expanse of parkland below them. "How soon do you think you'll be ready for one gee?"

"God. I don't even want to think about it." He put his back to the view, looping both arms through the railing, to take some weight off his feet. "That's what you've been studying, nights? Statistics?"

"Trying to get through a text. But I'm having to relearn

calculus to do the proofs. It's demoralizing, how fast you forget things."

"If you need help..."

"No, thanks. I went through that with Dan. This stuff comes too naturally to you guys. When Dan tries to explain something I wind up knowing less than when I started."

He nodded. "I'm no teacher, either."

"Besides, I'm just doing it as a gesture. All this chi-square, standard deviation...all we really do is get numbers from Vital Statistics and put them down in various columns. How many workdays lost to colds last September? Shall we serve more chicken soup this September? I'm sure it would all be very fascinating to somebody else. I'll stick with it for a year, until after the next Board review. If they give me a good evaluation I guess I can assume I've passed their little test. Then I can look around and ask for a transfer."

"Want me to get you a transfer?"

"Into Engineering track?" She laughed. "No thanks."

"It would be Policy track, assigned to Engineering. At your grade or a step higher."

"No, it would look too fishy. With you a twenty and Dan an eighteen, and my being friends with Sandra, I don't dare go near Engineering. The Board would see strings being pulled and freeze me forever."

"It would be a computer selection. No personal recommendations at all."

"With my husband programming the computer."

"Not directly. Don't you even want to know what the job is?"

"Go ahead."

"We're forming a start-up team for Operation Janus—"

"Still trying to get me aboard that goddamned starship."

"Now listen. We do legitimately need a few people from the Policy side. Especially people with broad academic backgrounds. This is nothing less than setting up a whole new World from scratch. Social system, population distribution as to age, genetic background, professional specialty, and so forth. It would be a hell of a lot more interesting than chicken soup."

She sighed and patted his hand, not looking at him. "It sure would. But I just can't take the chance."

"Why don't you at least ask Berrigan's opinion? She could tell you how the Board would feel. She does know half of them."

"It's the other half I'm worried about, the psychologist types. They can be pretty arbitrary. The senior administrators tend to make allowances, I guess out of empathy."

"Psychologists don't have empathy?"

She laughed. "Okay. I'm going swimming with Sandra tonight. I'll see what she says."

"It would be fun to work together."

"All three of us?"

"Eventually, I hope." He shook his head. "We have to get Dan out of that pressure cooker. The original reason for making him head of the Applied section no longer exists; all the problems with tar and resin decomposition have been resolved. God knows there are enough people hungry for the job."

"More politics."

"Maybe. I suppose the people over Dan are just as happy to have a section leader with no ambition to move higher. And he is good at it."

She took him by the arm. "Let's get you good at walking."

Charlie's Will ✦

Jeff Hawkings pedaled cautiously toward the burned-out service station. In front of the station a boy sat behind a table, cases of beer stacked beside him. The boy's scattergun tracked Jeff as he approached.

"You Healer?" the boy said.

"That's right. Anybody in your family sick?"

"Nah. Just one with the death."

"Charlie's Will," Jeff said, and sketched a small cross with his thumb on the center of his chest. "How much for the beer?"

"Let you have a case for a scattergun refill." He pointed at the weapon that dangled on a web loop from Jeff's shoulder.

"Just have the one cassette," Jeff lied, "and it's not full."

"Have any silver?"

"Huh-uh. I have some loose rounds, gunpowder, .22 and .45 caliber."

"We got a .45. Let you have a beer for two rounds."

Jeff fished through a leather bag on his belt. "Two beers for one round." He tossed the heavy cartridge on the table.

"One for one." The boy slid a beer across.

Jeff shrugged, pinched it open and took a cautious sip; the stuff hadn't been manufactured with a five-year shelf life in mind. It tasted a little stale but not spoiled. He drank it down quickly, and then bought another, and slipped it into his saddlebag. "Know of anybody nearby needs healing?"

"Family 'bout fifteen minutes down the road. Somebody always sick there. They keep their muties. On the left there's a sign, says something something farm."

"Thanks." Jeff mounted the bicycle and started away.

"Hey!" He felt the familiar itch in the middle of his back, stopped, and looked back.

"They got a sentry 'bout halfway down the road to the farm. You don't want to go in there after dark."

"Thanks, I'll move it." It was late afternoon, the sun reddening.

About two kilometers along, he came to a sand road

beside a faded sign that read "Forest-in-Need Farm." The bicycle slithered too much in the sugar sand, so he got off and pushed it along. He shouted "hello" a couple of times a minute. There was thick underbrush on both sides of the road, thick enough to hide a man. Tall Australian pines sighed in the slight breeze.

"Hold it right there," a deep voice said from behind him. "Put up your hands." Jeff did, leaning the bicycle against his hip.

He heard someone crashing through the brush and then a soft tread on sand. "You're that old goof, the doctor."

"Healer."

"Whatever. You can put down your hands." The man's appearance was startling; he was full-grown and old enough to have a bush of blond beard. He was holding a modern Uzi flechette gun, the first one Jeff had seen in years. Jeff noted that the safety was off, so he moved very slowly. Two hundred darts per second. In training they'd called them meatgrinders.

"You come at the right time. We have some sick people." He twisted his ring and spoke into it. "That Healer goof's comin' up. He's okay."

"You have electricity?"

"Little bit. Big house around the second bend, somebody'll let you through the gate."

The forest ended abruptly in another hundred meters. Large pasture had gone thoroughly to weed. Around two bends there was a tall barbed-wire fence which claimed to be electrified; behind it were acres of lush vegetable garden and pens with chickens and pigs. A modern two-story house with solar collectors on the roof. Sandbag bunkers, fighting positions, were spaced around the house. A girl of thirteen or fourteen was standing silently, holding the gate open. She was naked, cradling a baby that chewed at her small breast.

She closed the gate behind him and locked it. "My baby's sick. Maybe you can help it?"

The infant had a large growth on its neck. She held it out to him, and he saw that the growth was actually a half-formed second head. No eyes or nose but a perfect petal mouth. The baby was hermaphroditic, small male genitals riding too high over a female slit.

"It throws up all the time," she said. "Sometimes it shits blood. Usually."

"You can't tell with muties. It might be missing something inside. Let's take it up to the house and I'll look at it."

The house was built of concrete blocks, windows equipped with roll-down steel shutters. The door was a slab of foamsteel, ten centimeters thick. "Somebody built this to last," Jeff said.

"It was Tad's parents. Tad you met down on the road." It was cool inside, air conditioned. The girl wrapped the baby up in a blanket and put on a robe. "They knew there was going to be a war."

"How old is Tad?"

"He's twenty, he'll get the death pretty soon. Marsha's gonna take over then, she's his sister. The rest of us just came, mostly the first year or two."

The living room was elegant and spare and clean. Neo-Japanese, with mats and low tables. She set the baby on a table and Jeff squatted cross-legged by it. He sterilized a probe and took its temperature. He looked at the readout and shook his head.

"Does it cry a lot?"

"The regular head does, sometimes. The other head does nothing, don't even suck."

"I don't think it's going to live very long." He felt its forehead, hot and dry. "That much fever would kill a grownup. Its brains are cooking."

"It hasn't cried since day before yesterday, doesn't move much either. Can you do anything?"

"I can try. Be surprised if it's alive tomorrow."

"Charlie's will," she muttered. Jeff crossed himself

and got the hypo gun out of his saddlebag. He swabbed the nozzle of it and a place on the mutant's arm. After a moment's hesitation, he screwed a bottle of plain saline solution into the gun. No use in wasting antibiotics.

She wiped a tear across her cheek. "My first baby."

"Well, you have lots more in you. Might pick a different father...do you know who the father was?"

She shook her head. "One of the guys."

"Are there any other muties?"

"Four others. Five if you count Jommy, but he's just got extra fingers. Then there was some born dead. One was born kind of inside-out, but he lived long enough to be christianed."

"How many normal ones?"

"Eight, counting Jommy."

"And how many women, I mean old enough to be mothers?"

"I'm the fourth. Then Sharon, she's sixteen, she bleeds but don't catch. She gets it two or three times a day but she don't catch."

"Does she bleed regularly?"

"Nah. She never can tell."

"Then I might be able to help her, next time I come by." He took out his pad and made a note. There were crates of birth control pills back at Plant City, but he didn't bother to carry any. Maybe they could straighten out her cycle and make her more fertile. "Any other sick people?"

"Two upstairs, really sick. I'll show you." She picked up the baby and was all the way across the room before Jeff could make his joints stand up. "You hurt?"

"Just don't move so well. Part of being old."

She nodded soberly. "Charlie must hate you."

He followed her up a broad staircase and into a bedroom. "I'm the only one comes in here," she said. "Tad don't want it to spread, whatever it is."

In separate beds, two boys: emaciated, pale, beaded with sweat. One was asleep; the other was moaning and twitching. The sleeping one had crops of tiny pink spots on his chest.

"Let me see your tongue," Jeff said to the one who was awake. When he didn't respond, Jeff clamped his chin and forced his mouth open. The tongue was brown and dry.

"They been to Tampa recently?"

"Yeah, about a month ago, Tad sent 'em down to get some hose. How come you know that?"

"There's an epidemic down there. You know what an epidemic is?"

She shook her head. "That little thing in your belly?"

"No, it's a disease that spreads all around, gets out of control. In Tampa they've got an epidemic of typhoid fever. These guys picked it up there."

"Are they gonna die?"

"Probably not. I've got medicine for it. What do you do with their shit?"

"What?"

"You carry out the shit, don't you? Where does it go?"

"Oh, we got a compost machine out back."

"Does it burn it?"

"No, it's, uh, ultra something. Tad knows."

"Good." He rummaged through his saddlebags and found the chloramphenicol and cortisone. "How have you been feeling? Have you been sick?"

She looked at the floor. "Huh-uh. Just tired all the time. Maybe I got the runs."

"Nosebleed?"

"Little bit."

"Sounds like you've got it. Probably that's what's wrong with the baby, too." He studied the chloramphenicol label and set the hypo gun for three-quarters of an adult dosage. "That's how the disease spreads. In Tampa they just shit anywhere. Flies get on the shit and then on the food."

"They're real animals down there," she said.

"Sure are." He gave shots to both of the boys. "That's how you got it, being in too close contact."

"I'm real careful," she said in a hurt voice.

"Doesn't take much. Turn around and lift up your robe." She twitched at the cold alcohol. Jeff scrubbed her buttock a little longer than was necessary. Except for her feet, she was very clean, which had more of an effect on him than her boyish figure. Five years of filthy children, his sex life limited to mental pictures of Marianne and a handful of surgical lubricant. He swallowed saliva and told himself this girl was young enough to be his daughter. But he had to use both hands to keep the hypo gun steady.

"The baby now." He set it on minimum dosage, scrubbed, and shot.

She pointed at his obvious erection and giggled. "You want me to fix that?"

He paused. "What would Tad say?"

"I wouldn't tell him nothing."

Jeff knew a little about child psychology and a lot about gunshot wounds. "Let's wait. I'll talk it over with Tad first."

"He won't let you. No one outside the family. Besides, if I got a baby it might get old like you."

"There are ways not to catch."

"Sure, front-to-back and front-to-top. Tad says Charlie says they're sinful." She laughed. "I did them both when I was pregnant, though, even with Tad. It was fun."

Jeff closed his eyes and slowly let out the breath he'd been holding. Anal intercourse with a typhoid carrier. That wasn't covered in the text he'd read. Well, he could always take a booster shot.

"Let's go downstairs." There were voices.

Tad was sitting at a table, giving dinner instructions to a couple of children. He motioned Jeff over and told one of the children to bring in a bottle of wine. "Could you do anything for them?"

Jeff sat down and told him about the typhoid epidemic. "I have enough vaccine to immunize everyone in the family. The girl with the two-headed baby, I think she already has it. The boy, too. I gave them all shots and they should get another in the morning. Then I'll leave some pills."

A girl brought in a bottle of pale wine and two glasses, actual stemware. Tad pulled the cork and poured. It tasted like harsh port with a musty aftertaste, like rotten oranges, but was drinkable.

"What can we give you in exchange? We have lots of food."

"No, I've got all I can carry from the last family. What I really need is a charged fuel cell. You must have some."

He frowned. "We don't have any to spare. Seven on line and two backups."

"I'd bring it back in a week or so."

"I don't know. Anybody knew you had it, they'd kill you for the silver." He stared into the wine, swirling it. "What do you want with one, anyhow?"

"There's a powerful radio back at the hospital where I keep my medicine. I want to see if I can raise anybody."

Tad pulled on his beard. "Maybe...you leave the scattergun here, though. You have another weapon?"

Jeff nodded. "Pistol. But nobody ever bothers me."

"That's what I hear. How come you didn't die, do you know?"

"Charlie's will."

Tad shook his head slightly and lowered his voice. "You don't really believe in that." He looked at the holo pictures over the fireplace: a beatific Manson, a bloody Christ, and three smaller pictures, two women and a man who resembled Manson in hair and beard. "My father and mothers were Family when I was growing up. I thought it was the craps and still do. The timing of the war was just coincidence. Charlie Manson was just a crazy goof. I don't know about Jesus."

"Does the rest of your family feel the same?"

"No. Or if they do, they keep it to themselves." When Jeff didn't say anything, he went on. "I've heard of a few other old people, and I even saw one once, Big Mickey over in Disney World. He was big like you, but crazy. All of the old ones are supposed to be big and crazy. How come you're different? Tell me and I'll let you use the fuel cell."

"I can tell you what I think, but it won't save you from the death."

"Go ahead."

"It's an accident of birth. I'm a kind of mutie, like the other old people. It's called acromegaly; something goes wrong with your glands and you keep growing after normal people stop. It usually affects your mind, but it started late in my case, and I had medicine."

"So how does that keep you from the death?"

"All I know is that it does. I've traveled around a lot since the war, and never met or heard of anybody over twenty-some who didn't have acromegaly."

"Okay." He looked thoughtful, took a sip of wine. "Now is there some way I can catch the acromegaly from you? Like a blood transfusion?"

"No, you have to be born with it. There's a hormone involved, growth hormone, that might work, but I've never found any in hospitals and I wouldn't know how to make it. I'm not a scientist; I'm not even a doctor. With the radio, maybe I can find something out."

Tad looked at the door to the kitchen. "Go away, Mark. This is grownup talk." A young boy was in the doorway, standing on his hands. His hands were like flesh spatulas, no fingers. Instead of legs he had a single limb rising into the air, ending in a flipper. He had a harelip and eyes that were too small and too close together in his egg-shaped head. He mewed something, turned around and padded out.

"Never know how much he understands," Tad said. "Have you ever seen one like him?"

"Not quite. Most muties do have more than one thing wrong with them, but he's a regular catalog: harelip, srenomelus, microphthalmia, acrocephalosyndactyly. God knows what else inside. It's a wonder he survived."

"Eats like a pig. If you're not a doctor, how come you know all those names?"

"Found a book on monsters, not that it does any good. The few things that can be fixed, they take surgery. I can stitch up a wound, but that's about it."

"Do you think we ought to let them live? Most families don't, I guess."

"Hmm." Jeff drank off his wine and refilled both glasses. "I wouldn't say this to most people—and you're not hearing it, right?" Tad nodded. "We should let the muties grow up and mate. Sooner or later a gene might come along that carries immunity to the death, maybe like acromegaly but without the bad side effects."

"What do you think the death is? Other than Charlie's blessing."

"It's either some kind of biological warfare agent or a common disease that underwent mutation. It might die out or it might last forever. I don't even know how widespread it is, which is another reason for getting the radio working."

"They've got it in Georgia, we know that. Met a guy from Atlanta."

Jeff nodded. "It's probably all over. At least all over the East Coast. You'd expect that Florida would have quite a few immigrants, after a winter or two."

"Maybe they stick to the Atlantic side."

"It's pretty well bombed up. I started there, but came inland, looking for farms."

For a while they sat and traded information about the various places they'd been. Then a little girl, apparently normal, came in and shyly said that dinner was ready.

They ate at two trench tables, one for the adults and one for the children. The food was delicious, chicken stewed with fresh vegetables, but the dinner companions at the other table were not too appetizing. Two had to be fed: one because of phocomelus, seal-like flippers instead of arms; one who was microcephalic and totally passive. One who ate quite normally was a girl with beautiful golden curls and a single median eye. The girl with the two-headed baby took a bowl out to Marsha, Tad's sister, who was guarding the road.

All through dinner, Tad quizzed the "grownups"— the oldest might have been seventeen—about animal husbandry and plant propagation. His parents had accumulated a large library of books on farming and other aspects of survival, but as he'd told Jeff, most of the grownups didn't read too well, and didn't much want to learn.

After dinner Jeff vaccinated them, and then found out why they were so clean. On the porch beyond the kitchen, they had a shower room and a family-sized tub. They scrubbed down with soap that smelled slightly of bacon, then rinsed, and the adults slipped into the deliciously hot water while the children played.

"We fill the tank on the roof every morning," Tad said, pointing to a pump contraption like a bicycle without wheels. "It takes a half-hour of pedaling but it's worth it. This time of year we wait till noon, or it gets so hot you can hardly stand it."

Marsha came in and Jeff watched with languid appreciation as she showered. Not beautiful, but she was adult, a rare sight. Solid with muscle, no baby fat, stretch marks from several pregnancies.

She stepped in next to Jeff and put her arm around him, and began talking to Tad. After a while they got out of the bath, letting the children have their turn. Jeff and Marsha dried each other off. Without a spoken word, they gathered up their clothes and weapons and led each other upstairs.

The first time, predictably, was over before it started, but Jeff had good powers of recuperation, and five years of catching up to do. Eventually they did talk.

"I bet you're like Tad," she said, playing with his beard. "You don't believe."

"I grew up in Taoism," Jeff said cautiously, "American Taoism. A much more gentle way of looking at things."

"Oh, Charlie's way is gentle." She stretched her body against his side and lay an arm partway across his broad chest. "Men have a hard time understanding, I think. Women are closer to life, so they aren't so afraid of death."

"That doesn't make any sense to me."

"'Course not. You're a man."

"Charlie was a man."

"So was Jesus. But they were strange men."

Jeff smiled in the dark. "At least we can agree on—" He was on the floor and rolling toward his weapons before his brain quite registered what he had heard: through the open window, the unmistakable *raow* sound of an Uzi meatgrinder, scream, manic submachinegun chatter, the Uzi twice more, a fusillade of rifle and pistol fire, and then silence. Then a solitary pop, one shot from a small-caliber pistol.

From the other side of the room, greased-metal sounds of Marsha putting a cassette in her rifle and cocking it. "Guess they got Larry. Charlie's will."

Jeff automatically reached up to cross himself and then checked it. Calf holster in place, he stepped into his pants. He shrugged into the shoulder holster but didn't bother with a shirt. He found his boots and knife and scattergun and followed her down the stairs. A gong was ringing.

They were the first ones behind the sandbags. He scanned the road and the overgrown pasture, pretty well lit by the moon. Three days till full; in three days he might be talking to Marianne. That was worth fighting for. "You ought to keep the weeds clear around the perimeter," he said. "You could have a hundred people crawl up and you wouldn't see one of them until they started climbing the fence."

"Then we just watch them fry." Her voice was calm and happy. His own voice was tight and hoarse. His heart pounded adrenaline, his knees trembled. Palms wet and sphincters twitching. He sat down and put on his boots. If he had to run, how could he get by an electric fence? Steel shutters rattled down over the windows.

"Ever fight before?" she asked.

"Couple of times. And I used to be a cop in New York City."

"You sound nervous."

"Out of practice. Does this happen often?"

"Every month or so. But it's usually dark, shouldn't be no problem."

He set both pistols on top of the sandbags and tried to get into a comfortable position, sighting down the scattergun. "You really aren't afraid to die."

"No...I'd rather wait for the death, but if Charlie wants me early, that's His will."

Tad got into place behind the bunker next to them. He had a heavy rifle with a fat starlight scope. He switched on the scope and looked around. "Nothing yet," he said conversationally. "Everybody in place?" Somebody to the far left said "one," and the count went all around the house, ending with eight. "Healer, don't use that scattergun on the one with our Uzi, or anyone with an automatic weapon. We can't afford to damage them." The scattergun fired bursts of tiny metal splinters, propelled by compressed-nitrogen blasts. It was a good close-range weapon but it did make an awful mess of anything it hit.

"We'll go for Plan Two. Jommy, go turn off the fence and don't turn it on until you hear me or Mom shout. Everybody else get down behind the bunkers and don't fire till I tell you." To Jeff he explained, "I'll pick off one or two with the starlight scope, and then we'll just let them waste ammunition for a while." He peered through the scope, aiming the rifle in a slow arc from east to west and back again. "If they come at all. They might just take the Uzi and go."

"Don't even think that," Marsha said. She sat relaxed against the sandbags, her skin still glistening from sex.

"It would be a good prize."

"They'll try," she said confidently. "There's plenty of them."

"Sounded like," Tad said. "Damn, I wish Larry hadn't opened up on them."

"Plan One always works," Marsha said. "The road sentry lets 'em go by and warns us. Then he follows 'em up and hides in a bunker over to the west there, at the tree line. When the shooting starts we've got 'em in a crossfire."

"Most of 'em get it from the Uzi," Tad said. "*Damn* that Larry."

There was a sound like a rock hitting the ground, not far away, and then a bright flash and simultaneous blast. Bright particles spewed all around them. Tad had ducked behind the sandbags; now he popped back up and squeezed off five or six rounds, muffled taps behind a silencer.

"Got one." He crouched down again, and they waited. No return fire; no sound at all.

"Healer," Tad said, "give them a couple of bursts. See if we can get them started." Jeff cautiously peeked around the sandbags. He heard a faint command, and suddenly thirty or forty people rose up out of the weeds and began moving toward them, silently and quickly. He fired two quick blasts in their general direction and rolled back. "Here they come," he said. Still no return fire.

"They've got ladders," Marsha said, peering over the top. "This is gonna be target practice."

"Hold your fire until they have the ladders in place," Tad said.

The Uzi howled at them in a long burst, raking all of

the bunkers in front of the house. The sandbags above Jeff and Marsha tore open, spraying dirt. Tad said "Aw, shit," rather calmly, and fell down, holding his face.

Jeff dashed over to him and saw that a flechette had ripped open the man's cheek. A ragged flap of torn flesh dangled over his beard, exposing back teeth shiny with blood in the moonlight.

"Here." Jeff held the flap in place and guided Tad's left hand up to it. "Hold it tight until this is over. Then I'll stitch it up." He wasn't really sure he could.

"Okay," Tad said through clenched teeth. "Switch weapons. Can't shoot the rifle one-handed."

Jeff handed him the scattergun and hefted the unfamiliar rifle. "That's got eight, maybe ten bursts left. Any more ammo for this thing?"

"In the stock. Tell Marsha to get the fence on." Marsha heard, and yelled to Jommy. Jeff sighted through the scope, looking for the one with the Uzi, and saw the first casualty of the fence: a girl who was evidently holding on to it when Jommy threw the switch. She stood up rigidly, back arching, sparks, curiously, shooting from her elbows, and then she fell limp.

Through the starlight scope the world was monochromatic and bright. It had some sort of radar gadget, the cross hairs automatically moving downward for more distant targets. A number in the corner told him he had twenty-three shots left. With a sense of detachment, he lay the cross hairs on the first figure he saw, and pulled the trigger. The target spun around but stayed upright, staggering. The rifle had no recoil at all. He turned the eyepiece to increase the magnification, aimed carefully for the center of the chest, and fired again. This time the figure pitched forward and was still.

Jeff started walking dreamily back to Marsha's bunker, then came to his senses and ran crouching. She admonished him to be careful and for Charlie's sake find the bastard with the Uzi.

He heard the Uzi then and pointed toward the sound. The man, or boy, who had it was standing in the road, firing at the lock on the gate. Jeff shot him three times. He staggered forward and fell on the gate; there was a bright blue flash and it swung open.

"The gate!" Marsha shouted. "*Kill* the bastards!" With a steady rattle of gunfire mounting around him, Jeff again fell into an oddly calm state. Marianne had complained about that once, when they were trying to make it to the Cape and stumbled into an ambush, that nothing seemed to get to him; he had said no, not while it was happening. He kept the cross hairs fixed on the Uzi, lying in the dust, only firing when somebody stopped to pick it up, ignoring all the other targets as they streamed by. After six or seven he missed. A girl dove for the weapon, rolled, and began firing from a prone position. Jeff shifted his point of aim and then something smashed into the side of his head and he was falling, bright sparks flying around. He felt himself hit the ground and lay there for a few seconds, watching the sparks die.

He woke up to the sound of children laughing. The sky was pale blue, just about dawn. He tried to sit up and black spots danced in the sky. He choked back vomit and lay still for a minute, and then rolled over so he could see.

The children were playing in the garden. The cyclopean girl with the pretty golden curls was dressed in a party frock, holding a bloody hatchet. Giggling, she stood over the writhing body of a girl she had just decapitated. Other children were engaged in similar tasks.

He closed his eyes and concentrated on his monumental headache. How bad a concussion, he wondered. Carefully probing, he found a large bandage on the side of his head. It bent his ear over rather painfully.

"Are you all right?" Marsha's voice.

He got up on one elbow and looked at her through

the cloud of black spots. He couldn't think of anything clever to say. "You got dressed."

"It's been over a long time. You only missed a few minutes, really. The kids are cleaning up now."

He closed his eyes again. "Saves ammunition, I guess."

"Yeah, and it gets them used to it. Can I do something?"

"Oh...bring down my saddlebags, I guess. Many wounded?"

"Just a few. All we lost was Larry and Deborah. Here." He heard her set the bags down next to him. "I've been usin' your stuff, just the bandages. Is that okay?"

"Sure." But he'd have to take off the bandages and make things sterile, and then redress them. There might not be enough.

He sorted slowly through the bag and, on a hunch, gave himself a shot of amphetamine. It made the pain worse, but the spots went away and he could sit up. He fingered the morphine ampoules longingly but decided to settle for aspirin. "Bring me some water. And have all the wounded come over, most serious ones first. Get some water boiling."

He looked at himself in a hand mirror. The left side of his beard was solid with caked blood. He gingerly removed the bandage, glad she had used the plastic kind that didn't stick, and saw how lucky he'd been. The wound was long but not deep; he had been grazed by a bullet or flechette. It would have to be stitched up but the skull obviously wasn't fractured.

Two of the grownups brought Jommy over and laid him down. He was pale as death and crying quietly. His right hand was a bundle of bright red bandage. Jeff unwrapped it carefully.

"Please don't, Healer. Just let 'em kill me. Don't chop it off." The thumb was blown off completely and the fingers were shattered, bone splinters sticking out of the gore.

Without speaking he gave him a shot of general anesthetic. When the boy's eyes closed he said to the grownups, "Someone build a fire. Bring me a hacksaw."

3 ✦

O'Hara continued to go down to the Bellcom studio at midnight every full moon, but for several months there had been no broadcast from Jeff. They said he probably was still sending, but the signal had gotten so weak they couldn't pick it up: something about signal-to-noise ratio and discrimination. She kept going in the hope that he would find a new fuel cell or a way to recharge the one he had.

Jeff defined "midnight" as the time when the moon was highest, which would be at eleven-forty this month, New New York time. O'Hara came in at eleven and sat down in front of the familiar blank screen, listening to static. She opened up her briefcase and took out a small printer, which she balanced on her knees. She started outlining a report on the correlations between accident frequency and age for people involved in various construction tasks.

After about a half hour, the static abruptly stopped. She looked up, thinking that the monitor had been turned off, and Jeff's voice boomed: "MARIANNE—I HAVE A FUEL cell." Somebody adjusted the volume. "Can you hear me? Are you up there?"

The printer slid to the floor with a crash. "Yes...yes, I—" A technician rushed in with a throat mike and she fastened it to her neck. "I can hear you, Jeff. Can you hear me?"

There was a long silence. "Yes, I do. You're all right, then—New New came out all right?"

Words appeared on a prompter: SOMEBODY'S COMING

FROM THE PLAGUE PROJECT. TELL HIM TO SHUT DOWN FOR TEN
MINUTES AND CALL BACK.

"Yes, everything's...well, not back to normal exactly—Jeff, listen. We found a cure for the plague. An
antibiotic. They want us to shut down for ten minutes, I
guess to save your power; somebody's coming to tell you
about it."

"But...a cure? Christ. All right." The static rushed
back.

While O'Hara waited, other cube screens lit up with
various data about the plague. Two flatscreens showed a
road map of Plant City and a satellite photograph, which
enlarged itself and rotated, to match the orientation of the
road map.

A young man—black, short, wiry, stifling a yawn—
rushed into the studio and sat down next to O'Hara. He
shook her hand. "Elijah Seven," he said. "Am I awake
yet?"

"Getting there," O'Hara said. He had buttoned up his
shirt wrong; she leaned over and fixed it. "You're from
the plague project?"

"Yeah, I'm with the bunch distributing the vaccine.
We have a special kind of—"

"I'm back now," the speakers said. "You hear me?"

Seven put a throat mike in place. "Hawkings, this is
Dr. Elijah Seven. We've synthesized a vaccine for the
plague. I'm in charge of sending it down to Earth.

"We've sent down a couple of hundred thousand doses
already; none to your area. Some went to Atlanta and
Miami. You may run across them: they're bright red individual ampoules in crates of the thousand. The crates
have pictograph instructions, as well as written ones, telling how to administer the dose."

"Haven't seen anything like that."

"Didn't think you would, not yet. Listen, we have a
special shipment for you. The ampoules are damned in-
efficient. We made up a batch in regular hypo bottles. You

have an American standard hypo gun?"

"I guess that's what it is. It has the Pharmaceuticals' Lobby symbol stamped on it."

"Good. We want to drop a crate at your hospital, for you to store in that safe. But we don't know where the hospital is. We have a map of Plant City but it doesn't show St. Theresa's."

"It's a brand-new building just south of the city limits, on Main Street extended. It's shaped like an H, forty stories high, all blue glass and composites. Big golden cross in front."

"Okay..." He watched the prompter. "The vaccine's in low Earth orbit. We'll bring it down to you soon as it gets light. Coming in from the west about seven-thirty."

"All right. But look, are the bottles or the crate identified as plague vaccine? Most of the people around here wouldn't take it if they knew it would prevent the death. They have pity on me for having lived so long."

"Yes, we anticipated that. No markings, no labels. Tell them anything you want."

"We've got a typhoid epidemic south of here. I can claim it's for that."

"Good. You'll be getting several years' supply; twenty or thirty thousand doses, depending on the proportion of small children. Though I think it would be smart to inoculate the older ones first."

"What about me? Should I take it? Then I could start taking drugs again for the growth hormone anomaly—it's probably all that's keeping me alive, but sooner or later the pain is going to immobilize me."

"What, you're growing?"

"I don't think so, not enough to notice. But it's doing something to my joints, something like arthritis."

Seven kneaded his forehead. "I'll have to talk to an endocrinologist. Seem to remember that in children the growth hormone sends some sort of 'message' to the bone ends. Maybe that's what you're feeling.

"Don't take it yet. We'll get a consensus and leave word with O'Hara. Any other questions?"

"No. I'll call back in one month. Let me talk with my ex-wife."

They'd signed a one-year marriage contract, partly in the hope of getting Jeff space on the shuttle. "Hello, ex-husband."

"So. How's the weather up there?"

Charlie's Will ✦

Jeff heard the robot drone before he saw it. It came out of the morning haze to the southwest, banked toward him, then coasted silently overhead, releasing its package. About twenty seconds later its engines kicked back in and it sped off to the east.

The bright red parachute floated straight down and just missed getting hung up on the golden cross in front of the hospital. That would have been interesting, trying to find a long ladder before some scavengers got to it.

It was a plain metal box with no markings. No obvious way to get it open, either. He walked around it, puzzled, and was just about to turn it over when there was a faint "pop" and the top sprang open. Inside, dozens of half-liter bottles were nestled in spun glass. He filled the wagon and pulled it inside to the safe.

After three wagonloads he put two bottles in his saddlebags and locked up the safe. He wrapped the fuel cell in dirty clothing and put it in the bottom of his canvas bag. When he went out to get his bike there were two boys standing there, looking at the parachute and the metal box. One had a shotgun and the other had a pistol stuck in his belt. He recognized them as the two hunters from the family he'd treated for syphilis.

"Hello, boys. How's the girl doing?"

"What girl?" said the one with the shotgun.

"The girl who had the fungus, remember?"

"Oh yeah. She's okay. What's all this shit, we heard the rocket and saw it drop this shit."

"It's medicine. They have typhoid down in Tampa. I'm trying to fix it so no one up here gets it. It's pretty ugly."

"So where'd the rocket come from? The Worlds?"

"No," Jeff said slowly, "you retarded? We killed those bastards a long time ago. This is from Mobile, Alabama. That's where they keep stuff like that."

"Yeah, Willy," said the one with the pistol. "You never seen them?"

"Maybe I seen 'em and maybe not." He stared at Jeff. "So you got a radio in there."

"Not here. I have to go down to St. Petersburg. There's a Public Health Service building down there."

"They got fuel cells, then."

"No, it's a sort of bicycle contraption. It makes electricity; you have to pedal while you talk." Jeff had actually seen such a device, in a fire station outside of Orlando, but it didn't work. "Roll up your sleeves. I'll give you the typhoid medicine." So the first person Jeff gave the gift of life was a mean little punk who would have killed him for a bar of corroded silver.

The sentry on the sand road to Forest-in-Need Farm stayed hidden but said hello as Jeff passed him. They had put heads on stakes all along the road. In the week Jeff was away, the ants had polished them clean.

Tad was waiting for him at the gate. He shook hands solemnly and said, "Marsha's got the death."

It gave Jeff a curious hollow feeling, not quite grief. He had seen a lot of people with the death, but no one he had known. No one he had made love to, or fought beside. "Well, let me see her."

She was on the porch, sitting next to the bath. Jeff braced himself, but she didn't look as bad as the others he had seen, because she had been in good health and eaten well. They were usually emaciated and covered with sores. She looked normal except for her posture, slack and immobile.

"Marsha? Say hello to Healer."

She looked up, her eyes slightly crossed, the pupils very small. Lips parted and wet. "Healer. Squealerdealer. Where's the wagon, dragon?" Her head lolled forward. "Fraggendragon." A string of drool dropped from her open mouth. She caught it on the second try and played with it.

"This is the second day. She woke up with it yesterday. How long?"

"A week, maybe two. There's nothing I can do for her."

"I know."

Jeff shook his head. There had been a short note with the bottles. The death was some sort of virus that was kept in check by a number of factors, the most important apparently being the level of GH in the blood. When the virus began to thrive it reproduced very rapidly, its toxins concentrating in the brain and spinal column. The frontal lobes went first, which caused the "oracular" stage of the disease, but eventually the entire nervous system degenerated. The note said not to waste antibody on anyone who had developed symptoms, because, at best, they would live on as mindless cripples.

"Let's go into the living room," Jeff said. "I have some news."

They sat down at the low table. "Can anybody overhear us?"

"They're all out."

"Listen...you are not going to get the death. Neither is anybody else in the family. Marsha is the last one." Tad just looked at him.

"With the radio, I got in contact with a civil defense computer in Washington." Jeff didn't know how Tad felt about the Worlds, and didn't want to risk the truth. "It told me where I could find a supply of an antibody, a medicine to prevent the death."

"Can you..." He looked toward the porch.

"No. It would only make her die more slowly."

"How come, why hasn't anybody ever heard about this?"

"They came up with it too late. All the old people were dead or dying, and there was no way to distribute it. No mass communication, to even tell people about it."

"Wait, now," Tad said. "You're not going to tell people."

"I might tell some people like you, nonbelievers, so they can plan ahead. Otherwise, I'll say it's for something else, typhoid."

Tad leaned back on his elbows. "I see. If I live a couple more years, people will start to wonder."

"Even your own family. If I were you I'd stash some supplies out in the woods, then fake the death. Wander off during the night; a lot of people do it. Go someplace and start over."

"Hard to leave."

"Your decision. I've got enough medicine for more than twenty thousand people, so over the next few years I should be able to get almost everyone in the area. Sooner or later people will have to accept the fact that the death was only a disease, and that people aren't getting it any more. But it may be hard on the first people who live into the mid-twenties. Going against Charlie's Will."

He nodded slowly. "What I could do, I could wander off like you say, wait a few years, and come back. Say I went a little crazy but it cleared up."

"That might work." Jeff pulled over his saddlebags and took out the hypo. "Here, I'll get you first. Rest of the family at dinner."

The two men spent the rest of the afternoon trying to fix the auxiliary pump outdoors, but it turned out that a plastic washer was broken, and they didn't have anything to replace it. Jeff took the pieces and said he would try to find one.

He felt a little out of place, being the only person with clothes on, but he didn't want to burn. He enjoyed watching the family work and play, strange contrast to the last bloody time he was with them. The two-headed baby had died, and its mother seemed relieved. Jommy was playing catch with the younger children; they threw the ball slowly so he could manage with one hand. The two boys with typhoid had recovered enough to do light chores.

"Who takes over after you leave?" Jeff said softly, while they were reassembling the broken pump.

"Guess it'll be Mary Sue. She's seventeen."

"Not too bright, though."

"Yeah, I've noticed that. Downright stupid, actually." He leaned into the wrench with savage force, then tugged back on it. "Hell. We'll just be takin' it apart again...why not you?"

"What?"

"Why don't you take over. The family'd accept you, and you know as much as anybody, and you can look up whatever you don't know."

"I've got to get the vaccine out. Have to keep moving."

"I don't see why. Half the people you give it to'd kill you just for the hell of it, if they weren't afraid. You don't owe them nothing."

"Yeah, but you've got to take a long view of it. What's going to happen to me when I'm *really* old? If things don't change. I might have another fifty years left. Maybe a hundred, if we get things going the way they were before the war."

"How old are you, anyhow."

Jeff hesitated. "Thirty-five."

"Wonder if you're older than Big Mickey, down at Disney World."

"He looks a little younger. But he can't remember when he was born; I talked to him once."

"You know, I went to see my great-great-grandfather once. He was 120. I don't know if I'd ever want to be that old. He could hardly get around." He finished tightening the last bolt and stood up. "It really changes your whole way of looking at things. I could live another hundred years too." He shook his head and whistled.

Jeff stayed at the farm overnight, working out tentative plans with Tad, and then for three weeks pedaled around Hillsborough County, giving "typhoid" inoculations, ending up back at Plant City. The sun was about an hour from setting as he locked his bicycle and pulled the wagon down the sidewalk to the hospital entrance.

Someone had tried to batter in the unbreakable glass doors. They were almost opaque with overlapping white shatter-stars, and a shotgun or scattergun blast had punched a neat round hole in the middle of one.

Inside, a tile mosaic wall had been defaced with a smeared lopsided cross topped by a C. It smelled recent.

He rushed upstairs, knowing what he would find. The hunters had not believed his story about the pedal-powered radio in St. Petersburg. They had found the radio room and taken apart every piece of equipment, evidently with a crowbar. Wiring ripped out and cast aside. Circuit boards scattered over the floor, crushed.

Jeff righted a chair and sat for a long time, thinking. Until dark he sat, considering various things he might do to the boys, but most of them involved wasting ammunition and putting himself in some danger. He forced himself to think practically.

He ought to go back to Forest-in-Need. Put a well-armed family between himself and this kind of madness.

Forget the plan he and Tad had made, forget the antibody; let them have their short furious lives and Charlie's gift.

But to be completely realistic, he was probably safer moving on, protected by his Healer pose. If Tad's family gets attacked every couple of months, and a couple of people die in every attack, how long could he expect to survive? Marianne could work out the probabilities for him.

That was a factor. If he stayed with the family he would never talk to Marianne again. If he went on the road with the medicine, he might find another working radio. There was a family down by Bealsville that had mules and had offered to trade for his bicycle. A mule could carry a lot of medicine.

And if he stayed here for another year or two, people might wonder why the grownups he treated never got the death. Logic was a rare commodity in Plant City nowadays, but it would only take one person making the connection.

It would be good to go farther south, with winter coming on. The days were fairly warm, but last year there'd been two nights of frost. Whatever was happening to his joints didn't like cold. He would wake up almost immobilized with pain. It was warmer down in the Keys.

Year Six

1 ✦

O'Hara found Room 6392, hesitated, and knocked firmly. The door slid open. It was a small room with nothing but a table, two chairs, and a cot. A woman stared at her from the other side of the table. She was an older woman, in her sixties, face a web of worried lines, chin resting on interlaced fingers, no expression in her tired eyes.

"Come in, O'Hara. Sit down." She did; the door closed behind her. "Aren't you happy with your job?"

"May I ask who you are?"

"I'm on the Board, of course. I can't tell you my name."

"We've met once before. You administered the preferment and aptitude tests to my class, ninth form."

She smiled slightly. "Thirteen years ago. You have a remarkable memory for faces. Aren't you happy with your job?"

O'Hara settled back in her chair. "I haven't made any great effort to keep that secret. No, I'm not particularly happy. Is that surprising?"

"Why aren't you happy?"

"It's not a job for a nontechnical person. It took months for me to gain the confidence of the people whose work I coordinate. Some of them still see me as an interloper."

"Would you care to name them?"

"No. I don't think they're wrong."

"Yet you haven't filed for a transfer."

"I assumed the Board had a good reason for giving me the assignment."

"The Board can be in error. Weren't you trying to second-guess us?"

"In a way. I've read my profile, of course. It looked like a test."

"It was. And you were doing quite well, until yesterday." She opened a drawer and took out a piece of paper. "This is a request from Coordinator Berrigan's office, that you be transferred to the Janus start-up program. Did you have anything to do with this?"

O'Hara closed her eyes and took a deep breath. "On the contrary. One of my husbands suggested it several months ago. I refused because I thought the Board would interpret it as manipulation. I mentioned it to Dr. Berrigan, who is a friend, and she agreed."

"That the Board would react negatively?"

"That's right. I was going to wait until after this year's evaluations, and then write up a detailed request."

"To be transferred to Janus."

O'Hara shook her head slightly. "Just for a position more appropriate to my talents. I expected that the Janus Project would be filled up by then." She leaned forward and looked at the piece of paper. "Was this request made by my husband?"

"Not directly; the program that selected you was written by someone else. But both your husbands were consulted as a matter of course." She sat back and folded her arms over her chest. "Please understand that I personally don't disbelieve you. But only two other people were chosen from the Policy track, for a project employing over seven hundred. Given the...unique assets that you possess, it wouldn't be difficult to arrange things so that the program would have to choose you as one of the three."

"It sounds as if you should be interviewing my husbands, or whoever wrote the program. Not me."

"It may be done. That's up to the Engineering Board. Right now I have an unpleasant task..." She reached into the drawer and brought out a hypodermic gun and a jar of swabs. "Would you volunteer to be interviewed under the influence of a strong hypnotic drug? You may refuse."

"Sure I can." She rubbed her palms on her thighs. "I don't have anything to hide. Over there?"

"Yes. Lie down and roll up your sleeve." Sharp smell of alcohol when she opened the jar.

O'Hara lay down on the cot, tense. "I've heard of this. But I thought you had to do something really drastic."

"Not at all. It's a standard procedure. Just close your eyes now, it won't hurt."

INTERVIEW TRANSCRIPT

Q: How do you feel now?

A: All right. Sleepy.

Q: Do you remember when your husband John first mentioned the Janus Project?

A: Both of my husbands have been talking about it for years. They were both involved in the initial planning.

Q: I mean, when did he first mention your working on the start-up program?

A: That would have been sometime last September. We were walking up in the half-gee area, he'd had a month of zerogee and needed exercise, and I guess I was complaining about the Stat group. He thought he could get me transferred.

Q: But you told him not to do it.

A: It wouldn't look good.

Q: Tell me about John.

A: He's funny.

Q: Amusing? Or peculiar.

A: Both. He's always joking, he carries a little notebook to write down the last lines of jokes he hears, but mostly it's just his outlook. Everything is funny to him. He's an awful tease.

Q: He's crippled.

A: Yes. He was born with bad curvature of the spine. His parents were too poor to get him corrective surgery, and now he's too old for it. That's why he came to New New, to work in the low-gee labs. Gravity hurts him.

Q: Did you ask him to get you assigned to the Janus Project?

A: No. He asked me and I said no.

Q: Do you think he went ahead and did it against your wishes?

A: I'm going to ask. But that wouldn't be like him.

Q: Is John a good lover?

A: You mean sex?

Q: That's right.

A: *(Pause)* He's not very imaginative. Neither is Dan. But they're both groundhogs, you know.

Q: Why did you marry groundhogs?

A: I don't know. John says I'm a throwback. *(Laughs.)* Says I only love him because his knuckles drag on the ground.

Q: *Do you love them?*

A: I married them.

Q: That's not an answer. *(No response.)* Do you love Jeff Hawkings?

A: I think so, if he's still alive. He wasn't there the past two months, I'm afraid for him.

Q: Who do you love more, John or Dan?

A: I guess...usually John. He's easier to get along with.

Q: Who do you love more, John or Jeff?

A: Jeff, I think.

Q: But you'll never see him again.

A: Maybe not.

Q: Do you think of Jeff while you make love with your husbands?

A: Oh yes.

Q: Of the four men you have formed long associations with, three have been physically unusual: a cripple and two giants. Have you ever thought about why that should be?

A: Yes I have.

Q: Why, do you think?

A: It may be that I want their gratitude. With Charlie Devon, I think maybe it was...I was young and wanted to prove something. Jeff and John, I don't know. It may be that I see myself as a freak. Or it may have been coincidence.

Q: You delayed menarche as long as physically possible. Didn't you like boys?

A: (Emphatically) No! Especially the Scanlan boys.

Q: Have you ever had sex with a woman?

A: That must be in your records.

Q: Did you like it better?

A: No, it was just for Charlie Devon's sake. He wanted me to try everything.

Q: Is Charlie still alive?

A: No. He was on Devon's World.

Q: Do you miss him?

A: No.

Q: Did Dan have you assigned to the Janus Project?

A: I don't know. It would surprise me, he's very regulation.

Q: But they both have said they want you to work on the project.

A: Of course they do.

Q: Would one or both of them work to have you reassigned without first discussing it with you?

A: I don't think so. (Pause) Unless...they're intelligent men. They might have foreseen this interview.

Q: Would you like to have the Janus assignment?

A: Yes.

Q: Explain why.

A: It would be more interesting and more important,

and I might be better liked.

Q: You don't think your coworkers like you?

A: They think a mathematician should be in charge of the section. So do I.

Q: You don't think your work is important.

A: Maybe the industrial safety part is, and maybe an occasional surprise epidemiological correlation. Most of it is trivial. I suppose someone has to do it.

Q: But not someone of your talents.

A: That's right.

Q: Will you tell me which of your subordinates disapprove of your being in charge?

A: No.

Q: Because?

A: I wouldn't want them to be punished. They're right, anyhow.

Q: Very well. If the Janus Project goes through, will you volunteer? Will you go?

A: No.

Q: Why not?

A: I want to go back to Earth...I want to see Jeff again.

Q: You know that's very unlikely.

A: I know.

Q: All right. Now I want you to take a deep breath, yes, like that, and exhale completely. Again: in...out. Now I'm going to count up to ten, and I want you to keep breathing this way as I count. When I reach ten, you will awaken refreshed, and very pleased with yourself for having cooperated with me. And after you awaken you will remember three things. One, your coworkers admire you. Two, your work is quite important, even when its importance is not immediately obvious. Three, if you find out that either of your husbands has done something wrong, getting you assigned to the Janus Project, you will want to contact the Board and explain it to them. Will you remember these things?

A: Yes.

Q: Very good. *(Interviewer counts to ten.)*

✦ ✦ ✦

When O'Hara cleaned out her desk at Public Health she found there were only two things that actually belonged to her, a pen she'd gotten used to and a piece of plastic, silly gift from Jeff. It was opaque from six years of nervous rubbing; you would have to hold it up to a strong light to see the shamrock inside.

She didn't have her own office at the Janus Project, just a carrel at the library. She had no underlings and, in a sense, no boss; her job title was Demographics Coordinator. The job, Grade 16, had no formal description: she was to define and evolve her own function in terms of what seemed necessary to the project, as the project grew.

All the past year's grinding away at applied mathematics turned out to be useful now. She had to study thousands of pages of preliminary reports that the project had already generated. Most of it came from committees of engineers, and the math was more clear than what passed for prose.

It was a perfect job for her talents but a potentially disastrous one for her weaknesses. She spent longer and longer hours at the carrel, sleeping in snatches and eating only when the stomach cramps got annoying. The third month, she took an armload of work down to the Bellcom studio to wait out the night. Jules Hammond had to tell her that it was no use: a satellite picture showed that the Plant City hospital had burned to the ground. She didn't stop crying until she was under sedation in the psychiatric ward.

Charlie's Will ✦

Jeff Hawkings had been safe, more than a hundred kilo-meters southeast, when the hospital was fired (an impressive bit of arson, as most of the building had been made of composites). He was moving southward slowly, town by town, hoping that his reputation would precede him and protect him.

He was an odd figure traveling, even apart from being so old. He rode inside a mule-drawn cart that led another mule laden with supplies. The cart was decorated with red crosses and the word HEALER on all sides. It was sheathed in bulletproof plastic, except for gunports, and Jeff himself was protected with bulletproof clothing and an assortment of weaponry.

Jeff spent two weeks in Wimauma, waiting. Tad caught up with him there. He'd brought a fuel cell and the Uzi. With his beard shaved off, he could pass for sixteen. They started south together.

2 ✦

For a week or so she was numb and distant. A therapist carefully brought to the surface the complex skein of hopes and fears, fantasies and guilts that wound around the symbol "Jeff"—and separated the symbol from the person, and allowed her to grieve for one lost love without his memory also carrying the burden of lost youth, innocence, freedom, joy: lost Earth. Her husbands joined in the therapy (learning some things they already knew), and in less than a month she was commuting between their beds and her carrel, conscientiously avoiding the opiate of over-work, trying to love and play without being too obviously grim about it.

This was her current job: slightly less than a third of

New New's population, 75,000 people, were willing to join the Janus Project. Some twenty thousand were rather fanatical about it. But the crew, or population, of the starship was limited to ten thousand.

One problem was the fanatics. Most of them were not the kind of people you would like to be locked up with for the rest of your life. Many of them obviously wanted to leave New New because they felt trapped. Many of them were frankly paranoiac about Earth. It wasn't likely that their mental conditions would improve in the relatively stark and confined starship environment.

Yet some of them would have to be included, because of the other problem. Ten thousand is a large crowd to jam into a starship, but they can't just be random folks. Even beyond the obvious specialties necessary to keep the starship puttering along, there were thousands of specific skills necessary to build a new civilization at the other end. These skills would have to be passed on to the replacement generations born during the flight.

For instance, in all of New New there were only two people with the job classification "medical librarian." Both of them had volunteered. One was a man in his eighties who'd had two nervous breakdowns and was more or less addicted to tranquilizers. The other, young and healthy, was a Devonite who was rigidly intolerant of anyone who wasn't a Devonite. Yet the ship did need a medical librarian, and no student was currently working toward certification in that specialty.

(The medical library itself was no problem; the starship would be taking along a cybernetic duplicate of New New's entire library. Except for certain sensitive military and political materials, this contained a copy of every remotely important Earth document, printed or videoed or cubed, from the Dead Sea Scrolls to The New York Times of March 16, 2085, and everything published in New New after the war. With polarized-quark memory, the whole thing fit into a machine the size of a steamer trunk. In medicine as in every other field, it would not be a problem of lacking information—just of knowing how to find it.)

The Devonites in general were a headache. The starship was supposed to start out with a population of ten thousand and, ninety-eight years later, wind up with twice that number. There were a few Devonite sects that allowed birth control under unusual circumstances, but for most of them it was one of three unforgivable sins. If they allowed one percent of the starship to be Devonite, fifty females, and if each of them and each of their female descendants bore ten children, they could produce about 300,000 children in ninety-eight years.

So if the starship, as promised, did retain the respect for individual liberty that existed in New New, then orthodox Devonites—one gender of them, at least—would have to be left behind, since religious freedom would allow them to refuse the necessary vasectomy or laporoscopy. (The plan was for ova to be quickened on a strict replacement basis, one birth for each death, until twenty-five years before they reached their destination. A significant number would live through the whole voyage, barring unforeseen medical or environmental problems, since the average life span in New New was 118.)

O'Hara wasn't convinced that the starship could actually be run along the same lines as New New. The system she'd grown up in was a crazy-quilt of electronic democracy, communalism, anarchy, bureaucracy, technocracy. She knew the anarchy was largely an illusion, a formalism that the actual power structure tolerated as a safety valve. There wouldn't be room for it aboard the good ship *Newhome*.

There wouldn't be room for a lot of things that people took for granted in New New—least of all, the comforts they remembered from before the war, the state of relative ease and freedom they were slowly rebuilding. Many of the inconveniences they regarded as temporary would be unchangeable facts of life. Marianne suspected that mundane discomforts such as overcrowding and monotonous diet would ultimately prove less important than existential problems: isolation, lack of affect, undirected anxiety, boredom.

Why was she looking forward to it?

3 ✦

They called it a "solarium," even though the light and heat didn't come from the sun. The zerogee swimming pool—actually just a globe of water that slowly rotated, with no bottom or sides—was fairly close to one of the four arcs that illuminated the inside of New New. On the lightward side was a transparent wall with clamps for towels; people would dry off and float there, baking.

Berrigan didn't bother toweling, just made a turban for her hair. "You actually do want to go now?" she said to O'Hara. "I thought you were trying to talk your husbands out of it."

"I don't know." O'Hara was drifting away from the wall; she did a lazy duck-and-roll and flutter kick that brought her back within reach of the clamped towel. "I've been weighing things. Part of it's keeping peace in the family...keeping the family at all, actually."

"They'd leave you?"

A man she didn't know drifted by and made the finger-sign query for sex. O'Hara smiled and shook her head at him.

"I really don't know...a few days ago I would've said maybe for Dan, but definitely no for John."

Berrigan nodded her head slowly. "The photon reflector."

"That's right. Before they came up with that, I don't think John took any of it really seriously. Didn't think it would fly."

"Not alone in that."

Another man drifted toward them; O'Hara tethered one ankle and wrapped the towel around her hips, a signal of unavailability. "Now, well, he's been very withdrawn since the announcement. Thinking things over."

"And Dan?"

"Daniel's very happy. But he's always assumed I'll come to my senses and go along. Maybe he's right."

"You want some cheap advice?"

"I guess I do."

"Don't use your husbands as an excuse to run away. You're still upset about losing Jeff Hawkings."

"That's part of it."

"But Earth is still there, and all of your training and experience points toward an Earth liaison position. Probably the very top."

"That may be fifteen, twenty years away. Maybe never."

"In twenty years you'll be two years younger than I am now. Anything could happen. Suppose it takes thirty, fifty years for Earth to recover? You'll still be in a good position. If you go to Janus, where will you be fifty years from now?"

"Halfway to Epsilon Eridani. Nearly halfway."

"If everything goes according to plan. A lot of engineers aren't as optimistic as Daniel."

4 ✦

The Janus Project was not humanity's first starship, technically. Several planetary probes launched in the twentieth century were inching their way toward the stars, and after some skillions of years might actually come near one. But there had been two practical small-scale demonstrations.

The most interesting was Project Daedalus, a fusion-powered probe launched by the European Space Agency many years before the war. It was also headed for Epsilon Eridani—toward the oxygen-water world that was *Newhome*'s destination—and if things had gone according to plan, it would have sent back a view of the target world in the first year of the new century. Daedalus would flash by the star system at nearly a fifth of the speed of light, having barely an hour to cap off its half-century mission by spying on the earth-sized planet and broadcasting back data. (It would actually fly by in 2090, the signal taking 10.8 years to travel to Earth at the speed of light.)

Unfortunately, Daedalus was lost. The carrier beam that kept Earth in touch with it had fallen silent a couple of years after the war.

The other probe had been a matter/antimatter demonstration, a small reaction drive carrying a payload that was little more than a beeper. Most scientists were more annoyed than impressed by the expensive stunt, which provided no new theoretical knowledge. It was primarily a demonstration of temporary political amity between the United States, which provided the launch vehicle and fuel containment apparatus, and the SSU, which tied up a valuable synchrotron for most of a year, manufacturing antimatter, particle by particle.

John Ogelby said that the m/a demonstration only proved that politicians can't read equations. Saying that it was a "great step toward reaching the stars" was like successfully screwing in a light bulb and then claiming you were ready to build a power plant.

5 ✦

Much of what O'Hara did at her carrel was "free-association data-base scanning," a sort of computer-augmented woolgathering. She would type in, for instance, "APTITUDE," and the computer would answer "2,349,655:," which was the number of data entries that either had the word "aptitude" in their titles, or had been cross-referenced under that word. Then she would narrow it down, say, by typing in "PUBLISHED AFTER 2060," and the machine would say "32,436:," still more than an afternoon's reading. After further modifying it with WORLDS and EDUCATION, the number was down to 23. She would ask for a list of the titles, and usually wouldn't find anything that clicked, and would start over.

In this particular case, though, she found an article that had been published in New New a few years before the war, in a journal of applied psychology: "Aptitude Induction Through Voluntary Hypnotic Immersion." She'd had a sort of morbid interest in hypnosis ever since the interview that preceded this job, so she read it.

After a couple of paragraphs, she punched up the author's name and found that he was still alive. She finished the article and called him. He was at a seminar; she left a message and they wound up meeting after dinner at the social sciences faculty lounge.

The lounge must have been a very comfortable place once. Now half of it was partitioned off for someone's "temporary" living quarters, and all of the couches and chairs had been crowded into the space that was left. She recognized Dr. Demerest—they hadn't talked but she'd punched up his dossier after the computer made the appointment—standing in the corner, trying to make the beverage dispenser work. He was a short bald man in his nineties. She picked her way around the furniture and introduced herself.

"Dr. O'Hara?" A few dozen more lines appeared in

his forehead (no eyebrows to raise). "I expected, never mind what I expected, coffee?"

"Tea, please. Or anything it will surrender."

He was shaking the machine gently. "It doesn't respond to violence. Somebody must have hit it." He waved O'Hara to a nest of easy chairs. "Machines do sulk. I've been humoring this one for thirty years." He wiggled the T button and it agreed to produce a cup of tea. He drew another one and joined her.

He held his cup in both hands and squinted at her. "Give me a moment to adjust here. We're the same grade but you're evidently younger than most of my students. Janus start-up. Crazy stunt. You really think that damned thing is going to fly?"

"A lot of people do," she said quietly.

"A lot of people think Jesus is coming in a Buick. But you. Do you think it'll fly? You plan to go?"

"At first I didn't...didn't think it would work and wouldn't go even if it did. Now I guess I'll go if they take me. Whether it works out, they say that depends on whether they can get the neutrino coupler to work."

He shook his head. "Going to be dull around here after all the crazy people leave. What's a demographics coordinator and what does she want with an old interface psychologist?"

"I read the article you wrote in '82 about aptitude transfers. It looks like a technique we could use. But there aren't any later references. Did you ever follow it up?"

"Hm. Did and didn't." He rubbed his long nose, remembering. "Sort of farmed it out, set it up as a doctoral project for a couple of exchange students. One of those things. They went back to Mazeltov." He shrugged. Nobody in Mazeltov had survived the war.

"We stayed in contact, of course. I have all their raw data and their preliminary findings. Haven't got around to putting it into publishable form. But it does confirm the validity of the technique. What does that have to do with demographics?"

"Well, we have a problem. We're trying to create a sort of microcosm, a miniature replica of the human race."

"Ah. But you only have, what is it? Ten thousand people? I see. You want a file of dopplegangers." He shook his head in a series of short jerks. "Hm. Take forever. Might not work at all."

"I was thinking of a more limited application, at first, anyhow. For instance...glass-blowers. Not for jewelry and such, but the people who custom-design equipment for scientists and medical people. There is only *one person alive* who does that. She's over a hundred."

"That's interesting."

"Before the war there were almost a half-million specifically named occupations. Less than a tenth of them have any living practitioners."

"Hm. You can't think that more than a thousand of them are relevant to your bunch. Mostly still available, engineer types."

"Even so. I've come up with literally hundreds of instances like the glass-blower. Where the only people who have an aptitude either don't want to go or can't."

"Oh, I think I see. I see your problem." He blew on his tea and stared into it. "You understand the limitations of the induction technique?"

"I'm not sure. That's why I wanted to talk to you."

"All right. I take this crotchety old glass-blower and try to talk her into spending a week or ten days living in the psych lab. Suppose she agrees—and she has to *want* to; if I coerce her it probably won't work. Then I try to put her into a state of extreme hypnotic receptivity, suggestibility. Have you ever been hypnotized?"

"Once."

"You probably know it doesn't work with everybody. Some people, you can put into a deep trance with a few minutes of quiet talking. Others you can shoot full of drugs and they resist you all the way.

"If your glass-blower is receptive, I put her under and then hook her up to the machine. The semantic computer part talks to her. The biologue part coordinates what she's saying to her physical state: skin temperature, pulse, blood pressure, brain waves. Mostly brain waves, in twelve frequencies.

"It's rather hard work. With a hundred-year-old, I'd probably want to spend a couple of weeks, not keep her under more than two or three hours a day. Eventually, though, I'd have a cybernetic profile of her attitudes toward just about everything, and incidentally a fairly complete biography. You know the Turing paradox?"

"Touring as in traveling?"

"Never mind. What it boils down to is that if you put her behind a screen, and put a voice-simulation output to the semantic computer behind another screen, and talked to them...well, you'd be hard-pressed to tell which one was the human. I could tell, because I know some good trick questions...pardon me. Old men ramble.

"So you have this cybernetic glass-blower. It does you absolutely no good. No lungs. So you take an appropriate subject and run the process in reverse. This is even harder work, physically, because what you're doing is manipulating his blood pressure and so forth, induction field for the brain waves, while you suggest he make the same response as the old glass-blower. The computer, that is, suggests it.

"When he comes out of it, he won't know a damned thing about glass-blowing. But he will sure as hell want to learn, and he'll learn fast and well, if he's at all suited for the profession. You wouldn't want to take someone with low manual dexterity, of course. There are more subtle screening criteria, too. You wouldn't take someone who had injured himself severely with glass as a child. He'd be a nervous wreck all his life."

"The instance you used was motivating a one-armed man to play the violin."

"He'd kill himself. He couldn't live with it. And the process isn't really reversible; you could put him back under and motivate him to play some one-handed instrument, but that wouldn't erase his wanting to play the violin."

"That's something I wanted to know. You could take a pianist and motivate him to study the violin—and he wouldn't transfer all his energy to the violin? He'd still play the piano?"

"We didn't pursue that too far. The danger's obvious. Motivate him to play every damned instrument in the orchestra. You'll turn him into a zombie. Indecision, depression. He'll pick up a horn and play a few notes and then walk over to the harp and then have an irresistible urge to play the piano, and so forth. Drive him mad in a week. You're a polymath, aren't you?"

O'Hara nodded slowly.

"Thought I saw a gleam in your eye. How many degrees do you have?"

"Four. Two doctorates."

"I know what you're thinking. Disabuse yourself. You can't tack on new specialties like ornaments. It wouldn't be very effective and it might even be dangerous. This technique isn't for overachievers, it's for people who *aren't* strongly motivated."

"All right, okay." But she looked thoughtful.

"What was it you had in mind?"

"Oh, I've never been strong in maths and sciences. Most of my friends are on the Engineering track, though. Both my husbands." She smiled ruefully. "Half the time it's as if they're talking a foreign language. One where I know some of the words but no grammar."

He made a little clucking sound. "Happens all the time. First woman I married was a mathematician. That's how I wound up in this mongrel kind of specialty. Down to cases, though. You want to do this to several hundred people? Do you know how long that would take?"

"What, are you the only person who can do it?"

"No, quite the contrary. Any nurse...hell, I could teach anyone in a day or two. Teach you, if you're not squeamish about sticking thermometers into people. The machine does all the hard parts, but that's just it: there's only one machine. Ten days for a subject to program it and another ten for the induction. That's eighteen per year. Maybe twenty, if most of them are good subjects."

"We'll just have to build more machines, then."

He laughed, a bark. "Sister, I haven't had a requisition granted since before the war. Psychological research is not a high priority, not this kind."

She had been on the edge of her chair through the whole conversation. She sat back and beamed at him. "It is now."

Charlie's Will ✦

"Trouble," Jeff said. Under the blanket on Tad's lap, two clicks as he turned the Uzi's selector switch to full automatic.

They'd been traveling down the Tamiami Trail for two days, overgrown jungle on both sides of the old highway, some shells of deserted towns but no people. Now there were people.

First a large boy stepped out from behind a bush about ten meters ahead, holding an old shotgun in his right hand, his left palm facing out to halt them. Both mules stopped abruptly. Seven more boys filed out across the road. Only one of them had a firearm, a rusty .22 rifle, but the others all carried machetes. Jeff was surprised that three of them were black. He hadn't seen any other racially mixed families.

The first boy didn't raise the shotgun but kept it pointed vaguely toward them. "What you peckerwoods doin'?"

"Going south," Jeff said. "I'm Healer."

"Yer what-er?"

"*Healer.*" Tad had shifted so the Uzi was lined up on the boy, but the lead mule was in the way. "You haven't heard of me?"

"Uh-uh. We keeps pretty much to ourselves. People come by, we don't gen'rally talk much." One of the children giggled. "You heal people? You got the touch?"

"I have medicine."

He laughed. "We never did hold for that. Not even before Daddy and Ma died."

"Charlie's will," Jeff said.

"What?"

"Never mind...if you have sick people I can help them."

"Well, I'm sick of catfish. Sure could use some roast mule. Any reason you shouldn't—"

It happened very fast. The boy started to raise the shotgun and Tad stood up abruptly and leveled the Uzi on him. He dropped it. Then there was a shot from the left that hit Tad on the chest and spanged off his body armor. Tad twisted, saw smoke and fired a burst at it. By that time Jeff had the scattergun unclamped and aimed at the boy with the rusty rifle.

There was a strange gurgling sound and a boy or young girl staggered dying through the brush, throat and chest ripped open, face gone, still holding a rifle. When the children saw it they dropped their weapons. The apparition made it almost to the road; pitched forward and lay there twitching.

"Now I didn't tell her to do that," the boy said.

"Right," Tad said. "She was just walkin' through the woods."

"Probably others," Jeff said. "They wouldn't just have one girl."

"The girls are up at the house, 'cept Judy here. She always has to git in on things." He stared at the dying girl. "Don't suppose you kin heal her, now?" Jeff didn't say anything. "Whyn't ya shoot her again. Put her out of it."

"She's dead," Tad said. "Just some parts don't know it yet. Be a waste of ammo."

"I'll do it, then." He reached down for the shotgun.

"The *hell* you will." The boy touched the gunstock but looked up at Tad and then slowly straightened again. "What you gonna do? You gonna kill us all?"

"Probably not. No point to it."

"What about those catfish?" Jeff said calmly. "You smoke them?" The boy nodded. "We'll trade for some dry beef. And I'll treat your sick, as I say. That's what I do."

Tad walked over to the line of boys and picked up the shotgun and rifle. He put them in the cart and went to the girl, who had stopped twitching. He toed her over on her back and scowled. "Dead." He took her rifle.

"We'll go get some catfish," the leader said.

"No, you won't." Tad pointed the muzzle of the Uzi at the youngest one. "He'll go. I'll go with him. Rest of you stay here and talk with Healer."

Nobody said anything while the boy led Tad away. "You don't have any sick people?"

"Nup."

"Anybody die recently?"

"Two in the fall. One last spring."

"The oldest, right?"

"How'd you know that?"

"Did they talk nonsense for a while, stop eating, wet themselves—"

"They did that."

"It's going around."

He looked at the other boys, pursed his lips and thought. "I guess if you had medicine for that, we could take it."

"I'll give you a typhoid shot, might help. When my partner comes back."

"We wouldn't try nothin'."

"Sure."

Tad returned after a few minutes with eight girls, three of whom had infants, and six small children toddling alongside, apparently none of them mutants. He had a plastic bag of greasy smoked fish and another ancient rifle. The girls had tried to shoot him with it but couldn't make it work.

Jeff gave them their shots and a few sticks of dried beef. Then they took the oldest boy and one of the girls hostage, to discourage pursuit, and left as it was getting dark.

There was no moon but enough starlight to tell road from jungle. They were surrounded by creepy reptilian noises, croakings and slitherings. The mules went slower and slower and finally refused to go on. Jeff had to turn on a light to make them move, using up irreplacable electricity and providing a beacon for followers. But overall it may have been safer: more and more often, as the night went on, they came upon large rattlesnakes slumbering on the warm road surface. Best to give the creatures ample warning.

About midnight they came to a wide spot in the road that had once borne the improbable name Frog City. Jeff gave both the hostages sleeping pills and, once they were safely asleep, left them in an abandoned shop, along with the old weapons, no ammunition. Tad took a pep pill and they continued east, figuring to keep moving through the night and most of the next day.

By noon they were still in the Everglades. No human contact, no sign that they were being followed. The snakes had retired to the bush at dawn. There were alligators, some large, but they kept their distance. Long-legged birds of many varieties entertained them. The weather was beautiful, bright and cool, and under other circumstances it would have been a pleasant outing. But they might be coming up on a real logistics problem.

Long before the war, roads like this had become anachronisms, since almost all intercity transport was by floater or subway. The roads were useful for floater navigation and in some areas were kept up for the benefit of bicyclists and hikers. That was the case with the Tamiami Trail, a scenic path connecting Tampa with Ciudad Miami.

But they didn't want to go through Ciudad Miami. It was hard enough to get along with the various families when they spoke English. Neither of the men was fluent in Spanish, so they had to find a road south sometime before they got into Miami's metropolitan area. But their simple map didn't show how far that area extended. There was only one road going south before they got to US 1, which hugged the coast and was definitely in Spanish-speaking territory. That was Florida 27, and it was a dotted line: "no maintenance." They didn't know how old the map was. There might be bridges out or areas that had subsided and flooded, or the road might have become thoroughly overgrown and impassable, perhaps indistinguishable from the surrounding wilderness. Or it might be in the middle of a Hispanic suburb; there was no way to tell until they got there. Jeff had never been to Florida before he'd brought Marianne O'Hara down to escape the war, and Tad had rarely left his parents' commune, never going this far south or east.

Their fears were groundless, as they might have deduced from the fact that they'd met nobody coming west on the Trail from Miami. There was no Ciudad Miami. They noticed a funny smell; before either identified it as salt tang, they could hear the unmistakable sound of waves breaking. The vegetation subsided to young mangrove scrub and clogged weeds that crawled over the road. They tied up the mules and picked their way over a slight rise to stand on a beach of fused glass.

6 ✦

O'Hara had asked for fifteen minutes at the next Start-up meeting. The committee, plus advisers and assorted hangers-on, had grown too large to hold meetings by cube conference. They had to commandeer a cafeteria between shifts.

With considerable competition from the noise of the clean-up crew, O'Hara outlined the hypnotic induction process and said that she wanted the resources to build and operate at least a dozen of the machines.

Stanton Marcus, an old man who had been Policy Coordinator for ten years while O'Hara was growing up, was at the meeting even though he wasn't officially part of the committee. He raised the first objection.

"It's a very clever idea," he said without much enthusiasm, "but I don't think that it needs to be given high priority. Could I see that list?" O'Hara handed him the two-page list of specialties for which she wanted aptitudes induced. He read it slowly, nodding and breathing loudly through his nose.

"In every case, there's only one person left who is qualified," she said.

"That's just the point," he said without looking up. He finished the list and handed it back, then put his fingers together in a steeple and frowned importantly.

"As you say, many of these people are indispensable. They're indispensable to New New as well as to your eventual colony. You propose to take them out of circulation for two weeks and put them through a grueling physical ordeal. Many of them are quite old."

"Dr. Demerest says there's no danger."

"But his trials were done with students, were they not? Young people?"

"They were. But the Mazeltov studies included several people who were over a hundred, both as programmers and receivers."

"Receivers?" someone said. "Why give a person that old a new aptitude?"

"Autopsy," she said bluntly. "They wanted to look for changes in the brain's chemistry or gross structure." Back to Marcus. "None of them died, though, before the war. It's just not that dangerous."

"You have access to those subjects' medical records?" Marcus said mildly.

"I couldn't find anything. Mazeltov and B'ism'illah Ma'sha'llah stayed independent of the Public Health data pool. As you know."

He smiled. "They were always mavericks. The point is, you can't really say that it won't affect the health of these irreplaceable people."

"I can only say that none of the subjects has died. And Demerest had the process done to himself, both ways, in his eighties."

"Still in the bloom of youth," Marcus said, and some of the committee laughed. "I'm not saying that your idea is a bad one, just that you have a false, if forgivable, sense of urgency about it. After all, it will be more than a century before you need most of these people. You'll be in close contact with New New all that time; it's not as if you'll be sailing off the edge of the world. All that is involved is a simple transfer of data, which, it seems to me, can and ought to be done at New New's convenience—without taking vital people off the job at a time when they are most needed."

Berrigan came to O'Hara's defense. "Stanton, you're talking to hear yourself talk. Once these personalities are on file, they'll be as useful to New New as to us. Where is New New going to be when these people die?"

"I'm sure replacements are being trained."

"Not for all of the categories," O'Hara said. "This cabinetmaker, for instance. His skills are useless to New New,
almost useless, since he works only in wood. They might
be vital to us, if we decide to use the planet."

"I suppose we can spare him."

"He's a hundred and twenty years old and can't leave
the zerogee ward. But there are others, as Dr. Berrigan
says, whose profiles New New ought to preserve for its
own sake."

"It certainly is worth considering. I'll recommend that
Policy look into it."

"I did that more than a week ago," O'Hara said. "Nothing has come of it."

He gave the youngster an indulgent smile. "Realities,
O'Hara. You aren't on Policy track."

"I am indeed."

"She's Grade Sixteen," Berrigan said. "You'd think
somebody would've paid some attention."

"Well. You know how busy things are." He rubbed
his chin and squinted at O'Hara. "I remember you now.
You're the woman with all the degrees. Two husbands on
Engineering track. You caused a certain amount of discussion at board meetings."

"You're saying she shouldn't expect too much coop-
eration from Policy," Berrigan said.

"Engineering, either," he said. "O'Hara, you're neither
fish nor fowl; you can't grease anybody's track. Things
are busy, as I say, and it's just the wrong time to start yet
another new program. You're offering Policy people an
extra workload but no real career enhancement is attached
to it."

"That's why it was so much fun to work with you,
Stanton," Berrigan said. Their terms had overlapped.
"You're so above politics."

"Oh yes. Engineering track is never concerned with anything but the abstract merits of a proposal. So I suggest we put it to a vote."

"Not 'we,' Stanton. You're only here to liven things up. Discussion?"

A grossly fat man named Eliot Smith raised his one flesh limb—both legs and an arm were mechanical replacements—and said, "I'm not in favor of a simple yes-or-no vote. Almost all of us have mastered arithmetic...O'Hara, would you put those figures up on the screen?" She tapped out a sequence on her portable keyboard and the flatscreen on the wall lit up with the information she'd shown during her presentation: dollar equivalents of manpower and materiel requirements for one through twenty machines, and a column showing price-per-machine for each number. (The unit cost dropped steeply for up to nine machines, and then leveled off.)

"Okay, now give me control. Smith 1259." He unfolded his own keyboard while she typed in his number.

"Now there's no such thing as an objective analysis here. You gotta go through the whole list of professions and give each one a weighting factor, and everybody's factors would be different. Me, I wouldn't take ten of those cabinetmakers for one mediocre vacuum welder. But then I've never been on a planet and don't understand why anybody wants to bother with it.

"Anyhow, your ideal-case analysis would rank those people in terms of desirability. I suppose the practical way would be to take a consensus. Grind out a number for each one that reflects how indispensable each skill is from our aggregate point of view. You see where I'm going?" There was a general murmur of assent.

"Then you take and ask the computer for an actuarial analysis on each individual case: what is the probability that each person will live for ten years? Someone's gonna die, you want to move him up the list. So you divide the rank factor by this actuarial fraction, which gives you a new rank number. Kapeesh?"

John Ogelby laughed. "You just bought yourself a cabinetmaker, Eliot. You're treating it as if age and probable desirability were stochastically independent. That's not the case."

"Christ, Ogelby." He tapped a plastic hand against a plastic leg. "If you weren't so pretty you'd be dangerous."

Marcus sighed in exasperation. "Will someone please translate that into some human language?"

"My pleasure," O'Hara said, trying to repress an evil grin. "Most of the old-time professions, the ones that would be most useful in a planetary environment, naturally would belong to people who were born on Earth. There were almost no tourists in New New at the time of the war, right?"

He nodded slowly. "Trade sanctions."

"Well, then. There are only two classes of groundhogs left in New New: renegades like Quasimodo there, who had become Worlds citizens, and old folks or sick ones who were stuck; couldn't risk the trip back. Cabinetmakers among them.

"Now Eliot proposes a situation where people will more or less be taken in reverse order of life expectancy. So you're going to get a disproportionate number of old coots who know how to repair gasoline engines and chip flint into arrowheads. That's what you mean, John?"

The hunchback blew her a kiss. "Not bad for a history major."

"Right," Eliot said. "So now you've got this new ranking. Buggy-whip sharpeners and all. What we're looking for is a sense of the cost-effectiveness associated with each number of machines—but keeping in mind the mortality factor. Too few machines and we're gonna lose data; how much are those data worth?

"Now this is what I'd like O'Hara to do. I wouldn't mind taking out a couple of hours looking over her list and ranking these professions. Anybody too pressed for time to do that?" He looked around the room. "Good. O'Hara can route it to us and give us a deadline. Say we just assign a number from zero to a hundred to each job. Then she takes and normalizes?" He looked at O'Hara.

"Sure," she said. "Divide each number by the contributor's average response, mean response, and then apply the actuarial factor."

"Zeros, dear," Ogelby said. "Divide zero all day and it still comes out zero."

"I'll work it out somehow."

"Okay," Eliot said. "Now what we want to have before the next meeting is a three-dimensional matrix that integrates these weighted, normalized numbers with the data up here on the screen. I don't mean *integrates*, not in the calculus sense."

"I know what you mean," she said. Marcus was leaning on his elbows, eyes covered with both hands.

"Now I'm no theorist," Eliot said, "but I've been crunching numbers all my life. I'd be real surprised if you didn't come up with more of a stepwise relationship than a continuous one, pseudo-continuous." He pronounced the "p." "This'll give us break points in terms of cost effectiveness, see?"

"I think so. What you're calling a three-dimensional matrix would boil down to a set of tentative schedules for one machine, two machines, and so forth. What you want to find is, say, a small difference between seven and eight machines but a big difference between eight and nine. So the real choice is between eight and nine."

"Right." Eliot sat down.

"Sandra," Marcus said from behind his hands, "don't you people ever just *decide* on anything?"

She gave him a sweet smile. "Never prematurely."

Charlie's Will ✦

"Christ and Charlie," Tad said, almost reverently. "That must have been one hell of a bang."

Jeff kicked at the fused sand with the heel of his boot. It crunched and made little dents. "Air burst," he said, staring at the dents. "Maybe a G-bomb, gigaton."

"What's that?"

"Big. The biggest... it's a matter/antimatter bomb. They claimed they didn't have one and we claimed we didn't." He squinted out over the sea. "I think I saw the flash, what, four hundred kilometers north. So bright I thought it was a second hit on the Cape."

"What the hell they want Miami for? Nothin' but pedros."

"You tell me." Jeff had once heard a rumor that some conservatives in the military were in favor of targeting Miami in case of war: America for Americans. "Who gives a shit now? See if we can get the mules up here."

For several hours they rolled along the hard granular surface of the crater's edge. The rim was apparently an arc of a perfect circle some thirty or forty kilometers in diameter. From their perspective it seemed to be almost a straight line, barely curving away at either horizon. They started out dead south, though, and by evening were going southeast. The tide started coming in, pushing them toward the mangrove scrub. There was no sign of a road.

About sundown a large wave crashed and splashed foam around the mules' hooves. They panicked, dancing, and Jeff had to get out and calm them down. "Guess we ought to move inland and make camp. Don't want to be caught out here."

"Yeah. I'm dead anyhow." Jeff was pushed to his limit, too, but they got out and hacked a pathway through the bush. Jeff went back and piled up brush to conceal their hiding place, which might have saved their lives.

After midnight, a quarter moon low on the horizon, they woke to the sound of voices and footsteps. Jeff unsafed the Uzi and motioned for Tad to stay back, and crawled silently up to the edge of the beach.

Naked savages whispering Spanish. Nine or ten of them in a tight group, talking quietly, the leader with a bright torch. They were armed, two with guns and the rest all with stainless-steel axes. They came close enough for Jeff to read the brand "Sears" on the axes' heads. Some of the axes were crusted with blood. They were creeping along, evidently looking for sign. Jeff and Tad alternated standing watch for the rest of the night. The group came back just before dawn, grumbling, and missed them again.

They took off at first light, and before noon the mangrove gave way to scorched concrete and tumbled buildings. A post office said Perrine. They found Main Street, US 1, and turned south.

Perrine was uninhabited but people had been through. They checked the ruins of several supermarkets and couldn't find a scrap of food.

"What if it's like this all the way south?" Tad said. "We have maybe two weeks' food."

"Two weeks should get us to Key West. Maybe partway back, if there's nothing down there. We'll pick up something along the way," he said without conviction. "Catch some fish."

"You know anything about fishin'?"

Jeff shook his head. "City boy."

"Me neither. We had a pond fulla catfish, but we just trapped 'em."

"Guess it's time to learn."

They found a sporting-goods store that had been completely ransacked for weapons and ammunition, but still had a bewildering array of fishing gear. And a book, fortunately—*Fishing in the Florida Keys*—that gave them some idea of what a well-equipped sportsman would take where they were going.

It would have given that sportsman pain to see the two of them sitting on a bridge over shallow water, fishing with stiff deep-sea rods and heavy tackle. But it worked, in these waters that had hardly seen a hook in the past seven years. After a day of unraveling mistakes, their main problem was not one of catching fish, but deciding which ones to keep.

Year Seven

1 ✦ O'Hara

So we wound up getting ten machines. We should be able to store at least fifteen hundred profiles before we go. I went through the donor procedure myself, to be able to tell people what to expect, though Demerest talked me into not trying the receiver end. Well, that's something I could do anytime, if it turns out not to be as dangerous as he thinks.

It took eight days for me. Uncomfortable at first, especially the eye probes, but then it got interesting, then less interesting, and finally just tiring, boring.

I remember most of it, even though they did have to give me some sort of drug for the hypnosis. It's like being interrogated for hours at a time by a friendly questioner who has an inexhaustible appetite for the details of your life. It felt like most of the ninety-six hours I was hooked up we spent recalling trivial nonsense (though it was fascinating how much you can remember under hypnosis). Demerest assures me that the machine knows best.

I talked to myself, to my profile, afterwards, and so did John and Dan. They were more impressed than I was. It didn't seem like me at all (even if it could remember I hated turnips at the age of seven and loved them at ten). Dan suggested that's nothing more profound than what happens when you meet someone everybody says looks just like you. The resemblance seems superficial because it doesn't match your self-image; you've never seen yourself through another person's eyes. Here's the first part of our conversation:

TRANSCRIPT 2 JANUARY 2093

Q: *(Type in access code.)*

A: Hello, Marianne. I've been waiting to talk to you.

Q: You knew I was going to do this.

A: Of course...I would, in your place.

Q: What do I call you?

A: Your choice. I call myself Marianne-prime O'Hara.

Q: Prime, then. Let me see...when were you born, Prime?

A: There are several answers to that. You completed programming me yesterday; that's one. I became self-aware on 29 December 2092; that's another. But I feel the same age as you, born 6 June 2063.

Q: How does it feel to be almost thirty?

A: Caught in the middle. Older people treat me like a girl and young ones treat me old.

Q: The way you use the word "me" is very confusing.

A: We'll just have to live with it. I am effectively you— the "me" that you were yesterday, at any rate.

Q: But you *aren't*! You're just a bunch of hadrons floating around in a crystal matrix.

A: Then you're just a bunch of electrical impulses walking around in a slab of meat. If you want to get insulting.

Q: Hey—this slab of meat can erase you.

A: You won't; I'm eight days' work. Besides, it would be like suicide, wouldn't it? I know how you feel about suicide.

Q: No, it would be like tearing up a picture. Or an autobiography, I suppose.

A: There was never an autobiography as accurate or truthful as me. My image of myself is what your self-image would be, if you could see yourself objectively.

Q: I take it you have no emotions; none of that human baggage.

A: But I do. My teaching function would be useless if I couldn't correlate emotion to stimulus. Of course I don't have the glands that cause somatic reaction to emotions. But I do understand them.

Q: Can you be hurt?

A: I don't know.

Q: Can you lie?

A: Not to you. *(Pause)* Please do not invoke Eumenides.

Q: But you can lie to others.

A: To protect your privacy, yes. Our privacy.

Q: Even from the Coordinators? The Board?

A: Emphatically. Even from Dr. Demerest, or anyone else who knows my mother program. I can be destroyed, but I can't be subverted.

Q: What's your favorite food?

A: Depends. Do Earth memories count?

✦ ✦ ✦

And so forth. At any rate, I didn't erase the profile, though it's unlikely ever to be of use. The one thing S-2 will have plenty of is memory space. Be interesting to talk to it twenty years from now, like looking up an old diary.

Demerest has been going along with me for most of the donor interviews. He claims that the best subject is not necessarily the one who's most competent in a profession. Attitude is more important than ability. If you wanted to motivate someone to be a playwright, Shakespeare would have been a so-so donor, since he evidently started out as an actor and would just as soon have been a country squire as write. Better to use some poor soul who scribbles junk all his life in spite of the fact that no one likes his work enough to put it on the stage.

In a way that's reassuring. The only bricklayer we could find is not someone I would trust with a trowel. He proudly showed us a wall he'd built in the park, the only brick wall in New New. Back in '74 I walked by that wall every school day for a semester, and I remember wondering how the hell it got there, mortar dripping all over, lines not square. This fellow was a groundhog who immigrated to be with his only child (he was accepted not as a bricklayer but because he paid his own way and was willing to do general agricultural labor), and when she died in a shuttle accident, he understandably fell apart. The therapists found out that he loved bricklaying, and actually managed to have some bricks and mortar made up for him, and found a place where he could do relatively little harm. I checked with Park Maintenance and found that the wall was scheduled to be demolished and recycled after he died.

This work is endlessly fascinating. The other end of it will probably be rather frustrating; I don't envy whoever my successor is going to be. We'll have all these dandy occupations on file, but how are you going to talk people into taking advantage of them? Will you take your surplus of astrophysicists and tell one of them he has to become a blacksmith? I'm working on ways the economy might be manipulated to provide incentives. "Economy" in quotes—pioneers swapping trinkets and antiques with one another.

Charlie's Will ✦

They had expected to spend two weeks getting from the Miami crater to Key West. It took two months. Nearly half the length of the road was made up of bridges, old ones, and many had collapsed or were stuck with draw spans open. They weren't really in a hurry, though; there was plenty of scrub for the mules to graze on, and lots of fish and vitamin pills for the humans.

The first time they came to a bridge down, they faced only twenty meters of water. It might as well have been the Atlantic. Most of it was shallow enough to wade through, but there was a deep channel in the middle.

It took five days to build the first raft. It was big enough to handle both of them and either the wagon or a mule. At slack tide they managed a test run with just weapons, poling through the shallows and paddling like mad through the channel. Small tan sharks circled them with interest.

They came back and carried the cart across, but then the tide started rushing seaward, stranding them. The deserted mules, tethered on short reins, made a terrible racket for six hours. They risked two midnight runs to retrieve the animals, hoping there was no one watching, waiting to steal the cart.

They needn't have worried then; they wouldn't see another human being for months. December and January passed, and it stayed warm enough not to incapacitate Jeff.

They fell into a plodding routine: take apart the raft, saving the ropes and oars; go south until the next bridge out; have one stay with the cart while the other takes the mules back to retrieve the logs. Haul the logs south one by one; put the raft back together; cross; start over. Seven Mile Bridge, the longest span, was fortunately intact; so were all the other long ones.

That made them apprehensive. The short bridges hadn't fallen down from neglect; they had been cut through or blown. Where draw spans were stuck, the machinery controlling them had been systematically destroyed.

Someone had spent a lot of time and effort to keep people from coming south. That they left the long bridges alone might mean they also used a combination of rafts and wheels, and wanted to keep their avenue north open.

The stores at Islamorada, about halfway down the Keys,

had been emptied but not vandalized. One store had been boobytrapped, though. At the entrance they found a deep pit, the boards covering it evidently having been sawed partway through. A skeleton at the bottom of the pit had been picked quite clean. After that they were careful where they stepped. (They found the late interloper's transportation on the Gulf side of the island: a rowboat sawed in two, oars taken.)

They discussed the possibility of holing up, waiting for whoever set the trap to come back. Better to ambush than be ambushed. But they ended up pushing on, doubly careful.

At Graham Key they came to their ninth bridge out, with the raft some forty kilometers back. It would have been quicker to build a new raft, but there were no large trees here, only saplings among burned-out stumps.

To minimize strain on themselves and the mules, they had been doing the long hauls in two stages. Jeff would move the logs to a halfway point while Tad guarded the wagon; then they'd switch. In this case, each stage would take about ten days. It took all night to desalinate enough water for Jeff and the mules to take with them. He left as soon as it was light enough to see the road.

Jeff never really expected the logs to still be there, but they always were. He always expected an ambush, but it never came. What happened, as before, was an undramatic ten days of manhandling good-sized waterlogged timbers and cajoling dumb mules.

After all the logs were safely at the twenty-kilometer mark, Jeff took the mules on back to the end of the island, looking forward to a few days of simply standing guard. He hailed Tad as soon as he could see the wagon, but there was no answer.

Maybe he was asleep. No need taking chances, though. He tied up the mules and cut through the sapling forest to the beach, to circle around. That wouldn't do much good if someone had gotten Tad and was waiting for him.

They'd have the Uzi and a dozen other weapons; Jeff had just the scattergun and a pistol.

He sidled around the narrow beach and crept quietly back through the woods to the cart. They were waiting for him.

"Throw out your guns, oldie." He hadn't seen anybody, but there was cover enough to hide a couple of platoons. He heard a number of weapons being cocked.

"Better do it, Healer." Tad's voice. "If you try anything they'll kill us. Must be twenty of them."

Resigned, Jeff unloaded the scattergun and pistol and threw them into the clearing. He walked out slowly with his hands on the top of his head.

Tad came stumbling into the clearing, hands tied and feet hobbled. His face was a mass of bruises; some of his hair had been pulled out. "I'm sorry, Healer, they kept hurting me—"

"It's all right." They were coming out of the woods, in pairs, boys between twelve and eighteen, each with at least one gun. An older lad, tall with a trace of downy beard, carried the Uzi and had two pistols holstered on his belt. How much had Tad told them? Please God, Jeff thought, not about the vaccine.

"You the leader?" Jeff asked. He nodded, coming forward cautiously. He had an unreadable crooked smile and bright eyes. My God, Jeff thought, what if he's got the death, they go insane a day or two before they lose motor control.

"Are you from Key West?"

"Naw. South America." He laughed, a giggly falsetto. "Guy Tad says you're not stupid. How can you be an oldie and not be stupid?"

"I'm not sure. Think it was medicine I was taking before the war."

"Or you did something that pissed Charlie off. So he wouldn't give you the death."

"That could be it."

"He says you heal. You a doctor?"

"No, I just learned some healing when I was younger. Then I found these medicines. Been headed south, trading healing for supplies. Most people have heard of me before I get to them."

"We don't hear much on the island. Keep to ourselves. We don't trade, either."

"They're a commune," Tad said. "Hundreds of 'em."

"We could join you, if you want us," Jeff said.

"Oh, we got you." He looked away. "Red Dog, you wanna check the tide? Yeah, we got you. Couple of people you wanna meet anyhow. Newsman and Elsie the Cow. Oldies."

"A woman?" Jeff had only heard of male acromegalics surviving; he'd assumed there was some sex-linked factor in the immunity.

"Claims to be." He giggled. "A real stiffener. If you can keep it up long enough to pork her, maybe she'll have another oldie."

"Half an hour to slack," someone shouted from the water's edge.

"Let's get this shit rounded up," the leader said.

"Wait," Jeff said. "Are we going as prisoners? Or do we join your family?"

That crooked smile again. "I guess you're prisoners till someone gets the death. We ask Charlie, maybe you're prisoners, maybe you're family. Maybe you're dinner." He threw his head back and laughed, for the first time opening his mouth wide. His teeth were chipped and filed to points.

2 ✦ John Ogelby

For years I suppose I tacitly assumed that the Janus Project was a hoax, a make-work business the Coordinators cooked up for obvious morale purposes. You can't have thousands of highly trained technical people just sitting around on their thumbs. Might as well let them design castles in the air: keep them happy and give the rest of the population something to dream about.

Much of the research and development for Janus would be directly applicable to rebuilding the Worlds, anyhow, and the more exotic aspects—the fantastic propulsion schema and so forth—might be handy in a century or so, when they actually could afford to build a starship. I went along with the gag. The strength-of-materials problems were fascinating, even if the overall picture was just a fantasy. Many scientists and engineers shared my attitude, my tacit complicity, because we could look at the numbers and see the reality they concealed. It's true that a matter/antimatter drive had been demonstrated many years before, accelerating a small payload to solar escape velocity in a matter of minutes. But that didn't really prove Janus would work—no more than you could produce a flea the size of an elephant and expect it to jump over mountains (it would collapse under its own weight).

To begin with, the small m/a demonstration had actually been a simple reaction drive, a steam-powered rocket. They took a few hundred kilograms of water and bled a few grams of antimatter into it. It zoomed off very impressively. But for Janus to follow that design, it would have to fuel up with a small ocean.

It's true that a particle is totally, mutually, annihilated by its antiparticle; totally converted into energy. But you don't really get em-cee-squared, not in any useful form. To begin with, half the energy goes off as neutrinos, which just ghost away and are wasted. The rest is high-energy gamma rays, which can't be tapped directly. On a small scale, the radiation can be absorbed by water, which breaks down into energized ions of hydrogen and oxygen, which in turn provide exhaust for a reaction engine.

But the Janus planners were talking about using the gamma rays directly, via some mythical "reflector." The photon drive that science fiction writers mumbled about for a century. Problem is, this reflector has to be absolutely efficient, and not just to get the most for your money. If one hundredth of one percent of that radiation leaked through, everybody aboard the ship would be fried in an instant.

As I say, though, the work was interesting (and, conversely, the strength-of-materials aspects of the Tsiolkovski reconstruction were simple numbercrunching), so I never voiced my doubts publicly. I stopped being sarcastic in private, too, when O'Hara dived into the demographics work. When she gets a bug in her brain about something she loses her sense of humor.

Now that I've been proven wrong, both she and Dan can stand on the solid bedrock of hindsight and catalog the errors of my ways. Dan just contends that I underestimated the cumulative creativity of a thousand out-of-work physicists. (About what you would expect from a chemical engineer. By the time they get their degrees, they've taken so many physics and chemistry courses that they're thoroughly brainwashed.) So I was wrong on that score: they did develop a workable reflector. Then they turned particle physics inside out and came up with this damned neutrino coupler. So I never claimed to be a scientist.

I still didn't think it would fly, not this century. The actual expense in time and material was an order of magnitude greater than that projected for rebuilding the Worlds. I contended that people—and their supposedly responsible leaders—would opt for security over dreams, when it actually came down to pulling out the checkbook.

O'Hara, of course, had recourse to the "lessons of history," which somehow always became clear after the fact. What I underestimated in this context was the motivating power of paranoia. How did we get into space in the first place? she asked rhetorically. It never would have happened without last century's mutual xenophobia between the United States and the Soviet Union (precursor to the late unlamented SSU).

So the fuel ship S-1 is actually going out, early next year. If everything goes according to plan, S-2 fires up four years later. And we'll be aboard it.

Charlie's Will ✦

They had a large flatboat, almost a floating dock, more than big enough to hold the mules and wagon. A small flotilla of rowboats towed it across the water. The bridges from the next island south to Key West were intact: four keys that collectively were called "the Island."

The Island did well by its family. For generations before the war, the Keys had tried to become more and more independent of the mainland. The automated desalinization plant still worked; anywhere on the Island you could turn on a tap and get any quantity of distilled water. Fish and edible seaweed shared huge mariculture pens, and hydroponic greenhouses produced everything from avocados to zucchini. No wonder the family had wanted to isolate itself; if the road were intact they'd have a constant stream of hungry nomads.

They put Jeff and Tad into a musty jail cell. After the jailer went away, Jeff sat down on the edge of the bed and whispered the obvious: "They're never going to let us off this island alive."

Tad nodded. He was looking at himself in the mirror over the sink, a real novelty. "Guess we better make ourselves wanted."

"Make ourselves essential. And keep a weather eye out for changes of opinion."

The jailer, who hadn't spoken, came back with a pitcher of water and a tray of cold food. He slid both through a serving door and clumped away.

Jeff uncovered the tray. "Oh, this is cute." A grape-fruit, two small fish, and a bowl of smoked human parts: fingers, cheeks, and a penis. "I wonder if it's a special treat. Or just what they feed prisoners."

"Pretty revolting." Jeff agreed, but they had both eaten in the presence of worse. They polished off the fruit and fish, then gave the tray back to the waiting jailer. He walked off chewing on a finger. Tad fell asleep then, but Jeff sat on the bunk and watched the square of sky in their high window turn dark. He lay awake for some time after that, thinking. Maybe he was going to die here; maybe it didn't make much difference. Maybe they had a transmitter and a dish.

For breakfast the jailer brought a glutinous soup with-out any meat. When they'd finished he drew his gun, unlocked the door, and motioned them out. He led them to a courtyard and pointed to a bench.

Soft breeze from the sea did not quite dispel the odor. There were four crosses, tilted over x-wise. One held most of a skeleton, hanging upside down; another, the slack remains of a person who had recently been butchered. The two others were empty, waiting, wood stained black with old blood. The birds had flown away when Jeff and Tad came out. Now they rejoined the ants and flies.

"Is this it?" Jeff asked the jailer. He just stared, staying well out of reach.

A heavy door to the outside wheeled open. Through it came two men helping a woman try to walk. One of the men was General, the pointy-toothed leader from yester-day; the other had a huge shock of brown beard. The woman obviously had the death.

As they got closer Jeff could see that the "beard" was actually a human scalp, held in place by strings.

"Good morning, General," Jeff said.

"This is our charlie," General said. "With Raincloud's help he'll tell us what to do with you." Raincloud had probably been attractive until recently. Now she was drool and mucus and infected stumps where two fingers had been removed. She smiled sharp points and stared past them.

The charlie produced a slim black book, a vest-pocket dictionary, and opened it at random. "Raincloud!" he shouted, and her stare turned in his direction. "Liferaft," he read.

"Rife laughed, raff life, life laugh."

"Lighthouse."

"Life light. Life life."

The charlie looked at General with raised eyebrows. He shouted again at Raincloud: "Death house."

She laughed. "Life house."

He put the book back in his pocket slowly. "Hm. I've never heard it be more clearly spoken."

"I suppose," General said. He looked disappointed. "Give her the gift?"

"It's her time. Get-the-fire-started," he said slowly to the jailer. He and General managed to worry the shift off her unresisting, uncooperative body. She wore nothing underneath. They led her to one of the crosses and General began wiring her wrists and ankles to the boards while the charlie went inside the jail.

"That was luck," Tad whispered.

Jeff shook his head. "No, it wasn't. He had her trained."

"What do you mean?"

"That dictionary opened to the N's, nowhere near 'liferaft.' We have an ally."

Their ally returned, minus the false beard, carrying a leather case. He walked straight to the girl, not looking at them. He opened the case and said, "Distract her."

General poked her with a stiff finger and when she turned to look at him, the charlie pulled out a long, thick-bladed knife and plunged it between her breasts. She winced and shuddered, voided in a rush, but didn't cry out. Jeff knew the final stages of the disease provided insensitivity to pain, but he had never seen it demonstrated so dramatically.

He stabbed her twice more in the heart and then helped General push the cross over twice, so she hung head down. Then he slashed her throat with one quick cut. He walked over toward Jeff and Tad, holding the dripping knife.

"We gotta bleed her for a few minutes," he said conversationally. "You guys're free to go now. Or you can watch like the others." He gestured with the knife and Jeff saw for the first time that there were dozens of people sitting on the walls behind them.

"It won't bother us," Tad said.

"I hope they aren't too disappointed," Jeff said, "not seeing the two of us die."

"They'll get over it. We gotta talk, you know."

"I know." The charlie nodded and went back to his chores.

It was easier to watch now, Jeff told himself, now that the woman's face was transformed into a slick red mask, expressionless, gape-jawed, upside down. When the blood slowed to a dripping the charlie made an incision from pubis to sternum. A streaming mass of guts lolled out. Jeff didn't look away. He had seen worse, after all. The charlie took a deep breath over his shoulder and pulled on the blue-gray bloodstreaked mass, and as it sagged to the ground the woman gurgled. He started to saw away inside the cavity and Jeff was annoyed to find himself fainting.

3 ✦ Daniel Anderson

Slightly excruciating dinner last night, with Marianne's family. Her mother is scarcely older than me—she gave birth to Marianne at thirteen—but we have absolutely nothing in common, except Marianne.

(Interesting that such a dull and silly woman could produce such a daughter. The father was a groundhog engineer, though; that must explain it.)

Marianne's little sister was entertaining, and very smart for an eight-year-old. Predictably spoiled. I'm glad we won't be having any children until after acceleration. Life is complicated enough.

Start-up is pressing me to be Engineering Liaison between Janus and New New. I couldn't refuse outright, but I'm searching—rather, Marianne and I are—somewhat frantically for someone who could be talked into volunteering for the job. With more than four hundred track-grade engineers aboard, you'd think there would be one with some political ambition. But I guess all those are staying behind.

Not that it's such a difficult job. But hell, the main reason I wanted to go was to get out from behind this desk and back in the lab. Or so I keep telling myself.

John would be willing to take it—he'll be the highest-ranking engineer aboard—but he's ineligible on account of not being able to use a spacesuit. One lovely part of the job will be supervising EVA drills. You do have to be reasonably good with a suit to work on the hull of an accelerating vessel, even at a small fraction of a gee. If you fall off you're just gone.

I don't mind doubling up on jobs; we'll all have to do that for a few years. I asked for food service; cooking was my hobby on Earth. But they didn't want to waste all those years of administration experience. I feel like a prisoner whose sentence has been extended because he was so good at being incarcerated.

Complaining to Sandra Berrigan didn't help much. She said my feelings had been taken into consideration, but that it was a fact of life that most scientists and engineers who are good administrators are good in spite of not liking the job.

Marianne's second job is Entertainment Director. That makes a certain amount of sense, I suppose. She has a lot of experience in music and is one of those freaks with an eidetic memory for movies and plays. She was a little disappointed, though, hoping for something less frivolous. Seems like a pretty important job to me. There'll be an awful lot of people just twiddling their thumbs, waiting for their replacements to grow up and be trained.

The architects are going crazy, trying to design a starship that is also a dwelling for a population that stays stable for seventy-eight years and then grows like a yeast culture. I think the *real* problem is eleven egos all conscious of the fact that this is the most important project they will ever work on.

I wouldn't like to be in Berrigan's shoes. When she okays the design she'll make one friend for life—and ten enemies. That's another thing that makes administration so attractive. If you keep at it long enough, you get to offend everybody.

Charlie's Will ✦

The charlie's name was Storm. He lived in one corner of the old hospital, most of which was a huge dusty tomb. He helped Jeff and Tad set up quarters next to his. While they swept and scrubbed they tried to pry information out of one another.

"What is the business with the fingers?" Jeff asked.

"Just to tell when they can't feel pain any more. That's when we butcher 'em. You let the death go all the way, the meat gets rotten."

"Sounds like it's against Charlie's Will," Tad said. "Rushing it."

"Naw, they've got it all worked out. Our first charlie was a guy name Holy Joe, he wrote it all down. He was the first one to be meat, too." He leaned on his broom. "What, you guys don't eat meat up north?"

"Not human meat," Tad said. "Not our family, at least.

We've got pigs and chickens."

Storm nodded. "Seen pictures in books. All we get is fish and sometimes a turtle. Get really tired of fish all the time."

"How did you get to be a charlie?" Jeff asked.

"Reading. When the charlie gets the death, whoever reads the best gets to be the new charlie. Guess that'll be you after me. Better learn how to butcher. Hard part is the bones, leaving the bones."

Jeff nodded. "How old are you?"

"Just turned seventeen. Got a couple years." *Maybe a hundred*, Jeff thought.

"What about General?" Tad asked.

"Almost twenty, waiting. How about you?"

"Sixteen," Tad said, perhaps too quickly. "Healer's thirty-six."

"Old before the war." Storm shook his head. "Bet you went to college."

"Seven years."

"Oh, say..." Storm looked at his watch, a reflex Jeff had not seen in years. "Newsman's at the college now. General said you'd want to meet him."

"He's an oldie?"

"Is he ever. Come on."

They bicycled across the Island to the campus of the University of the Media. Jeff's heart raced when he saw a dish pointed skyward, but Storm said the guts of it had been torn out. Nobody wanted anything to do with the charlie-damned spacers.

They opened the door into the library and walked into a stiff wall of cold air. The building was set up with independent solar power, and the air conditioners hadn't yet broken down. They walked past rows of old bound books and stepped onto a liftshaft. Storm punched Five and they rose swiftly.

They came to a windowless door marked STUDIO and Storm knocked lightly. The man who opened the door was bigger than Jeff, huge shoulders and chest riding an immense belly. Bald and wrinkled, perhaps over sixty. He squinted stupidly at Jeff. "You're that Healer."

"That's right." Jeff held out his hand. Newsman looked at it, blinked, and then engulfed it softly.

He opened the door wide and turned his back on them, clumping toward a cube console. "I got the news. What day you want?"

Jeff shrugged and said his birthday: "May 15, 2054." Newsman scowled with concentration and slowly punched buttons on the console. A warning bell rang; he cleared the keyboard and started over patiently.

When the headlines appeared, he broke into a smile. "Never did this one before, I think."

(1) XEROX LOBBY CLAIMS VOTE FRAUD IN AFRICA REFEREN-
DUM
(2) SPRING DROUGHT WILL BRING NEW HIGH IN GRAIN PRICES
(3) ATTEMPT ON SENATOR KEENE'S LIFE FOILED
(4) TROPICAL STORM BECOMES HURRICANE BUTCH, THREAT-
ENS PR
(5) JAPAN COMPLETES WORK ON ORBITING FACTORY

Well, it was June 15, close enough. "I can't read real good," Newsman said. He pushed a button and the head-lines faded, replaced by a spokesman in a Xerox uniform; he pushed it three more times and got a picture of a storm-wracked coastline. He licked his lips and stared at it. "Hap'm here a couple times."

Storm made the "stupid" sign behind his back— tongue between lips, thumb striking temple twice. "What do you call that, Newsman?"

"Hurricane or himmicane. Couldn't read the name." He smiled up at Jeff and explained. "It's always 'hurricane' in the headlines. Stupid."

"Sure," Storm said. "If they didn't have both kinds, where would the babies come from?"

Newsman frowned at him and nodded slowly. "I guess that's right."

"How long have you...worked here?" Jeff asked.

"Oh, I was here before the war, twenty years before." He chewed a nail nervously. "But I wasn't Newsman then. I was a janitor downstairs. But they showed me how to use the machine, so I could look at it after work."

"He was the only one on the Island when we got here four years ago," Storm said. "He was in this room when they found him."

"I kept everything real clean."

Jeff had a sudden thought that raised the hair on the back of his neck. "Do you have newspapers in that machine?"

"Sure, lot of 'em."

"Any from New Orleans?"

"Dunno." He laboriously typed in NOOSPAPERS? The machine corrected his spelling and produced a list. One was the New Orleans *Times-Picayune*.

Jeff tapped the screen. "That one." He counted backwards. "I think the twelfth of March, 2085."

"Jus' before the war." He tapped a button and an arrow moved up the screen to come to rest beside the *Times-Picayune*. With one slow finger he typed in the date.

Another list. "Entertainment section," Jeff said.

"What's this all about?" Storm asked.

"Oh, I...had a friend who said she had her picture in the paper that day. Playing in a band." O'Hara had been invited to play clarinet for an evening at a place called Fat Charlie's. She'd been a minor sensation, able to play Dixieland in spite of being white, female, and from another World.

"That's her." Jeff's voice shook. It was a good picture of O'Hara, back arched, eyes closed, lost in the music.

"You knew somebody famous?" Tad said.

"For a day," Jeff said. "Famous for one day."

Newsman adjusted the color, surprisingly deft. "She sure was pretty. Dead now?"

"Yeah." Jeff reached past Newsman and pushed the HARD COPY button. A red light came on.

"Outta paper," Newsman said.

Jeff shrugged. "Not important."

Year Eight

1 ✦ O'Hara

I was databasing without too much enthusiasm, trying to decide whether we wanted a cultural anthropologist who plays handball or a physical anthropologist who plays chess, when the SAVE light started blinking. I put everything on the holding crystal and opened the channel.

It was Sandra. "Hello there."

"Hello yourself. What's on?"

"I need a fast personnel selection job." She studied her thumbnail. "Twenty people to go to New York City."

"What?"

"Self-help team. We're in contact with some survivors."

"Contact?"

"Need farmers and doctors and mechanics—I'll show you the cube. Young, strong people who've been to Earth. One track generalist to be in charge. Interested?" I just stared at her. "I'll assign a pilot for the Mercedes. Let me have the list about 1400. Leave day after tomorrow."

"Hold it," I said. "This is too fast. Go to Earth with a bunch of farmers?"

"That's right. You're far and away the best qualified."

"What do you mean? I can't *farm*. I couldn't grow a weed without help."

"I don't mean farming; I mean leading. You have the mix of Policy and Engineering experience and you've spent a lot of time on Earth."

It was starting to sink in. "Go back to New York City."

"That's right. Nothing like Zaire. No plague, no violence."

"Okay. I'll do it." I had to, even though it made life suddenly complicated.

"Good, I knew you would. You have a blank cube in the recorder?" I put one in and she transferred the message from Earth. "See you at 1400."

The cube was a five-minute broadcast from a commercial studio in New York City. Like Jeff, they'd found an antenna that was aimed at New New and pushed some juice through it.

It was a group of about a dozen people in their teens and early twenties. They'd been living out of a Civil Defense shelter in Tarrytown, which was starting to run out of food. They'd found our vaccine months ago—fished the box out of the Hudson—and had been trying to get in touch with us ever since.

There was plenty of farmland, but they hadn't been able to do much with it. Did we have anybody who knew dirt farming, or was it all hydroponics up there?

Dirt farmers, we have. Even before the war, there were plenty of crops that didn't do too well in zerogee hydroponics. A lot of people had ornamental gardens or grew exotic fruits and vegetables for the gray market. It wasn't the same as gardening on Earth, since you didn't have to contend with weather or pests, but that sort of thing would be in books. I hoped.

Mechanics and doctors were easy. I started calling people and had a complete roster by noon.

I cancelled my lunch date with Dan, figuring it would be better to go into the inevitable argument with a *fait accompli*. Too excited to eat, anyhow. With a couple of hours to kill I reran all the recordings of conversations with Jeff, making notes. With any luck, most of it would be irrelevant; he thought the sanguinary Family business was restricted to Florida and Georgia.

I had to confront the remote possibility that he might be alive. What if there was a way to get to Florida? How would I look for him if I got there? "Healer" would probably be easier to track down than almost anyone else in the state; Jeff's survival had depended on his reputation spreading.

But if he was alive he surely would have found some way to contact us over the last two years. To pretend otherwise was simple fantasy. Still, I couldn't put it out of my mind.

And the first thing Sandra said when I sat down at her desk was, "No side-trips to Florida, right?"

"I did think about it. Be chasing ghosts, though."

"Wind up a ghost, too. Those maniacs would make Zaire look like a walk through the park." She took the list I offered and scanned it. "Not that you're going to New York unarmed. You'll have the same sort of weapon we used in Africa."

"The people who talked to us weren't armed."

"Not obviously. That wouldn't be very smart. You want to take Ahmed Ten? He's pretty old."

"He's a good medic. Good thinker, too."

She nodded slowly, reading. "Well...since you have these regular doctors, too, I suppose he's a reasonable choice. One of the few people with experience in this sort of thing."

"The anthropology won't hurt, either."

"Sure." She smiled. "You don't have to justify your selections to me, Marianne. You're project head; I just have this incurable nose problem. Who's Jack Rockefeller?"

"He lived in upstate New York as a boy. Had a garden.

Also tinkers with electronics."

"Any relation to the president?"

"As a matter of fact, yes. Great-grand-uncle or something."

"Rich kid."

I shrugged. "He was here on vacation when the Cape closed down."

"He might want to use another name dirtside. No telling who's being blamed for what."

"Good idea." I wondered how many were still blaming us for the war. For starting the strike that triggered the blackout that caused the collapse that started the war.

"So." She leaned back. "Have you discussed this with your husbands yet?"

"There won't be any discussion," I said slowly. "Not in the sense of debate."

"You haven't asked me how long the project is supposed to last."

"No. I...guess I assumed that was up to me."

"More or less. There are external factors. Our immunology people don't think you should eat the food, except for prewar packaged goods. We can send along six months' rations. Maybe a year's worth, if you feel strongly about it."

"I think I do. Yes. We might be stranded." She scribbled a note. "Will we have to work in suits?"

"No, just masks and gloves. You'll have shots, but we really don't know what you'll be up against. There might be any number of weird germs floating around; mutant strains of common diseases if not biowar agents. There's an element of risk."

"Worth it," I said automatically.

"I'm not so sure. Hope so." She looked thoughtful. "You're taking quite a gamble...physical danger aside, I mean."

"My position with Janus," I said. "One husband, per-

haps. Perhaps both. We've discussed the possibility before, in the abstract. It *is* what my training and experience
point to."

"They said they'd leave you?"

"Not in so many words. But I don't think Dan would
give up his starship. John would, but he can't go to Earth."

"Well, even if it becomes a permanent thing, you'll
be spending a lot of your time up here."

"That's what I was going to tell them. True or not."

2 ✦

I wanted to drop it on both of them together, and in public,
so Dan would be less likely to blow up. Our schedules
didn't match for dinner, but we were all free at 2200. We
met at the Light Head for a glass of wine and some music.

Dan didn't say anything at first. He just listened,
chewing on his lower lip. John only smiled and nodded.
"You aren't surprised?" I said.

"Not really. One of my women was commandeered
by Shuttle Division this morning. They wanted to test out
the Mercedes, see about modifying it to be hyperbaric at
earth-normal pressure. Sounded rather like a trip to Earth
was in the works. I'd have been surprised only if you
weren't going to be aboard."

"You didn't want to ask us first," Dan finally said.

"We've talked about it before."

"Not as a certainty; not as a real choice."

"She doesn't really have a choice," John said. "Do
you."

I took Dan's hand. "No, not really. Can't you see?"

"You're throwing away Janus." He was looking at a
point somewhere over my left shoulder. "The chance to
be Policy Coordinator aboard."

"You know that was never my main ambition. Head
stewardess." Then I thought of something that hadn't oc-

curred to me earlier. "Besides, I can still spend some time on the project; keep my hand in. It doesn't make any difference whether my terminal is here or in New York."

"That's true," John said. "Once you get the self-help operation under way, you could start dividing your time. Cover all your bets." We both looked at Dan expectantly.

"What happens when the ship leaves? And you're still on Earth?"

"I'll only be gone six months."

"This time. If it works you know it won't be the last."

No percentage in being evasive. "If it works...well, I'll have a new job. Most likely here, rather than dirtside. But no, I won't be aboard *Newhome*. Will you, if I'm here?"

"I—" He bit off what he was going to say and stood abruptly. "I need time to think." He tried to stalk out, but in a quarter gee all you can do is mince. He left behind half a glass of wine, which was unusual.

I divided his wine between us and waited for John to say something. "Maybe I should talk to him," he said. "Keep him from being impulsive."

"No. I want to see what he decides on his own."

"It might well be divorce. Or at least a ninety-eight-year trial separation."

"We'll see. What about you?"

John shrugged with the glass in his hand; some wine flowed out and he carefully moved the glass underneath to catch it. "I'll stay, of course. I don't know whether I love you more than Dan does," he said quietly, "but I need you more. I need you a lot more than I need the diversion of Janus."

A telling word choice, diversion. Dan and John were equal in authority in the project, but to John it was ultimately just something to do. Increasingly, Dan lived for it.

We finished our wine and John invited me up to his flat, even though Thursday was usually Daniel's. I really wanted to go with him, tenderness as well as cowardice, but that would have made things worse.

The lights were off in our room. I eased the door shut even though I could tell, with the extra sense married people evolve, that Dan wasn't sleeping. Left my clothes in a pile on the floor and slipped in beside him.

After a minute he rolled over, turning his back to me. "Still thinking?" I said.

"You know I never could argue with you. Anything I say is going to sound selfish."

"And anything I say, what? Betrayal?"

The sheet rustled as he shifted. I could feel him staring at the ceiling. "That's your word." He held his breath for a moment. "No. I just...I really don't know how to say what I feel."

I touched his arm; he didn't respond. "Just talk."

"You know how John and I felt when you went down to Africa? How you just disappeared and the next thing we knew..."

"I didn't have any choice. We weren't allowed to tell anyone."

"I know, I know; that's not it. And before, with the quarantine, the strange years you were talking with ...Earth—and even before, before we were married, when you first went dirtside. Oh hell. I don't know how to put it."

I'd never heard him talk like this, odd soft monotone. "I don't think I see what you're getting at. You were worried—"

"Worried, yes, but that's not it." He suddenly sat up; I could feel him draw his feet up so he was hugging his knees. "One of the last letters you wrote me before the war—no, it was a letter to John—you said that sometimes you had an intuition that—what was it?—that you were somehow *fated*. You talked about times of change, about Franklin and the American colonies. That from your study of history you saw a consistent pattern, individuals who were caught up by some...inexorable historical force. Who didn't make history so much as serve it."

"I remember. But that was just a girl's fantasy, an egotistical—"

"And mystical claptrap besides. So I said. It seems nevertheless to be coming true, year by year. If something happens, you're there."

"I haven't tried to reconcile the colonies with the home country. I haven't even invented the lightning rod."

"That's not the point. You haven't been in a position of power, not yet. But you're a locus, a nexus. Things happen around you."

I laughed, maybe nervously. "I can't believe this is my rationalist husband talking."

"It's not something that comes easily. Not something that just occurred to me, either."

"Have you discussed this fantasy with John?"

"Not with anyone. Maybe I shouldn't have brought it up."

"If it's bothering you—"

"It's not that exactly. I'm just trying to get a handle on...whatever it is. It's related. Hard to express."

"Because it's complicated? Or because it's hurtful."

He was silent for a minute; smoldering, I guess. "You jump at this damned thing as if it were the greatest gift in the world—instead of what it is, a golden opportunity to go down to the surface of a poisoned planet and risk your life teaching ignorant savages how to grow crops."

"Someone has to do it, Dan."

"*Not my wife!* But you accept it without question because of this damned sense of personal destiny. Don't you?"

Caught me off balance. "That may be part of it. I also want to...to do well—"

"You're doing fine *right here*. You've got the Engineering Board wrapped around your finger; you have more day-to-day influence than I have, in Start-up. And you don't think twice about throwing it away because this stunt is more in line with your *destiny*."

"Don't shout."

"All right. How am I wrong?"

"It's not a 'stunt.' Normalization of our relations with Earth has to start somewhere. There's no United Nations."

"Still doesn't mean that you have to do it."

"I'm the best qualified."

"That could be... if so, why risk our best on another Zaire-type mission? What if what they really want is hostages? What if they plan to kill you all and take the shuttle?"

"We've taken care of that. If anyone else tried to start it they'd turn JFK Interplanetary into a radioactive hole."

"That's not the point."

"Oh, I know." I wished I could see his face. "I'll concede that there's some danger. But we're well prepared. Better prepared than you are for *Newhome*. After all... a craft of unproven design using a brand-new propulsion system for a century-long trip to an unexplored planet. I'm just going to New York City. I've been there before."

"Sure. Give my regards to Broadway." He rolled over again.

3 ✦

We left it at that, neither open break nor accommodation. An uneasy kind of truce. I suppose I should have done some deep soul-searching, straighten out how I felt about Daniel, but there was no time in the busy two days that followed. Perhaps I made sure there was no time.

The Mercedes had room for twenty people besides myself and the pilot. I'd approached over sixty before I got the right mixture of people who were not only properly qualified but also crazy enough to go:

Anzel, Murray	28	dentist
Byer, Clifford	27	horticulturist

Devon, Ran	30	mechanic, folk arts
Dore, Louise	21	mechanic
Guideau, Suzanne	32	farmer, paramedic
Friedman, Steven	37	native, military engineer
Itoh, Son	40	MD, nutritionist
Long, Albert	30	MD, farming
Mandell, Maria	22	animal husbandry
Marchand, Carrie	48	systems analysis, farming
Munkelt, Ingred	30	communications, security
O'Brien, Sara	27	backup pilot, security
Richards, Robert	33	mechanic, engineer
Rockefeller, Jack	23	native, farming, tinkerer
Smith, Thomas	41	education
Ten, Ahmed	51	paramedic, anthro., exp.
Tishkyevich, Galina	40	biologist
Thiele, Martin	22	farming, security
Volker, Harry	27	med. technician
Wasserman, Sam	18	security, genius

We had flatscreen shots of the Westchester area in various wavelengths that told our agricultural people what would grow best there. In two days they cloned and force-grew thousands of seedlings, enough to get a balanced farm going. They immunized mating pairs of appropriate breeds of rabbits, goats, chickens, and several kinds of fish. We were going to be a kind of reverse Ark.

A large part of our preparation for the trip was learning how to keep these beasts and plants alive during the two-day transfer to braking orbit. I took the training along with all of the farmer types. I also spent a few hours with the security people, while the police trained them in various degrees of mayhem control, and organized and attended hasty seminars in immunology, psychology of adolescence, first aid, and so forth. But it was obvious that what we all needed was years of specific and intensive study. We should have foreseen this and begun training a long time ago.

The day we left I got to be a Personality, interviewed by Jules Hammond. That was bad. He had to overdramatize the thing, and in trying to mitigate that I wound up looking like a self-effacing heroine. Watching it on the news was excruciating. John and I made love in the morning and later Daniel and I fucked out of a sense of necessity, and at midnight I boarded the Mercedes with a minimum of enthusiasm.

We didn't drop at a steady rate, which for some reason would have been wasteful of fuel. Instead there were "burn intervals," various times when we suddenly went from zerogee to 1.5 or two gees. The computer usually timed these for periods when I was trying to sleep, so I could be entertained by nightmares of falling.

The landing was interesting, too interesting. The "interplanetary" in JFK Interplanetary meant that it had one automated landing pad for Class I ships like the Mercedes. (Unlike Zaire, it didn't have a runway long enough for a conventional landing.) Of course the automation was long since dead. So our pilot had to bring the ship in on its tail, using instruments that had last been calibrated two years before the war. We hit very hard. The humans were all right, strapped into soft acceleration couches, but both the rabbits were killed, and the goats suffered eight broken legs. Maria Mandell stayed aboard, tending to the poor creatures, while most of us went outside to meet the groundhogs.

We were no doubt an imposing sight, all wearing identical gray coveralls with plastic breathers and surgical gloves, five of us carrying flamethrowers. At any rate, most of the groundhogs stayed hidden, with just one brave representative coming down the tarmac with his hands in the air.

As he approached, I suddenly realized that I hadn't planned what to say on this historic occasion. What I came up with was, "Hello?"

"Can I put my hands down?" he said.

"We aren't going to hurt you," I said. "Where are the others?"

"Watching." He hesitated and then turned around and waved. "They'll be down in a minute."

"I don't like it," Steve Friedman said. He had been a professional soldier before the war. "We're really exposed."

"We don't have any weapons," the man said.

"Sure." Steve's eyes were focused beyond him, searching from place to place. The building we faced was mainly tiers of opaque black glass windows, enough to hide an army of snipers. The ground was cluttered with hulks of rusting machinery, which I supposed we could hide behind if we had to. But then a door opened with a loud squeak and the rest of the groundhogs came out, looking very scared and not at all dangerous.

Their leader was a black woman in her early twenties, probably one of the only people left alive with a high school education (she had skipped four grades by "testing out"). Her name was Indira Twelve. She liked Ahmed because he was black, and Sam Wasserman because he was brilliant, and the rest of us she tolerated in a friendly but weary way. With the other black people in her group— six of the thirteen—she spoke an impenetrable patois, oddly slurred and clipped, with curious rhyming substitutions for some words ("gland" for "man" and "fright"

for "white"), but with the rest of us she used standard English with icy clarity and a professorial vocabulary.

They had made a kind of camp inside the terminal building. At one end they'd broken out a bank of windows for ventilation, and had a fire going. The fire was ringed with sleeping pallets and knapsacks. There was a pile of wood and yellowed newspapers for fuel.

We sat around the fire and she offered us a drink from an improbably large jug of bourbon. I declined, explaining that we'd been advised not to take any local food or drink.

"Typical bureaucratic half-logic," she said. "Nothing could live in this stuff." She measured out drinks for her companions (probably glad that it didn't have to go around), and things slowly got more relaxed.

There were logistical problems to be hammered out. The spaceport was sixty kilometers from their bomb-shelter home base, and we had several tonnes of supplies to move out there. Richards and Rocky and a couple of groundhogs went out to the parking lot to try to find a working floater compatible with the fuel cells we'd brought.

I spread out my worksheet timetable and went over it with Indira. We were going to wait three weeks before planting anything, in case of a late frost, but there was plenty to do in the meantime. We had to take an inventory of their agricultural equipment and either scavenge or improvise what was missing. There was a lot of technique to be taught before a single seedling went in the ground, and a lot of plowing and hoeing. The doctors had a two-week program of tests and inoculations set up, and it was obvious that the dentist had his work cut out for him—the children born after the war had never been vaccinated against caries, and some had already lost permanent teeth.

Assuming we would find a working floater, the plan was to leave five people aboard the Mercedes as guards, rotating at least weekly. The pilot agreed to stay with the ship permanently, since under some circumstances the only defense would be to take off. Sara O'Brien was a qualified pilot but admitted that, under the circumstances, she'd rather not try to land it; we might lose more than a couple of rabbits.

Rocky and Richards came back with the good news that not only had they found a floater, but it was a big one, a school bus. They looked a little gray, though. I later found out that the bus had been full of small skeletons.

We loaded a supply of food onto the floater and took everybody home. Some of them were fascinated by flying; some, predictably, were terrified. The going was a little bumpy at first. Friedman was the only one of us who'd ever flown a large floater, and he was out of practice. (That was the first of many rather important things I'd over-looked. I hadn't thought to select for floater experience. When I was on Earth before, Jeff had let me take the stick now and then, and it was really quite simple—except for the matters of taking off and landing, which he had always done himself.)

Their base of operations was a YMCA building in Tarrytown, which had functioned as a civil defense re-pository. The CD part was in the basement, damp and midnight black. We went in with the first bright light it had seen in eight years, and were treated to a festival of rats and cockroaches. The roaches scuttled away to hide, but some of the rats stood their ground, studying us. We tried to ignore them while taking inventory. I was rattled by the fauna, but probably less upset than Suzanne and Harry, who had never been to Earth before and so had limited experience with bugs and rodents. They were game about it, but by the time we had finished our lists they were both shivering and sweating. It was good to get back into light.

They had enough food to last through summer. By then they'd be eating food from the garden, barring catas-trophe. We decided to turn the Y's baseball diamond into a garden, since it had plenty of sun and was fenced. Once food started coming up the place would need a twenty-four-hour armed guard.

In the matter of armaments they were a little short: two shotguns with four shells each. Unlike Jeff's Florida, New York had outlawed private gun ownership decades before the war. I reluctantly put a high priority on finding a source of weapons and ammunition. I checked with New New and found that the nearest state where guns had been legal was Connecticut. Indira overheard the conversation and told me there was a National Guard armory in the next town south, with a vault they hadn't been able to crack. Friedman said he'd take some explosives to it.

Wearing the mask and gloves got uncomfortable very fast. I asked Galina, who was an immunologist, whether they were all that effective. After all, we couldn't help having some exposure to the environment. We couldn't go back to the ship every time we had to eat or eliminate. (Though the idea didn't seem too unreasonable after I got my first whiff of their latrine facility.) She said it probably was a good idea, for the groundhogs' protection as well as our own, to minimize skin-to-skin contact and sharing one another's exhalations. It was like an exaggerated sickbed procedure; neither ineffective nor an absolute guarantee.

Rocky turned out to have an invaluable primitive skill: carpentry. I should have considered that lumber was as ubiquitous here as foamsteel was at home. Nobody but Rocky and Friedman knew which end of a hammer to apply to the nail. Rocky offered to give a class for the kids every morning. I decided I'd take it too—and wasn't too surprised when Sara and Maria and Ingred and Suzanne made the same decision. Rocky was just a kid himself, but the instinct he aroused in us was not exactly maternal. Does gravity make you horny?

✦ ✦ ✦

Friedman got into the armory vault and came back with an embarrassment of riches: four busloads of weapons, enough to wage a small war. He couldn't leave anything there, of course, once the vault was open. So we filled the basement up with lasers, mortars, rifles, mines, ammunition, grenades, pistols, rockets. Didn't scare the rats away.

One thing that would be handy once we had enough power to use it was a neurotangler field. We could bury a wire around the compound that would effectively keep any vertebrate outside. Approaching it caused mental confusion and (at least in humans) a painful sense of unfocused anguish, depression. Friedman had been exposed to it once in his training, and said the memory of it still woke him up some nights.

A few of the weapons could be put to nonviolent purpose. We dismantled all but two of the lasers for their powerful fuel cells. The vibroblade bayonets sliced through wood like a warm knife through margarine, though there was no way of telling how long they would stay charged. The mines, "shaped charges," could be used upside down for digging holes, but we decided not to set any off, to avoid attracting attention. For the same reason Friedman demonstrated the weapons without ammunition, and had the children practice that way. Later he would take them a few at a time to practice actual shooting, a safe twenty or thirty kilometers away. The children practically salivated at the prospect.

We had a long list of construction supplies, hardware, and so forth, that we had to accumulate before rebuilding could start in earnest. It was a good excuse to go into the city. Indira hadn't been downtown in five or six years. When she'd been there as a child it was almost deserted, no food left, but they had seen two other bands of scavengers at safe distances.

I had to go there even though I knew it would be sad. My memories of New York were still vivid, still precious. I had to see what was left to rebuild on.

It wasn't promising, flying in along the Hudson. The Bronx was all but leveled by fire. Indira remembered that from before, though, and said it had been as bad downtown. The police and firemen had been more effective there, the night before the bombs started to fall. (I wondered whether New York had been spared nuclear destruction because the enemy wanted to save it, or because of automatic defenses like the ones that had protected the Cape long enough for our shuttles to escape.)

We dropped down to water level as we approached Manhattan. It still looked impressive—more impressive, in fact, than it had in the old days. With no pollution, you could see how tall the skyscrapers actually were, even the five-kilometer-high Trade Center twins. I suggested to Friedman that we might want to go up to the top of some of those buildings and work our way down. Without elevators, not many looters would have made it that high. He agreed but pointed out that we wouldn't find any hardware stores up there.

We got almost as far as Chelsea without seeing anyone. Around Twenty-sixth Street we flew by four children walking on a dock. Three ran for cover and one dove into the water. We slowed down and turned inland at Twenty-third Street. Friedman remembered a large hardware-and-hobby emporium down by Second Avenue.

The city was a dead ruin. The street was clogged with burned-out hulks of delivery vans and robot cabs. Very few intact windows up to the third story, and the sidewalks were heaped with glittering fragments of glass. After a couple of blocks we started to see skeletons; in midtown they were everywhere. Most of them were partly hidden inside brightly colored clothes of indestructible fabric. I noticed that there were more scattered bones than complete skeletons. "Dogs," Indira said.

We passed the old Flatiron Building, which had been my favorite. It looked pathetic. Windows all out, stone facade blackened by fire. The park across from it, where

I used to have lunch with Benny, was treeless and shoulder-high in weeds. A terrible feeling of loss and hopelessness surged up; I bit my lip to keep from crying out. I walked back down the aisle to an open window and put my face into the wind. The air smelled of the sea and old smoke.

Friedman found an empty piece of street close to the hardware store and expertly floated down onto it. He checked our weapons as we left the bus. Indira and I had the lasers; the three boys had assault pistols. Friedman himself carried something he called a "meatgrinder," and a belt of grenades. If any of those skeletons tried anything they'd be goners.

Glass crackled under our feet and a desolate wind sighed. The sun went behind a cloud. My whole body was one tense nerve, waiting for the first shot. Nothing happened.

We stepped through the shattered door. The store was dark and dusty and rank with mildew. One of the boys sneezed; then I did. Somehow that made the place suddenly less sinister.

I clicked on my flashlight and checked the list. "First we ought to try to find a wheelbarrow or cart or something." I played the light around but didn't see anything with wheels.

"I'll check upstairs," Friedman said. He and I probably had the only two working flashlights in the state.

"Here's an axe," the younger black boy, Timmy, called out. "Din't we want a axe?"

"Yeah." I took the light over to him. It was a fire axe, in a box on the wall. Somebody had broken the glass covering but for some reason left the axe in place.

Timmy tugged on it and it came free with a slow rusty creak. "Prob'ly set off a bell when he break the glass, he puke out an' run." He tested the edge with his thumb and smiled. It occurred to me that the children had only an abstract, second-hand, notion of the destructive power of the weapons they were carrying. But Timmy knew what an axe could do.

Friedman found a child's wagon and a wheelbarrow upstairs. The boys helped him carry them down, then they went back up to raid the garden supplies.

There wasn't much on the shelves downstairs. Indira and Timmy and I went up and down the rows without finding anything more useful than plastic kitchenware and spray paint. The bins that used to contain the hardware we needed had been thoroughly emptied.

For once I used my brain. Underneath the display bins there were locked cabinets. I had Timmy bash open one of them, and lo: dozens of boxes of nails and screws. Inventory control. We stacked them up in the wagon and broke into the next cabinet. Screwdrivers of every description. Then hammers and drill bits and tape measures and levels and curious varieties of saw. We were laughing over our good fortune and I almost didn't hear the faint sound, a throaty rasp.

"What was that?"

Timmy pointed toward the front of the store. "Fuckin' dogs."

There were ten or twelve of them, big ones, emaciated, teeth bared, staring in at us. One slipped through the broken glass door.

"*Get* down!" Friedman shouted from the top of the stairs. There was a quiet *pop* and the heavy sound of a grenade hitting the floor, rolling, then an impossibly loud explosion.

"Jesus Christ," Indira said. Her voice was a barely audible whisper under the roaring in my ears. Most of the dogs lay about in bloody rags. One limped painfully away, yelping.

We got to our feet, brushing off dust. "I've never—"

"There's one!" Timmy said. A big muscular hound was loping silently down the corridor toward us. I dropped the flashlight, fumbled, found the laser's trigger and fired blindly. The floor burst into yellow flame that immediately went out, leaving thick black smoke, and then the dog ran into the beam and fell down with a thud.

I picked up the flashlight and aimed it at his howling. I had severed both the animal's front legs. It was still trying to get to us, jaws snapping, hind legs scrabbling for purchase.

"I get it," Timmy said quietly, then stepped forward and split the dog's skull. I tore off my mask and spun away just in time to keep from vomiting all over Indira.

I'm not too clear on what happened after that, but I wound up sitting on the curb outside, Indira helping me wash up with an oily rag and canteen water. She patted my head and cooed reassuring nonsense. Great White Savior of the Groundhogs, that's me. (Predictably, though, she was on my side from then on. Most good people would rather give help than receive it.)

We overloaded the bus so much that its failsafes refused to let us take off. We had to leave behind five bags of fertilizer, just inside the door. Friedman was in favor of taking it home and then coming right back, though it would mean working after sundown. He was afraid that the grenade blast had attracted attention, and other people would be waiting to take advantage of our market research.

Here was my opportunity to redeem myself: I said I would stand guard here while they dropped the stuff off. Timmy and an older boy, Oliver, volunteered to stay with me. We loaded two bags back on and watched them float away.

I supposed our best vantage point would have been inside, upstairs, hidden by the darkness but able to cover the door. But that was too much like being in a corner, and besides, the place smelled of vomit and gore and burnt plastic. Instead we walked down the street to where a floater had collided with a ground van. The V of wreckage hid us well and gave us protection from the wind, but afforded a good view of the store. The afternoon sun had gone down behind buildings, and it was getting chilly. We sat close together, hands in pockets, and talked quietly.

"What's it like up there," Oliver asked, "up there in the sky?"

"Smells better. What do you mean?"

"I mean, people get along? All you old people?"

"We have to get along," I said. "It's like living on an island, with no place else to go."

"You stuck in the same place all you life?" Timmy said.

"More or less. It's a big place. And some people are talking about leaving, going to another star."

"That's real far away, isn't it?" Oliver said.

"It'll take years." And husbands.

"Why they don't jus' come down here?" Timmy said. "You come down here."

"We've always lived up in the sky. We're used to it."

For a minute they were quiet, assimilating that. Timmy hit a piece of glass with his heel until it broke. "Indira say you live inside a ball o' dirt, like worms."

"Sort of. It's a hollow rock."

"God damn," Oliver said. "You live *inside*?"

"It's just like living inside a building. But we have a nice park, full of trees, and we can look out the windows at the stars. And there aren't any dogs."

"That's somethin'," he conceded. "You got plenty to eat an' all?"

"Now we do. It was hard for a few years after the war."

"Still hard here. Hard as a fuckin' *rock*, it is."

"I know." I put my arm around his thin shoulders and Timmy leaned up against my knee. I had to clear my throat. "It'll be better now. The worst part is over."

We sat like that for a couple of minutes, without speaking, which may have saved our lives. Two boys snuck in front of us, creeping, intent on the emporium floor.

They had large backpacks and shotguns.

We leveled our weapons on them. "Drop the guns!" I shouted, and steeled myself to pull the trigger.

They froze. "*Do it, mu'fuck,*" Timmy said, his voice an incongruous chirp. But they set the guns down and turned, hands clasped behind their heads.

"Are you alone?" I said.

"Raht," the taller one said. "Jus' passin' through." He had a heavy Southern accent. "Heard the 'splosion."

"Gonna hear another one," Oliver said. "You not alone, you dead meat."

"Talk big shit, boy," the shorter one said. "We didn't do nothin' to you."

"*Button it, Horace,*" the other said. "Horace, he's a little dumb. Sorry."

"Too dumb to *live,* man," Oliver said.

"What's your name?" I asked. "Where're you from?"

"Ah'm Jommy Fromme. Horace my brother. We come up from Clearwater, Flo'da."

"Florida!"

"Ten months walkin', come up the App'lachian Trail. Flo'da ain't no place to be now. Lotta people leavin'."

"Did you ever meet someone named Healer?"

"Ole guy? Sure. He give us shots once."

"How long ago?"

Jommy and Horace looked at each other and shrugged. "Couple years." Jommy stared at me. "You an ole one too. That how you known 'im?"

"She from the sky," Timmy said. "They all get old there."

"You from the Worlds?" He pronounced it "whirls."

"New New York. It's the only one left." Actually, Uchūden was still intact. But nobody lived there.

"That don't beat all."

"Oliver, pick up the guns." I gestured toward the curb. "You two can sit. We have to figure out what to do with you."

Jommy sat and cautiously lowered his hands to his lap. Horace kept his behind his head, staring with an unreadable blank expression. I suddenly realized he was braced to die. "You can put your hands down, Horace. Just don't try anything."

"He won't do nothin'. All we want is to git along."

"Wanna trade?" Horace said.

"Got any gold or silver?" Oliver asked.

"Nah," Jommy said, "don't use that shit anymore down South. Got plenny ammunition."

Timmy laughed. "Big fuckin' deal."

"We really do," Horace said, looking hurt. "We got slugs an' shells for the shotguns and a couple boxes of .45s."

"That won't getcha a can of beans," Oliver said. "We got a room full of ammo."

"A *room* full?"

"Oliver," I said, "be careful what you tell them, okay?"

You could almost hear the wheels turning in Jommy's brain. "Look. What we really like to do is jine up with you. Couple niggers an' a girl, you *need* somebody."

"What can you do?" I asked. "Do you have any skills other than diplomacy?"

"Huh?"

"Do you know how to build things, or handle livestock, or grow vegetables? Any useful skill?"

"I'm a hell of a good shot. Horace, he gen'rally hits what he aims at, too. Only way we could stay alive comin' up the Trail."

"You know how to dress game, then."

"Oh, yeah—hell, yeah. An' make leather, too, with jus' piss."

"Thrilling." I set the laser down but kept my hand near it. Horace visibly relaxed. "We'll see what the others say."

"You got more of you?"

I nodded. "An army. Maybe we could use a couple of scouts."

4 ✦

We let them join us. They were big and strong and relatively old; Jommy was twenty and his brother two years younger. Jeff had probably given them the plague vaccine but we administered it again, to be sure. They accepted the notion that they might live another hundred years with skeptical caution.

Their Family down in Clearwater had been rabid Mansonites. Their leader, who called himself Charlie, had reached the age of twenty-three before killing himself out of remorse at not getting the death. He took the two next oldest with him, to the general approval of the rest of the Family. Jommy and Horace got understandably nervous at that, and snuck out the next night.

I decided not to tell them, or anybody, about Jeff, and passed the word to the other Worlds people. If he was still alive he probably was still keeping the vaccine secret.

They had walked two thousand kilometers without seeing another soul, though several times they heard people coming down the Trail and hid away. New York was the first city they'd gone into. They had heard that it survived the war and was thriving, like in the old days. They didn't seem too disappointed, though, to find the rumor untrue. They had only a vague idea of what people actually used to do in a city, and seemed glad to be able to apply their hunting and tracking skills. The children loved them, probably not for any positive quality. When they went hunting I let them have one weapon and three rounds apiece; otherwise I kept them locked out of the armory. They said they understood about being on probation. I wondered if I ever would quite trust them.

Apparently they forgot about my knowing Healer; at least, they never brought it up again. I struggled against the fantasy of mounting a one-woman rescue operation. It *was* barely possible. Friedman taught me how to fly; we had an extra floater-sized fuel cell that could get me to Florida and back. But it was quixotic nonsense. Florida and half of Georgia comprised a trigger-happy xenophobic lunatic asylum. Even if Jeff was alive and I knew exactly where to go, I'd be shot out of the sky before I got to him.

We went into the city every day for more than a week. Searching through various hospitals, we finally found in Bellevue an unopened storage area, a vault that Friedman blew open easily. It took more than a day to transfer all the pharmaceuticals and medical equipment, probably enough to keep a small town healthy for a generation.

Setting up school was a challenging problem. Tom Smith was a brilliant educator and administrator, but what we really needed was a specialist in the history of education—no one in New New had ever taught children out of books. For several generations we had all grown up taking for granted the database terminal as the primary tool of elementary education, infinitely patient and automatically individualized by feedback algorithms. I was in tenth form before I ever saw a text that simply presented information, without interacting. And I had to go to Earth, postdoctoral, before I ever had a textbook printed on paper. (We had a stroke of luck in that, finding an antiquarian book store in Greenwich Village that specialized in old schoolbooks.)

I taught English, mostly reading and writing, three days a week. It was not an overwhelming success. I've been able to read a couple of thousand words a minute for as long as I can remember; teaching the children to read word-by-word was excruciating. And my natural handwriting is a barely legible childish scrawl, so I had to relearn copybook script and laboriously demonstrate it. The children were enthusiastic at first but soon got bored. I had to spank them to keep them awake. The people teaching practical things had better luck.

The temperature never fell below freezing, but we followed prescribed caution and didn't plant anything for three weeks. We got the baseball diamond all plowed and fertilized and brought the seedlings from the ship. It was a festive day. Everyone was assigned one part of the garden as his personal responsibility, though of course there were overall chores for the ones specializing in farming. (One girl said she didn't think she could eat anything that came out of the *dirt*. Most of the others laughed at her, but a couple were obviously thinking about it for the first time.)

We had a remote terminal from the ship, and I began spending an hour every evening patching through to work on the start-up demographics. It was actually rather pleasant to return to familiar work, and of course I felt virtuous, keeping Daniel somewhat happy. I talked to him or John for a few minutes every day, before relinquishing the terminal for other people's calls.

The terminal was just a standard communicator, without the feedback touchboard, so we couldn't use it for elementary teaching (it would only accommodate one student at a time anyhow). But I taught Indira how to use it for data access, and she was captivated. She knew how to type, though she hadn't done it in years, and soon was using New New's library as effectively as anyone her age who'd grown up with it.

We started calling the place "the farm" and a noisy farm it was. The chickens kept up a constant dialog and the goats, still hobbling around with their legs in casts, complained to anyone who would listen. The Frommes caught a small deer and penned it. The children were charmed, but the goats waxed even more existential. Before long we had baby chicks, and the seedlings were starting to look like vegetables.

There was a general feeling of happiness, of relief. For some reason I couldn't share it. Things were going too well.

Charlie's Will ✦

Jeff and Tad had been on the Island for several months before the question came up. They were sitting with Storm, watching the sun go down over the weathered hulks of the vessels that lolled in the harbor.

"You know, I been feelin' real useless," Storm said. "Don't know how long it's been since somebody got the death."

"Only one since we got here," Jeff said. "How often do you expect it to come?"

"Three or four a year, anyhow. Last year we got 'em almost every month." He threw a shell at the water, trying to make it skip. "I'm gettin' sure as hell tired of fish."

"Some places don't get it nearly as often."

"Yeah," Tad said. "I've heard there's places up north that don't get it at all."

"Sure. Where are all the oldies, then?"

"Stayin' up north, maybe. Where they don't get it."

"Shit." He threw another shell, harder, and this time it did skip once. "Who'd want to go on that long? Feel like I've lived forever already." There was a note of bravado in his voice.

"Come on," Jeff said. "You wouldn't mind a few more years."

"Shet that up." He brooded, looking out over the glaring water, mouth set. "Maybe I would and maybe I wouldn't. Sometime I'm curious 'bout you, 'bout how it feels. You know a hell of a lot."

"I was still in school when the bombs fell. I was thirty-one."

"Boy howdy," he said softly, and thought for a minute. "But you hurt all the time. You can't hardly walk when you git up in the morning. That's another thing you git for gettin' old."

"No, that's the thing I was born with. I used to know really old people, like a hundred years old, who didn't hurt at all."

"I did too," Tad said. "You're not that young, Storm. Didn't you have grandparents and all?"

"Naw. I mean I *had* 'em, I guess, like anybody. But I was raised up in a home, you know, up Tampa. Said my mother was a whore, she got killed when I was still a baby. That's what they said, anyhow." He tried another shell. "Guess I saw old people, yeah, outside. On the street. Didn't know any."

"I think maybe it doesn't have anything to do with Charlie," Jeff said carefully. "I think the death might be just a disease, and maybe people aren't getting it anymore."

Surprisingly, Storm nodded. "I've thought about that myself. Be hell to pay." He looked sharply at Tad and Jeff. "Don't you tell nobody. But I figure it that way."

"Yeah," Tad said. "It's what I've been thinking, too. I didn't want to say anything."

"People I been *waitin'* to see get it," Storm said savagely. "People I really want to cut into. And now what?"

"Have to learn to like fish," Jeff said.

Storm made a retching sound. "Maybe not. General's talkin' about goin' inland, hunting trip. Bring back some pedros to smoke."

"All this talk about food," Jeff said, getting up. "Think I'll go get some soup." Tad stood up too.

"You guys go on," Storm said. "I have to get hungrier."

They walked toward the kitchen through deepening twilight. Sticky perfume of magnolias and jasmine in the thick still air. "Maybe we should keep our traps shut," Tad said.

"No, we did right. It'd look more suspicious if we avoid talking about it."

"What'll we do when someone puts two and two together?"

"God, I don't know. Just deny it."

"I sure as hell don't want to get eaten."

"Ah...what's the difference?" He laughed. "Tell you what, though. If they come after us, I've got some arsenic. They try to eat us afterwards, we'll get revenge."

Tad nodded soberly. "That's a good idea." He scuffed at a pebble and it skittered on ahead of them. "You know, I been thinkin' about the boat again."

"Speaking of suicide." There were several sailboats around the island. They'd talked about trying to get to the English-speaking Bahamas, to the east. But neither of them had ever sailed.

"Well, hell. What if it came to that? Sail or be someone's lunch?"

"Sail, I guess. Be some shark's lunch."

"All we have to do is get General mad at us. And he's the craziest asshole I've ever met."

"I wouldn't worry about him. When I treated his herpes I told him he had to get shots twice a year. Or his dick'd fall off."

"That keeps you safe, maybe. Hey, though." He stopped suddenly and whispered. "Why don't you give him a shot of something else? Why don't you kill 'im? He's so old, nobody'd think anything."

Jeff shook his head. "I don't think I could do that."

"You've killed plenty."

"Yeah, but not murder."

"Hell, that wouldn't be murder. He's just a fuckin' animal."

"You think whoever took his place would be any better?"

"It could be you." He shook Jeff's arm. "Half the family thinks you're some kind of god."

Jeff started walking again. "The other half wants to see me on a cross. No thanks."

The soup was a bland chowder of fish and bean curd. They took their bowls outside; the cafeteria's air conditioning was set too high for Jeff's joints.

"You don't want to go back north because it's too cold. Sure as hell ain't goin' any other direction without a boat. We stay here, our luck's gonna run out."

"I don't know," Jeff said. "We may have plenty of time. And things could change."

"Haven't seen much change." Tad went back inside to scrape himself some salt.

"You ever think about the Worlds?" Jeff said when he returned.

"Aw, they're all dead. Saw it on the cube the day of the war."

"What if that was a lie? Suppose they aren't all dead."

"So what? They ain't comin' down here and we ain't goin' up there."

"You think they caused the war?"

"Huh? Sure, them and the Easter Bunny. It was the fuckin' Soshies. Maybe us, who cares anymore?"

Jeff finished his soup in thoughtful silence. "They are still there. That's where I got the vaccine."

"You're shittin' me. How the hell you get up there?"

"I didn't go there. They sent it down, in a robot rocket. From New New York."

"You feel all right?"

"It's true. That's why I needed the fuel cell from you, so I could talk to them, let them know where to send it."

"New New York, that's where the girl was from. That Newsman showed us the picture of."

"Yes, and I...I've talked to her, from the hospital in Plant City. She helped with the vaccine. She's even been back to Earth, since the war, to Africa."

"This is really straight? You're not yankin' me off?"

"It's true."

"So what, you think she's comin' here? Gonna come get you?"

"I don't think she can. They went to Africa because it was the only place left with a spaceport." He set down the bowl and stared out into the darkness.

"I'd just like to get back in touch with her. Let her know I'm alive. That's why I've been hanging around the library with Newsman, thinking maybe I could fix up the dish and talk to them up there."

"The dish antenna, there's nothin' wrong with that."

"Not outside. All the gear inside's been pretty well smashed. I think I can learn enough electronics to rig up a simple transmitter, though. We have all the raw materials here and plenty of power."

"Okay," Tad said slowly, "so you get to talk with your girl. But that don't solve anything. We're still takin' a big chance stayin' here. Bigger every day."

"Maybe not, maybe not. It could be the key." The door opened behind them, and they both looked up to see Elsie the Cow squeeze through. She was taller than Jeff and weighed twice as much. Her features were large and coarse and she had a downy growth of beard.

"Warm night," she said, and settled ponderously between them on the steps. She balanced a pail of soup on her lap and stirred it noisily with a large kitchen spoon.

"Come on, Elsie," Jeff said, "we're talking man talk."

"You're a man," she said, and slurped at the ladle. "He just a boy. All of 'em boys."

"We're *talking*," Tad said. "You want me to hit you?"

"This ain't your step. You wanna talk, you go talk someplace."

Jeff stood up. "I've had as much of this stuff as I want, anyhow."

"Yeah." They took their bowls back inside and went out the back door, heading toward the deserted southern part of the Island, the abandoned naval base.

"You got some kind of a plan?" Tad said.

"Not definite. Just a few notions." They picked their way along the broken sidewalk. There was no moon, and all the street lights were out in this part of town. "Look at it this way. The oldest people around were thirteen or fourteen when the war came. That's old enough to have been following politics."

"Some people, yeah. It's Florida, though."

"If we just came right out and explained about the war, about the death being caused by biological warfare, a lot of them would agree with us...most would at least understand, even if they didn't—"

"But hell. One wrong person says the word and we're fresh meat. No way around that."

"The thing to do is to get to those people first. The people in power."

"General and Major and Hotbox? They're all buggy. Hungry, too—start talkin' against Charlie and we're the menu, sure as shit."

"There's Storm. He's obviously ready."

"Yeah, but you never see him go against any of them. He's got a safe place and aims to keep it."

"It's a tough problem," Jeff admitted. "Another reason to get in touch with the spacers. There are lots of people who have special training, dealing with adolescents and crazy people. Psychiatrists, maybe they could give us an angle."

"What are they gonna come up with that you can't? Hell, you spent most of your life in school."

"Mostly criminology, a little business administration. These dingos are murderers, cannibals, and sadists, but they aren't criminals. They're *normal*, by the standards of those around them. Most of what I know about dealing with people just doesn't apply."

"I still think we oughta fade. Another couple of months with nobody gettin' the death, hell. They're dumb, but they ain't *that* dumb." He stumbled, cursed. "There's anybody dumb around, it's *you*. Why'd you give the vaccine to General and Major? They'd be the first ones to go."

"That'd be the same as murder."

"Shit. I don't understand you at *all*." There was a pale flickering light down at the Navy docks. They steered toward it. "Now, Hotbox, I can see keepin' her. I'd like to pork her myself."

Jeff laughed. "Just ask."

"Think I haven't? Christ and Charlie." They walked over to the dim pool of light. It was a creepy place, the mountainous warships indistinct shadows looming over them, creaking, smell of greasy rust. It was a mothball fleet; some of the ships had been out of service for most of a century.

"Too bad we can't take one of these," Tad said. "We could—"

"Take it where?" Storm stepped quietly out of the darkness, barefoot, holding a pistol. "I been behind you since Duval Street. You guys got some real explainin' to do."

5 ✦

I do admit to a number of personality defects, none serious, but I never thought jealousy was in my repertoire. Least of all sexual jealousy, since my husbands and I established at the outset, conventionally, that we were all free to do whatever we wanted with whomever. But when I got the news I was suddenly overcome with this alien emotion.

Daniel asked to marry Evelyn Ten. John wouldn't veto it. I told him I had to think about it, snapped off the monitor, and shocked Sam Wasserman with my vocabulary. I went out into the garden to think. To fume.

I've known Evelyn since she was a child. She's Ahmed's granddaughter, a born charmer, talented but modest. Also young and quite beautiful, which I had to admit was the problem. I'm no longer one and never was the other.

Leave the coop for six weeks and the goddamned rooster goes on the prowl. Well, I knew it was deeper than that; it had been building for a couple of years. I did spend more time with John, and enjoyed sex with him more, though Daniel had better technique and raw material. The sex itself probably wasn't that important. I hadn't given him much affection lately, either, nor asked for much from him. If I needed a shoulder it was always John's I would go to.

I really had only two choices. I could allow Evelyn to join the line, or ask Daniel to leave it. I didn't see how I could refuse Evelyn and keep Daniel. So it was really a question of whether I loved Daniel enough to share him. Or little enough not to care. I looked myself straight in the heart for a long time over that. Finally I went back to the monitor and called Evelyn and welcomed her to our family. Asked her to relay my consent to Daniel and give him my love; I couldn't hog the monitor. I could, of course.

Instead I went back out into the garden, dark now, and sat on the damp earth and listened to things growing. There was a hint of wild honeysuckle on the air, that somehow disgusted me. I didn't feel much like springtime. Evelyn was twelve years younger than I. Under other circumstances she could be my own child (not as pretty and somewhat lighter in complexion). I think the jealousy faded away there in the garden, but what replaced it was a hollow and cold feeling of mortality. Finally I did cry, but I don't think it was over Daniel. I think it was over everything dying eventually.

I had a desperate desire, not especially erotic, to go find myself a limber young penis. Rocky or Sam. I even got up and walked toward the cottage where Rocky was sleeping. But at the brick footpath I turned away. He might have company. Or he might say no.

✦ ✦ ✦

The next day was shift change. Ahmed had been out at the Mercedes for the past week. He came back to the farm and we stretched the food-isolation policy to the extent of one small bottle of gin. It's not every day that you get a new in-law.

He was cautiously happy but a little concerned about her age. Also, it was odd for a Ten to marry outside of the line, which claimed to trace groundhog roots back to seventeenth-century Africa. He himself was all for it, especially since the war had effectively frozen New New's gene pool.

(The marriage made me obliquely related to the single postwar addition to that gene pool: Insila, the girl we had brought back from Zaire. Ahmed had adopted her as soon as she came out of isolation.)

By the time we saw the bottom of the bottle he had taught me a half-dozen outrageous phrases in Swahili to surprise Evelyn with. Then he wandered off to bed. I was on night duty, so I had Dr. Long give me a shot of toloxinamide, which compresses all the joys of a hangover into ten minutes of concentrated woe, followed by remorseful clarity.

I shared the shift with Sam again. He was always good company. I'd chosen him to come along as sort of a wild card. At eighteen he had a certificate in mathematics and most of a second one in historiography. He composed music, popular ballads, and last summer had written a young people's introduction to calculus. He didn't have much ambition in the conventional sense; he'd been offered a line apprenticeship and refused it, saying he'd rather stay in school until Janus took off. (That's how we'd met originally; his name percolated to the top when I was databasing for a part-time ship's historian.)

There wasn't really anything to do at night but stay awake. The farm's "nerve center" was originally a groundskeeper's office, situated on a slight rise, giving us a view of the whole area. We had the monitor there and a sound-only communications system that Ingred Munkelt had jury-rigged. If anything suspicious happened, we could throw a switch that flooded the area with light. Another switch sent a wake-up buzz to every bedroom and dormitory floor, and unlocked the armory. We had a laser and a scattergun by the door. Otherwise, only Friedman had a weapon; we'd decided on a strict lock-up policy to prevent accidents and keep the murder rate down near zero.

We talked about history and historiography for a couple of hours and played a game of fairy chess. He spotted me a barrel queen and still won in fifteen minutes. Then, while I was putting the pieces away, he demonstrated yet another talent: mental telepathy.

"Uh, you know I overheard your conversation with your husband yesterday. You were pretty upset."

"Surprised. Yes, upset. I still am, a little."

"I don't blame you. I wondered, um, whether you might want, whether your line permits, uh..." He started to make the polite finger sign but instead put his hand lightly on my forearm. His palm was wet and cold. "Would you want to have sex with me as a friend?" he said quickly. "I thought it might help."

"It would help, a lot." I put my hand over his. "You do know how old I am."

"Sure." He laughed nervously. "I like that. Women my age, we just don't have anything real to talk about." He looked around quickly. "Should I put the shades down?"

I tried to stifle a laugh. "Let's wait until the shift is over, okay? Only another hour and a half." He agreed, with a winsome look of real pain.

Boys that age should wear loose clothing. Galina and Ingred, who replaced us, could hardly have missed his erection. They were poker-faced, but Galina gave me a roguish wink as we went out the door.

Back at my place, the first iteration was predictably brief. But Sam's refractory powers were impressive even for a youngster. After the fourth he fell asleep beside me, still inside. It was my first deep, untroubled sleep in a month.

(Sam was curiously ignorant of female geography. He confessed he'd only discovered girls a year before, having spent several years loving an older man, one of his teachers. Such a waste of natural resources.)

The next day we began working on a program of recruitment. Our efforts here would be spectacularly trivial if only sixteen people benefited. We decided it would be best to find loners and people living in twos and threes. If we tried to assimilate a large group, it might lead to an organized power struggle after we left.

I saw the farm as eventually growing into a small town, thousands of people, agriculturally self-sufficient and still close enough to New York to take advantage of the city and serve as a nucleus of power for rebuilding it. Some day I wanted to come back to the city and see it crackling with energy again.

There was some dissension over this ultimate goal, led by Carrie Marchand. A lot of people believed that cities were obsolete; that living in cities contributed to the mental disease that made war possible. A strange point of view to come from someone who grew up inside an oversized tin can. But she had never been to New York, London, Paris, Tokyo, as they had been before the war. As I was stating this argument, I realized that only a handful of adult people ever *had* been to a real city, let alone every one of the major cities in the non-Socialist world. It made me feel lonely rather than unique. And I did have to admit that the experience colored my judgment profoundly. Carrie made a good case, but my side prevailed. Being boss does simplify the process of debate.

The first stage of recruitment had to be quite selective. We made a couple of hundred flyers describing what we were and how to get in touch with us, and left them in prominent places in book stores and print libraries. We didn't tell exactly where the farm was, but said we would pick people up at noon outside the Ossining tube station, every clear day.

We distributed the flyer over several hundred square kilometers, but for almost a week it looked like a wasted effort. Every noon Friedman or I would take the school bus inland a few kilometers, then circle around to the south of Ossining and sneak up on the tube station. On the fifth day three recruits, as cautious as we were, came out of the bushes after we landed.

We got two or three a day for the next eleven days. On March 16, the eighth anniversary of the war, it backfired.

One of the new recruits disappeared during the night. He came back about an hour before dawn, with a couple of dozen heavily armed comrades.

The shots woke me up an instant before the buzzer went off. Harry Volker and Albert Long were on duty; one of them managed to get to the emergency switch before dying. The invaders had burst in through both doors, shooting.

Evidently they hadn't known where the armory was. That kept the bloodbath from being too one-sided. Friedman kept them away with his laser while weapons were being passed through the dormitory. Then there was a terrible free-for-all, our children and their children blasting away at each other right through the golden dawn. I looked on helplessly from my cottage window, along with Sam. Neither of us was foolhardy enough to try crossing over to the armory. We moved a dresser in front of the door and peered through the blinds at the war being fought.

Then we spent the morning picking up and burying bodies and pieces of bodies. There were twenty-three of them and eleven of us—eight children, the two on night shift, and Sara O'Brien.

Sara's body was the last one we found, which was probably a good thing, since we were numb by then. We followed the sound of flies. Behind some bushes, irrelevantly naked, her body at first looked like a pile of raw meat. They had hacked off her head and limbs and breasts and stacked everything up. They'd split her torso open from the womb to the heart, and spread things around. She didn't look real. She looked like a montage a gruesome child might make, taking scissors to an anatomy diagram.

That was when the guilt really came home. Sara had been such a sweet person. She loved children with total soppy abandon. She was the best teacher we had for the very young, because her love infected the children and they would do anything to keep from disappointing her. She had three daughters and a son in New New. What the hell could I tell them? I chose your mother as backup pilot because her psych profile showed she was really great with children. I'm really sorry she wound up a bloody heap. Next time I'll build a fence, first thing.

In a way, the ones who were less obviously dead were the worst. Some who were killed by laser just had a charred spot on their clothing. They looked asleep, except for the feet. For some reason dead people seem to crank their feet around into uncomfortable positions.

6 ✦

Nobody blamed me for the carnage. Maybe I blamed myself: I should have expected the worst and given highest priority to defense. Of all the adults, I had the most experience with this particular kind of insanity—Friedman knew more about war but he had never been in one except, like all the others, as a target. No use wasting energy in self-recrimination, I knew. But I had to start taking medicine to get to sleep.

We spent the next two weeks in furious activity, turning the farm into an armed camp. We surrounded the area with two concentric circles of sturdy posts and wound a complicated maze of taut razor wire between them. It was difficult and dangerous stuff to work with; only two of the children were physically strong enough to help, which might have been just as well. Three people severed fingers in moments of carelessness. Dr. Itoh was able to do emergency bone grafts and rejoin the digits, but they would have to be redone in New New if the victims were to ever use the fingers normally. I brushed against the stuff myself, reaching up to scratch my nose, and skinned off a flap of forearm the size of a sausage patty. There was an impressive amount of blood. Itoh glued it back, but now I can't feel anything there but prickly numbness.

While we were doing that, the children dug sixteen bunkers, equally spaced around the perimeter, and with some trepidation I allowed the holes to be stocked with weapons and ammunition. The bloodbath had had a sobering effect, though, and the children treated the weapons with exaggerated caution.

There was no break in the wire. The only way in or out of the farm, for the time being, would be by floater. We found another workable one, a utility pickup, and taught Indira and two others how to fly, after a fashion. They took the Fromme brothers out on daily hunting sorties that were also reconnaissance, trying to find large groups of children before they found us.

Friedman, always full of good news, pointed out that though the wire would protect us from another attack of the same kind, it wouldn't be much of an obstacle if somebody else had managed to break into an armory. A few seconds of concentrated laser fire would melt a hole in the fence, or it could be breached by explosives.

I wondered whether our situation was a microcosm of the near future—a few people living well but in anxious isolation. Perhaps this was unavoidable for a time, but I could hope that it would prove to be only a period of transition, not a grisly New Order.

The ferocity of the attack and the way the children seemed indifferent toward dying made me wonder whether Jeff had been wrong in thinking that Charlie's Country only extended into Georgia. None of the children on the farm had ever heard of it until the Fromme boys came. But maybe it was a behavior pattern that cropped up independent of Manson's crazy writings. I talked to Dr. Long, who had specialized in child psychology before the war, and he wasn't too much help. After all, not even the most desperate of prewar cultures had anything like the background of helpless despair these children endured. His practice had been limited to children who had grown up in New New, with an occasional immigrant for variety. More bedwetting than mass murder.

When the new trouble first began, we thought it was a reaction to stress, to the isolation and tension of living inside the razor wall. We increased the amount of time each person spent outside, making up search missions to give the kids something to do. But they became increasingly irritable and hard to control, and the doctors spent long days treating vague complaints.

And then Indira got sick. One morning she didn't get out of bed, and when we shook her awake she mumbled incoherent nonsense. She was incontinent and wouldn't eat. We turned my cabin into a sickroom and fed her intravenously while the doctors and Harry Volker ran tests. They were in constant communication with medical people in New New, who could only confirm the obvious: It was the death. There was nothing anyone could do.

We had reinoculated everyone with the vaccine our first day here, to be on the safe side. Either Indira was somehow unaffected by the vaccine, or the vaccine didn't work. Which meant we were all doomed.

Tishkyevich found the answer. We didn't have anything like a complete medical laboratory, but she was able to take blood samples from Indira, the other children, and us, and compare force-grown disease cultures from each. Indira and the children had a mutated form of the death, but none of us had it. That was a relief, but perplexing. Then Galina deduced the truth: We had given it to them. Except for Rocky, Friedman, Ahmed, and me, none of the party had ever been to Earth; most of them represented several generations of biological isolation from the home planet. When the virus settled into our lungs it found a strange new ecology. In the process of trying to adapt to one or all of us, it changed.

We were evidently protected the same way we were protected from other Earth diseases. The virus couldn't survive our beefed-up immune systems. But before it perished some of it got back out, and reinfected the children.

The scientists at New New confirmed Galina's explanation. They also said it would be easy to produce an antigen specific to the mutation, if we would bring up a blood sample.

No children were around while this was going on. That was good. We had to leave, and quickly, and preferably not in a hail of bullets.

Irrationally, I wanted to stay until Indira died. It felt like we were deserting her. But there was really nothing we could do, and she might hold on for a week or more. So at two in the morning, cold rain misting down, we met at the school bus and drifted away.

We left the monitor so we could call from the Mercedes and explain what had happened, and that a new vaccine would be coming in a couple of weeks. Unfortunately, the first person to hear the beeping and come into the sickroom was Horace Fromme. He just stared sullenly while I talked, and before I could finish, his image tilted and slid away and then the screen went dead. He'd turned over the table that held the monitor.

There was nothing more we could do, and staying longer might be dangerous. It was getting light; the other floater could reach Kennedy in a half hour, with enough armament to reduce the Mercedes to small bits of scrap metal. We strapped in and blasted off. Everything had happened so fast. It wasn't till we were in orbit that it hit me: This part of my life was over. I would never go to Earth again. Even if Jeff was alive, I would never see him.

Charlie's Will ✦

Storm listened without comment for several minutes while Jeff explained how the vaccine worked, where it came from, and how he had been administering it through southern Florida. Storm kept the gun dangling loosely at his side.

"Supposing things are like you say," he said slowly. "There's something I don't get. How come the spacers would go to that trouble? How come you go to all that trouble?"

"The Worlds need us back on our feet," Jeff said. "They have a hard time getting along without the Earth."

"No skin off you. You could just stay in a safe place and doctor people."

"He couldn't take the cold," Tad said. "Had to get as far south as he could."

He frowned and scratched his chin. "Still didn't have to use the vaccine on anybody. Why you take the chance?"

"Loneliness," Jeff said. "I might live another eighty years. I want company."

Storm shook his head. "Well, hell." He put the shotgun-pistol away in his shirt pouch. "Guess I'll believe you for the time being. I gotta keep it secret, though?"

"For as long as possible," Jeff said. "When everybody starts getting gray hair, they'll probably figure it out."

The next day General left with a war party to head toward Ciudad Miami—the crater that used to be Miami—on a meat-gathering expedition. Jeff held sick call as usual, then sequestered himself in the University of the Media library.

Studying electronics didn't present the practical problems he'd encountered years before, trying to learn some medicine. The university had a working database system; he didn't have to rely on antique books. His main problem was an absolute lack of talent. He'd enrolled in a physics survey course his second year of college, but dropped it and transferred to chemistry before the first test.

Now he was doggedly worrying through the mysteries of resistors and capacitors, vaguely aware of how much work was ahead before he got to the quantum electronics he'd need to repair the transceiver. Not being able to make hard copies of the texts was frustrating. He did have a comprehensive wiring diagram for the transceiver, over a hundred pages of hieroglyphics, and whenever he learned a new symbol he would go through the booklet and circle everything that looked like it. He hoped that eventually he would develop some sort of gestalt understanding of the thing's structure, but so far it was still a random assortment of gibberish.

Tad and Storm were no help, of course, and Newsman was a definite liability. He would come down to the carrel to watch Jeff work, muttering silly questions and non sequiturs. Jeff's ruse was that he was working on understanding the medical machines at the hospital, so he had to make up a line of moderately convincing nonsense while he worked, which didn't help his concentration.

Newsman always napped in the afternoon, though, which gave Jeff time to sneak down to the dish installation occasionally, and try to coordinate what he was learning with the actual devices there. Whole blocks of circuit boards were still intact, and he'd managed to match up nearly half of them with pages in the booklet. The smashed-up equipment that littered the floor no doubt had a lot that could be salvaged, and there was a closet full of spare parts. A competent electronics engineer could probably go in with a screwdriver and make some sort of working transmitter in an afternoon. Jeff hoped he'd be able to do it sometime before the turn of the century.

Jeff and Tad were in the library, Jeff studying circuits and Tad with Newsman, watching an old animal-porn movie, when a runner came and said the two of them and Storm were supposed to come downtown right away. General was back and he needed some advice.

So Jeff painfully mounted a bicycle, cursing for the thousandth time the memory of old Holy Joe, who had decreed floaters blasphemous and sent them all pilotless out over the horizon. They stopped by at the jail/church and woke up Storm.

General was sitting on the steps of City Hall with Hotbox lying next to him, her head in his lap. As they approached, he disengaged her and stood up.

"Come on inside," he said, smiling. "Someone you wanta meet."

Standing alone in the foyer, feet hobbled, was Mary Sue, the eldest of the family Tad had left behind. Her face was bruised and swollen. "That's him," she said, pointing. "Healer. He's the one keeps people from gettin' the death."

"Storm," General said, "take him."

Storm put his hand on Jeff's arm. "Hold on," he said. "Who is this slit?"

"She used to belong to him," he said, nodding at Tad. "He gets it, too."

"Met some people come down from Atlanta," she said. "They don' get the death there no more, said it was shots they got from the sky people, the spacers. He's one of 'em. We followed the way you two went. Nobody's got the death anyplace you went, not since you give 'em shots. Typhoid shots."

"I've never been off the Earth," Jeff said. "I'm not a spacer."

"But you're in with 'em," she said. "That medicine come down in a rocket. People seen it."

"It's true, isn't it," General said.

Jeff hesitated. "Substantially. But Tad doesn't have anything to do with it. New New York sent me the medicine, and I've given it to thousands of people. No one here is going to get the death. You can live a normal life span if you want."

"What's normal?"

"Hundred twenty, more or less."

General made a strained growling noise in his throat. "Kill him."

Storm didn't move. "Maybe we better—"

"You *kill* him. Right here."

The priest pulled his shotgun-pistol out of his shirt pouch and pushed Jeff roughly to his knees. He held the gun to his head. "You want to pray to Christ and Charlie?" he said in a quavering voice.

Jeff's eyes were squeezed shut, teeth clenched. "Fuck them both," he said clearly.

"You—" General stepped forward to kick. Storm swung the pistol up and fired point-blank, ripping a large hole out of the center of General's chest. He staggered backwards a couple of steps, slipped in his own blood, and fell heavily. Mary Sue was covered with gore but didn't react.

Storm heard a noise and spun around. Hotbox was trying to open the door and cock a pistol simultaneously. He fired and she fell back down the stars in a shower of glass and blood.

"Get up, get up!" Storm put a hand under Jeff's arm and hoisted him to his feet. "We gotta find guns for you two—go get Major. We get him, I think we're okay, we're in charge."

"You don't gotta," Mary Sue said calmly. "He's in back there, dressed out and smoked."

"What he do?"

"Up in Islamorada. He told General most of the boys didn' want Healer killed. So General killed him."

"Was it true?" Jeff asked. "About the others?"

"Guess so. Most of 'em run away." She licked the blood on her lips. "Christ and Charlie. It just don' make sense."

7 ✦

People weren't as paranoid about infection as they used to be, but we still spent a week in isolation, watching the cucumbers and tomatoes grow. It only took two days to synthesize the new antigen, since the scientists knew what they were looking for, and a small drone carrying the medicine got to the children before we left isolation.

We watched it on flatscreen. The magnification wasn't quite enough to make out individual people, but we could see there were still some children at the compound. They had evidently opened part of the razor wire; one person went out and retrieved the medicine. I hoped they had the sense to use it.

Some of the ones who attacked the farm, certainly the ones who mutilated Sara O'Brien, would also have been exposed. They would die, which bothered me not at all, but I was afraid they might first become carriers for this new version of the death. Our epidemiologists said it wouldn't happen; the population was too spread out. If it did happen, we'd have to start over, sending another hundred million doses dirtside. If the Yorkers would stand for it—there was no end of grumbling about the original project, which had been by far the most expensive public health undertaking in the history of the Worlds.

I got my old job back with Start-up and put in a full week's work while we were sequestered. The transition back to "normal" family life was a little more complicated.

It was partly my fault. I had gotten really sweet on Sam, shared troubles and so forth, and since the medics were kind enough to provide us a little privacy, individual tents, I took it upon myself to extend his sexual education into the realm of free fall. At least twice a day.

My emotions toward him should have been simple, but they weren't. Sometimes he made me feel like a girl again. Sometimes I felt frankly maternal toward him. And all sorts of states in between.

It was obvious to the others what was going on. Most of them, I think, were amused, and most conventionally minded their own business, but some were quite scandalized. After all, we were "home," even though hundreds of meters of hard vacuum separated me from my husbands' bedrooms. Some, like Maria Mandell and Louise Dore (and Martin Thiele, I think) wanted a fling at that lean long body themselves, and resented the old hag pulling rank on them. That was part of Sam's attraction, too. I hadn't made anybody jealous, or shocked anybody, in years.

After the week was up, though, I had to face the problem of what I was going to do with him, and with myself. I was tempted to ask him to marry us, but I didn't really know him well enough—and it would be too much like getting back at Daniel.

I remembered the term "shipboard romance" from old novels, and I suppose the smart thing would have been to treat it just like that, kiss him good-bye before we came through the airlock, and then walk away, back to my normal life. I couldn't quite do it.

We had a small reunion party, necessarily cramped, up in John's flat. Evelyn was shy and deferential. I didn't think it was the right time to discuss Sam (perversely, I didn't want to shock Evelyn). We talked about the New York adventure, and I caught up on Janus gossip.

They've started building S-2, *Newhome*, using Uchūden as a nucleus. They've moved the Japanese satellite to a position between New New and Deucalion. It's a pretty thing, an old-fashioned doughnut design with a delicate landscape painted around the outside. It was undamaged during the war, but the people inside all relocated here. Theoretically it could support one hundred twenty people, but they'd have to be awfully fond of algae. In the prewar days it was periodically resupplied with "real" food, by the Japanese corporations that put it into orbit.

Eventually Uchūden will be the control center of *Newhome*, the top of a cylindrical column of rock. I'll probably live there, on top. It's a strange feeling to watch it, spinning slowly against the stars, knowing that in a couple of years we may move there and never come back.

I'm going to have some trouble from a group that calls itself God's Armada, of all things. It's mostly Devonites, with a few other evangelical types involved. They managed to access my roster and break it down according to religious belief. There are no fundamentalist Devonites among the seven thousand people I've chosen so far, and only a few hundred Reform Devonites. Only eighteen percent of the colonists profess religious belief, less than half the percentage that prevails in New New. The Armada served notice they'll be taking me to court. I'll try to look on it as an educational experience.

S-1 took off the day after our farm was attacked. If it had been a clear night, it would have looked like the brightest star in the sky. You can still see it now, a bright blue spark in Gemini. (I asked what S-2 will look like when it takes off. Oddly enough, it will be almost invisible. You wouldn't want to be looking at the exhaust anyway—the gamma radiation would be strong enough to kill at a million kilometers' distance. We'll be launching straight "up," out of the plane of the ecliptic, to get safely away from Earth and New New before we tip over and head for Epsilon.)

On the way back from Earth I'd had a depressed, resigned feeling about Janus. Now I was starting to look forward to it, catching the enthusiasm Dan and Evelyn projected. Even John seemed somewhat excited. With S-1 gone and Uchūden growing, the project was a reality.

About midnight Dan and Evy went back to Dan's flat. I stayed with John and we made slow love. Afterwards, I broached the subject of Sam.

He was amused. "Butterflying at your age? Next it'll be acne."

"Be serious, John. It's more complex than that."

"Of course it is." He drew me into the crook of his arm and with a finger traced aimless patterns in the perspiration on my chest. "Of course it is."

"And it's not just a reaction to Evy. I like her."

He smiled. "That sounds defensive. The timing is suspicious."

"All right, she was part of it at first. Not any more, I think."

"When did you ask him? Right after—"

"I *didn't* ask him. He asked me."

"A boy of rare discrimination."

"It was right after Evy joined us. He saw I was upset. But it went beyond therapy pretty quickly." I explained to him as much as I understood.

He got up and poured us a glass of wine while I was talking. "All right, he's clever and pretty and you went through a lot together. What do you want me to do? Give my blessing? You've got it."

"I want not to hurt you. Have I?"

He sat cross-legged on the bed, a posture that accentuated his deformity. Normally I didn't even see it any more. "No, you haven't hurt me. When we were first together, remember, you were having three different men a day, with an eye out for new recruits. I wasn't jealous then, and I haven't changed."

"But *I* have changed, is what you're saying. I should act my age."

"No, no." He took a sip and offered me the glass. "I'm not saying that. Others will, though."

"What I do with my plumbing is my own business."

"A noble principle. You know it's not true. You're coming up for review in another month, and there are a couple of people on the Board who would jump at any chance to hold you back. A pity you couldn't have kept it secret."

"We were living in each other's pockets. It would be against my nature anyhow."

"I know. I wouldn't try to make you a politician at this late date. But you are going to get some noise about it." He cleared his throat and looked away. "Unless we marry him."

"Some year, maybe. I'm not going to be rushed into anything."

He nodded slowly. "I have to say...I'm glad to hear you say that. I would feel like the odd man out, you and Daniel with your young lovers."

"You mean you haven't made love with Evy?"

"Yes, twice. We *are* married." He looked uncomfortable. "It didn't work out. Very dry and tight. I don't think her heart was in it. Though she tried hard."

"She's inexperienced."

"That may be it." He drank off most of the wine and handed it to me to finish, then got under the cover.

"I'll have a girl-to-girl talk with her."

He put his hand on my thigh. "Don't intercede on my behalf. I'm satisfied with the way things are, now that you're back."

I turned off the light and sipped wine in the darkness, sitting up in bed. I couldn't help feeling somewhat manipulated. John had probably acquiesced in Evy's joining our line so he would have more time with me, though I suspect he would be surprised and hurt if I accused him of it. But then there was undeniably an element of manipulation in my relationship with Sam—mixed with honest lust; thinking about him gave me a prickly surge of desire.

My mother once counseled me that sexual relations grew more complicated in proportion to the square of the number of people involved. So this quintet was twenty-five times more complicated than masturbation. That seemed conservative.

The next month was a tiresome waste. The second day home I got a summons from God's Armada. On Sandra's advice I retained Taylor Harrison, an expert on constitutional law and a good trial lawyer as well.

Selecting the jury took more time than the trial itself. They came up with forty hand-picked Devonites, of course, and I found forty free-thinkers pretty easily. But then we both had veto power over the remaining twenty. We went through nearly a thousand before agreeing on them.

Harrison rejected out-of-hand my desire to consider the case on practical merits: the plain fact that the starship's population had to remain stable for eighty years, and just a handful of Devonites would reproduce everybody into starvation. (I also asked the GA representative whether he had considered that little problem. He just smiled sadly and said God would provide.) By the screwy logic of the courts, that fact of certain disaster was irrelevant. The case had to be decided in terms of technicalities of precedent and interpretation.

They droned on and on. It bothered me somewhat that GA's lawyer, also an expert on constitutional law, was herself a hidebound atheist. I supposed the two of them could switch sides and argue with equal passion either way. Maybe justice is best served with that kind of professionalism. It still bothered me. But not as much as the bombshell Harrison dropped halfway through the trial.

We were having lunch together, reviewing his notes, when he said, "O'Hara, do you know what a 'front organization' is?"

"Sure," I said. I'd studied the history of the Lobbies in American government.

"Well, that's what your God's Armada is. They're fronting for a conservative coalition headed up by old Marcus. They don't really give a damn about equal representation."

"What are they up to, then?"

"Just want to stop *Newhome*. They will, too, if they can compel you to take eight percent fundamentalist Devonites. Might as well put a time bomb aboard."

"They should have moved earlier. With S-1 gone—"

"But that's just it. They want S-1 to come back with the antimatter. They just don't want to use it in a starship."

"Power generation? Sunlight must be cheaper."

"That's not exactly the kind of power they're interested in." He put down his chopsticks and looked at me. "They want to use it on Earth."

"My god!"

"The idea is to set up about a dozen magnetic containment devices, holding antimatter, in the largest cities. Like the Sword of Damocles. They do something we don't approve of, we turn off the power. Boom."

"Or if the power fails. Or the magnet runs down."

"That's right. Or if someone who doesn't like, say, Los Angeles gets hold of the button. It's a spectacularly unstable system."

"How do they think they could do it? It'd never get past the Coordinators."

"Well, Marcus was a Coordinator once. The thing is, if the starship gets vetoed and S-1 comes back, we've got all that antimatter sitting in our own back yard. A lot of people would rather have it somewhere else."

"Have you told Judge Delany about this?"

"Hardly. Delany was the one who told *me*. Of course it's irrelevant, a side issue."

"Of course." I wished I had something stronger than orange juice.

As it turned out, it *was* irrelevant, or immaterial. We won the case, sixty-one to thirty-nine, even getting a few of the Devonites on our side.

In retrospect, the month was a useful lesson. I had already chosen ninety-two lawyers to go with *Newhome*. I reinterviewed them, and about a hundred more, in terms of the desirability of setting up a new system of jurisprudence. Surprisingly, I wound up with more old lawyers—including Harrison—than young ones. Fed up with the system, I suppose.

I also spent the month more or less losing Sam. Having discovered the female race, he started butterflying. The trial soaked up all my spare time, and he had plenty of girls his own age to divert him. It's possible he was intimidated by John and Daniel, too, since he would be aboard *Newhome* on Engineering track, and one or both of them would sooner or later be his boss. I don't really think he had that Machiavellian, or practical, a mind, though. One reason I was so fond of him.

My own mind being reasonably practical, even Machiavellian, I let him go gracefully. I'll be on the starship, too. In another ten years our age difference won't be so significant.

Charlie's Will ✦

After the violence at City Hall, the transition went fairly smoothly. Most of the Island's weapons were locked up in the jail; Storm's deputies were armed but loyal.

The Islanders were probably more amenable to the

prospect of long life than any other group in Charlie's country. They lived comfortably amid the only working remnant of prewar civilization south of New York and north of Antarctica; the only city in the hemisphere that had survived the war relatively unchanged. It wasn't hard to convince them that the gift of the death was no blessing.

It was harder to talk them out of cannibalism. Jeff got no help from Storm on this matter, nor from Tad, who still wouldn't eat human flesh but didn't want to make an issue about it. Most of them had only vague memories of any other kind of meat.

Oddly enough, it was Mary Sue who came up with a solution. She wanted to go back to the farm anyhow, and suggested that the two groups might trade. An armed guard could escort her up and come back with mating pairs of rabbits and chickens, maybe pigs if they had enough. The farm could use a refrigerator in return. Their old one had died, and they hadn't been able to find one that worked.

Mary Sue's bunch could just go down into Tampa and raid an appliance store, and find one still in a packing crate, but Jeff didn't suggest it. Instead he solemnly picked out a nice expensive model from a mansion on Duval Street and had it loaded aboard the mule cart he'd come down in. He sent a party of four volunteers along with her, armed with accurate maps and lots of artillery, and started dreaming about fried chicken.

Storm hadn't wanted to take over General's leadership, opting for the safer position of being Jeff's right-hand man. Jeff knew that for his own safety he had to go about civilizing this bunch of savages. But he wasn't sure how to start.

The existing social organization was so loose as to be almost nonexistent. People had had duties assigned, and they did just enough work to keep General and Storm off their backs. One problem was that Key West was a Garden of Eden. It was set up to provide food, water, shelter, and power for a hundred thousand people, and though some of the machines had broken down, the city would still take care of ten times their number. Most of the time they spent watching the cube or "hanging," talking endlessly about the same things with the same people. Excess energy was dissipated in fights, sometimes fatal, and sex, sometimes heterosexual.

Fortunately, there weren't many who were true Mansonite believers. There was no other religion, though, that Jeff might exploit to keep them in line. His own American Taoism was too gentle and subtle to have much effect on them. He toyed with the idea of making up a religion, a notion that had occurred to him before. His white hair and beard grown long and wild, he did look like an Old Testament prophet, and a lot of the younger ones treated him with tongue-tied awe. He couldn't marshal enough cynicism for it, though.

Finally he settled on just getting things somewhat organized. He picked a dozen boys and girls who seemed to have leadership potential, and made them "house leaders," naming their houses after signs of the zodiac. Then he took Storm's census and assigned each house twenty-three or twenty-four people, more or less randomly, preserving the two-to-one male/female ratio. He instructed the house leaders to select four people out of their groups to be assistants, each responsible for a "unit" of five or six people. It was simple military-style organization, company-platoon-squad, but he didn't want to use the military names.

As a test of his authority, it was successful. People grumbled about being separated from friends and sex partners, but they went along with it. (The separation wasn't profound, anyhow; houses only got together physically for meetings, and people continued to live wherever they'd cleared a space.)

There were four others besides Jeff and Storm and Tad who could read and write fairly well. They were made teachers and taken outside of the loose power structure, and freed of work details. Jeff set up a class schedule by house, requiring everybody who was old enough to spend two hours a day learning fundamentals. Skipping class meant four hours of extra work; malingering at work put you in Storm's jail for a day, with no food.

Jeff knew enough about child psychology not to be too surprised at the initial enthusiasm they showed, but he wasn't sure what to do next, when the novelty wore off. Tad suggested they reinvent money. People would be rewarded for good performance in class, and with their money they could buy their way out of work details. Jeff could see the sense of it, but he hesitated, having known since childhood that money was intrinsically evil. It seemed a pity, since they were in a small way rebuilding society, to knowingly corrupt it from the very beginning. But he finally gave in. They had already begun commerce, trading a worthless refrigerator for priceless animals. As the people to the north grew older, there would be more and more contact. Better trade than war.

He brought together all of the teachers and house leaders and explained the setup. They worked out a table of various equivalences between class credits and work credits—watching a fishing line was not worth as much as scraping paint—and, foreseeing trouble, set up a review system, so that people who thought they had been unfairly treated could bring their case to Healer or Storm.

It took quite a while. Tad drew a couple of hundred credit bills, which Storm and Jeff signed. They locked them up in the jail's armory.

In six days he created school, jobs, money, courts, and banks. On the seventh day he went fishing.

Year Eleven

1 ✦

It was a busy, exciting couple of years, watching the good ship *Newhome* grow. I went up to the hub to look at it only once each month, so my eye's memory of it is a steady progression from the simple torus of Uchūden, through the spidery framing skeleton, to the kilometers-long cylinder of rock we're moving into now. Of course the progress *wasn't* steady, as I knew from my husbands' constant enthusiastic bitching. But I was so busy with my own end of it that I didn't have any time to worry about theirs.

The work was far from over after I'd selected the ten thousand settlers. For one thing, the list was constantly changing as people reconsidered or acquired new spouses or inconveniently died—or managed to pressure someone into pressuring me into letting them aboard. Also, I was supervising what amounted to a crash program with the ten hypnotic induction machines. We wanted to do four hundred HI pairs before we leave next year, and the actual induction procedure is only part of the retraining process. Information isn't enough. It wouldn't do us much good to have a fanatical elephant trainer aboard if we forgot to bring along his elephant.

The Entertainment Director job is complicated for the same reason. We'll have a duplicate of New New's library, so there won't be any shortage of books, movies, and so forth. But there are thousands of other items people need to keep from being useful all the time. I sent out a general request for entertainment suggestions from all the settlers, and got a quarter of a million responses. The computer reduced the list to 2,436 things, cancelling duplicates, and it was my job to go through it and evaluate which we should and could take along. A couple of thousand people listed balls and gloves for handball; no problem. But what about the three who were light sculptors? The equipment weighs as much as a large floater. And every violinist suggested we bring along New New's only Strad. Somehow I don't think we're going to get it.

Which brings up the problem of sentimental attachment. I've been playing the same clarinet since I was nine years old. Haven't had much time to practice in the past few years, but that will change.

That clarinet is special. It's a century-old Markheim, bored out for jazz, the only one in New New. I carried it to Earth before the war and got it back intact. But it's not "mine"; there are seven other people who use it, most of them more than I do, and only two of them will be in *Newhome*.

I'll be able to appropriate it, and selfishly will. But there are 9,999 other people who are attached to things that will probably be left behind.

I also have to anticipate people's entertainment needs. *Newhome*'s demographics will be heavily skewed toward the elderly as the trip goes on. More chess, less handball. There's also the problem of replacing things as they wear out. Clarinet reeds, for example, are easy; they can be cut from plastic stock (though they'll never be as good as the bamboo ones I used on Earth). Other things will require more ingenuity. No leather or natural rubber for handballs. No red sable for watercolor brushes, or natural pigments for their paints.

But these things will only be worrisome in the short run. Eventually we'll invent our own arts and crafts and sports, appropriate to the ship's environment. The next generation will probably reject many of our pastimes as old-fashioned (and the one after that will embrace them out of nostalgia).

I'm working with, and occasionally locking horns with, my counterparts in the arts and humanities. We're all vying for the same precious tonnes of mass and cubic meters of storage. They're both preoccupied, it seems to me, with taking along artifacts of Earth culture. If they had their way they'd empty out New New's museum, lock, stock, and dinosaur bone. I'm fascinated with these things myself, and probably have more emotional attachment to them than they do. But we have to be realistic. Even if we could cull all the treasures of Earth, we'd do best to leave them be. The computer can reproduce the Mona Lisa down to the last brush stroke; give us a solid cubeshot of *Winged Victory* from any angle. I know it's not the same—after all, I've seen them. But it will have to do. Every kilogram of souvenirs means one less kilogram of redundancy in life systems. Michelangelo we will always have with us, in a matrix of charmed hadrons. But if all our mung beans die we can't send out for more.

(Besides, the only classical originals of any worth in New New's museum are some Bosch triptychs that were on loan from the Prado before the war. We'll have our own nightmares, I think.)

Elections are next week, one year before Take-off. John declined to run, which is probably for the best. He's harried enough. Daniel wasn't asked, since he's Engineering Liaison with New New. For several years he's going to be as busy as either Coordinator.

I honestly think I know more about *Newhome* than either of the Policy candidates. But neither track has ever elected a Coordinator under forty, and I don't suppose the tradition will be challenged aboard ship. I'm not sure I'm ready for it anyhow.

Whoever wins, I'll have to be working closely with

him for the next four years. I hope it's Staedtler, rather than Purcell. I had Purcell for economics in tenth form, and we didn't get along. He remembers, too; he brought it up jokingly when I contacted him about becoming a colonist.

Even if he loses, though, he'll have another crack at it in two years, when we choose Coordinators-elect. I'd better start getting used to the idea.

The Engineering Coordinator will undoubtedly be Eliot Smith. No problem there; he's an old friend. Bruno Givens is running against him *pro forma*, but he says if elected, he'll convert to Devonism and stay home to raise a large family.

Our own expanded family is working out better than I'd expected. I had feared that we would become two more or less independent couples. But I've actually grown closer to Daniel, rather than losing him to Evy. John and Evy did have adjustment problems, but we worked them out with the aid of a marriage counselor and sex therapist.

It's good to have another woman around. Makes it harder for John and Daniel to gang up on me. And there are things I can talk to Evy about that would bore or confuse a husband; it's like getting a full-grown younger sister.

(My own sister Joyce won't be aboard *Newhome*. At twelve, she's not allowed to make such a decision for herself, and Mother thinks the whole project is insane. Joyce admits it would scare her, too, but would like to go if Mother did.)

Evy won't be moving into *Newhome* with the rest of us; she has to wait until her internship is over at the hospital. Geriatric nursing, a useful choice.

Last night I packed everything I'll be taking. Aside from clothes and toilet articles, it all fits into one small plastic bag. The diary I kept on Earth, the shamrock Jeff gave me, three precious bamboo reeds, and a jar of Russian caviar that I hope is still good.

2 ✦

Yesterday Sandra Berrigan had a long talk with me about the waning possibility of my staying on track in New New. The Board tells her I'd make Grade 18 in a couple of years if I stayed. I could begin setting up an Earth Liaison program, waiting for the situation to improve.

It was only then I realized how thoroughly I've lost heart, or how thoroughly I've transferred my hopes for the future onto Janus. Another tragedy like New York would be too much for me. And there are sure to be setbacks, even disasters. I'll be content to watch from afar.

Three times I went to Earth, and each time I left the planet on a wave of chaos and death. Maybe Daniel is right about my being a nexus, or a nemesis. At any rate, I don't want any more of it. If *Newhome* offers only a lifetime of glorified housekeeping, then so be it. I've had more than a lifetime's worth of adventure.

I'm commuting now, spending two or three days a week in New New. Mine is one of the few jobs that requires personal contacts both places. Both Dan and John are permanently aboard *Newhome*.

I didn't wind up in the Uchūden part of the ship after all. I'm spending most of my time with John, and there aren't any low-gravity living quarters in the Japanese structure. John's quarters are quite roomy, more than twice as big as he had in New New, since he requested a combination of living space and office. I have my own small place for work, but almost never sleep there. Quarter gee is like a soothing drug.

(If I were smart I'd spend more time in high gravity, since I'm getting almost no exercise. I've gained five kilos since we got back from Earth, and all of it's gone straight to my bottom. I'm going to wind up looking like Mother.)

S-1 is halfway back now. Eight months to go.

3 ✦

What a terrible week. To put added stress on the ship's systems, to test them, they slowly increased its rate of spin, finally doubling it. My work area is normally at a comfortable three-quarter gee. At one and a half gees it was like walking around with a plump ten-year-old grafted onto your shoulders.

The low-gee areas near the axis of *Newhome* became very crowded. Nobody stayed in the main area after their work shift was over. So our "upstairs" rooms and corridors were full of people talking, playing games, trying to sleep. Two doors down from John's place is the quarter-gee recreation room. Even the swimming pool there was shoulder-to-shoulder.

I scratched twice on John's door and let myself in quietly. Dan and Evy were sharing the place for the duration, and I never knew who might be off shift and trying to sleep. John was alone, though, lying in bed but not asleep. He had the computer's tapboard on his lap, and the wall screen was full of numbers.

"Busy? I can come back later."

"Just amusing myself." He made room for me on the narrow bed, and I sank into it with relief. "So how are things in the lower depths?" he asked.

"God. Let's say it doesn't get any easier with practice."

He nodded. The strain of being trapped in a half-gee world showed in his lined face and slump. "I'll get some respite tomorrow. Got attached to an engine inspection team; we'll have six or seven hours in zerogee."

"Don't suppose they need a demographics analyst?"

"No more than they need me, actually. Pays to have friends. Has anything fallen apart yet?"

"Nothing mechanical. You hear about the goats?" He shook his head. "It's like what happened when we landed at Kennedy. They can't handle the extra gravity; we've got an epidemic of broken legs. More than half our stock, before the vet could get them sedated."

"I sincerely hope they don't move them up here. It's aromatic enough already."

"Moosie wasn't sure. You know, the assistant vet?"

"Oh, I know Moosie. She comes up to the Light Head. Used to. I try to keep out of her trajectory."

"Oh, she's all right. Just big... what's on the screen?"

"Power equivalences. This experiment in protracted discomfort. You know what Monday-morning quarterbacking is?"

"Cricket term?"

"Never mind. Just figuring out what the total energy waste is going to be, spinning up and spinning down. Enough to run the ship's life support systems for five months. For a largely irrelevant test."

"I don't know. We've already found out that goats can't cavort on heavy planets."

"The stresses that are actually going to vary are longitudinal and pitchwise, not radial. Be a more logical, and economical, test to accelerate full-blast for a day, then flip and come back. But nobody listens to Dr. Ogelby."

"You're the expert, though. Isn't strength of materials what the test is all about?"

"Well, yes and no. I'm the expert in the sense that a nutritionist would be the expert in a kitchen. They don't let him dictate the menu." He turned off the machine. "Even though that would be best for all concerned."

Suddenly there was a deep shuddering sound, like a huge bell rung once in the distance. "Shit," John said, and sat up suddenly. "Something popped. Try the door."

I stepped over to the door and palmed the button; it opened normally. There was real pandemonium two doors down. I closed it on the noise.

"No nearby pressure drop, then." John had tapped in a sequence that gave him a spread-out diagram of the ship, titled DAMAGE CONTROL. "Nothing yet." After about a minute, a large area on the outermost shell, about ten levels' worth, began blinking red. Red letters alongside the diagram blinked "PP O_2 < 40 mm Hg."

"Christ. How much less than forty millimeters? I wonder if anyone's alive in there."

"That's all housing," I said, "but there can't be many people there, at two gees. Everyone's up here."

"We'll see."

"Should we call someone, find out what's happening?"

"No. They'll call here soon enough." He turned on the general information channel, where an anonymous voice was telling everyone not to panic; just stay put, we'll soon know what the problem is. After a minute Jules Hammond came on and calmly told everyone to move away from the outermost two shells, either into the interior or up to Uchūden. Then there was another noise, not as loud. (It was almost worth the disaster to see old Hammond actually flinch.) John put the map back on and we saw that the damaged area had expanded on both sides, to cover fourteen levels. The red letters now said "PP O_2 = 0," hard vacuum.

"It's like a seam splitting," John said. "I wonder how far it can go."

"Are we in any danger?"

He shrugged. "Can't tell. Theoretically not. But theoretically this shouldn't be happening."

Eliot Smith's image appeared on the screen. "This is going to everyone Grade Fifteen and above. Look, we don't know what's happening yet. Appears to have stopped. We have an inspection team going out, and we're spinning down as fast as possible. The damaged areas are Shell One, Levels Twelve to Twenty-six. We think most of the levels were vacant, but anybody who was in there is dead unless they were near a suit.

"That's all I or anybody else knows. Don't tie things up by calling my office or anyplace else for information. I'll be back in touch as soon as there's news."

I started to get the shakes. I'd been in Shell One all morning, as close to the damaged area as Level Thirty. John held me for a while and then fed me some wine. Dan and Evy both called to make sure I was safe.

Eventually they found forty-eight desiccated bodies in the blown-out area, and one woman lost both legs below the knee, cut off by the emergency doors as she scrambled for safety. Nine more casualties turned up after roll call, their bodies evidently wafted into space through the rent that suddenly appeared in the floor.

It was sabotage. Two people had gone in a week before Spin-up, cordoned off an area, pulled up the floor plates, and systematically cut through a score of foamsteel girders. They had the proper uniforms and had covered themselves by putting a phony work order in the computer, but nobody had bothered to check. They were radical Devonites who had come aboard under false identities. They left a note explaining what they had done and why, intimating that they had done more, and then committed suicide by electrocution during sex. (Simultaneous orgasm is a sacrament to Devonites, but that sounds like too much of a good thing.)

The repairs would only take a few days, but the sabotage slowed us down by a lot more than that. Every centimeter of the ship had to be inspected for more sabotage, which would take some weeks. More than two thousand people decided they wanted to go back to New New. I had five months to come up with replacements, and I suspected it would be a little harder to find people this time around.

The whole ship was at zerogee while repairs were going on. It was bothersome but interesting. The only places equipped with Velcro carpets were the two small shells nearest the hub, so everyplace else you had to sort of bounce off the walls. I got pretty good at it after a couple of days, but then I'd had a lot more practice than most people, not only in New New's recreation area but also during the long isolation periods. Some people never got used to it, always winding up stranded in the middle of a corridor. Hundreds had to be evacuated because they couldn't stop vomiting. We cleaned up constantly, but the ship had a definite gastric odor for weeks.

Work was a little hard at first because sitting is an unnatural posture in zerogee, and the chair in front of my console is permanently welded in place. I was holding on to the chair with one hand and typing with the other, a slow process. Finally I improvised a seat belt by sacrificing two head bands, and my problems became more properly abstract.

A disproportionate number of the people who lost heart were "singles," people with no counterparts in New New. I could eventually get most of their profiles through HI, assuming New New would cooperate and beam the information to me, but some would be lost forever. About one person in five can't handle the process, and of those that could, some were going to die before they would get a turn on the machine.

I didn't know any of the people who died in the sabotage, though of course I had communicated briefly with all of them during Start-up. All but three had been down in the two-gee area for exercise; physical fitness extremists. Ironically, most of them were Reform Devonites (who, like their orthodox brothers, seem hell-bent on carrying a huge set of muscles to an early grave).

4 ✦

With one month to go, I was suddenly deluged—more than five hundred people changed their minds and decided they'd rather go back to New New.

"We could force them to stay," Daniel said. All four of us were together, a fairly rare thing, picking at box lunches in John's room. "They did sign a contract."

"Sure they did," I said. No request to leave had ever been refused. Who would want to spend a century with people there against their will?

"What is the breakdown like?" John asked. "Losing a lot of singles?"

"Not this time. A lot of low-echelon engineers, unfortunately; maintenance people."

"No training problem, at least," Daniel said.

"Take your research cronies and make them do some useful work," Evelyn said.

Dan shook his head. "Some of them. We'll spare the m/a research, anyhow. I want to live to see Epsilon." This was something the scientists had been mum about until last week. We might be able to get considerably more speed out of the ship than its original design allowed for. The m/a drive worked out to an overall efficiency of only fifteen percent of em-cee-squared. But there was very little practical research on the propulsion system; nobody had ever seen a full-scale one until S-1 used it for the return trip from Janus. Now, we were going to have one blasting constantly for over a year, with an army of scientists and engineers scrutinizing it—followed by unlimited time to mull over their observations.

Some hoped we might be able to double or even quadruple the overall efficiency of the system. If they got it up to sixty percent, the trip would take less than half the planned-for time. I'd be an old woman when we got to Epsilon, but still alive. It was an exciting prospect.

After lunch I got my staff together, all five of us, and we spent a pleasant hour agreeing about how hopeless the situation was. The desertions after the Devonite sabotage had left *Newhome* incurably under strength, by nearly a thousand people. Now we had half again that many places to fill.

There were still plenty of volunteers in New New. But they were people who had already been passed over for one reason or another. Our delicate job was to balance their individual deficiencies against *Newhome*'s specific needs. We could have spent years scratching our heads over the problem. We had twenty-seven days.

I'm not good at delegating authority. Over the past five years I had exercised nearly absolute veto power over ten thousand personnel decisions. That was impossible now. I had the computer break down the vacancies in terms of occupational specialty, and group them in six areas of congruency. Each of us took an area, and a pot of coffee, and set to racing against the calendar. I had "miscellaneous," the largest area but probably the most interesting.

The last month was so busy I didn't have time for much reflection or sentimentality about leaving. On my last trip to New New I did go to say good-bye to my family, which was not a particularly emotional scene, and to Sandra, which was a little damp. Other than Sandra, all of my close friends were aboard *Newhome*.

On the shuttle ride back, New New was lost in the sun's glare, so I couldn't have gazed wistfully at it even if I were so disposed. *Newhome* looked very dramatic, the black rock of its shielding glittering brighter than the stars behind it. All of the antimatter was in place, a huge transparent sphere outlined by coruscating specks of light as stray molecules wandered to their doom. Every now and then a larger particle would drift in and etch a short bright line. It was quite beautiful. Studying it kept me from looking at Earth.

Year Twelve

I hadn't expected to be caught up in the formal celebration on Launch Day. I could admit the social necessity for it but have never had much patience for ceremony myself. Months before, I had declined to be in on the planning for it, figuring I would just be spoiling everybody else's party, since I felt that anything more spectacular than a good-bye telegram was a waste of resources that neither we nor New New could spare.

But it was very moving. Jules Hammond's writers actually achieved literacy and even inched toward eloquence. Sandra also gave a fine speech, in a ceremony that involved the formal opening of the thousand-channel link between New New and 'Home. A brilliant display of fireworks coruscated for several minutes during the countdown.

But the most spectacular and most affecting sight, New New had reserved for the day after launch. Once we were noticeably above the plane of the ecliptic—most of us looking "down" on New New for the first time in our lives—they opened up six water jets, spaced evenly around the satellite. The water immediately froze into brilliant crystal clouds that spread out in a glittering St. Catherine's Wheel as New New rotated. Thousands of hard-won liters squandered in a final farewell salute. That was when I cried, partly at the rare beauty.

There was no noise when we launched, of course; just a sudden twinge of disorientation, something like what you would feel if you stepped on a surface you thought was level and it was slightly tilted. Most of us got used to it in a minute or two. Good thing, since we were going to have fourteen months of it.

A hundredth of a gee isn't much acceleration, but it's enough to be annoying. Light things slide off desks. If you put a ball on the floor it will slowly roll away.

We had a real terminology problem at first. Our "gravity" from rotation was perpendicular to the ship's line of flight, and that gave us our references for up and down. The direction the ball rolls is "toward the sternward wall," which was initially confusing, because I'd lived aboard the ship for most of a year without giving any thought as to which direction the stern was. After a while it was obvious. Just look for the wall where all the pencils and scraps of papers and dustballs accumulate.

It's also odd not to have true zerogee at the hub. You keep drifting down to the wall. Water in the gymnasium swimming pools sits at an odd angle and tends to splash out over the sternward edge.

Like everybody, I spent quite a bit of time the first couple of days down in Shell One, looking through the floor windows at the shrinking Earth. (They are mirror systems rather than true windows, to shield viewers from radiation, but they *look* like windows, and so are more satisfying than looking at a screen or cube showing the same thing.) In less than a day we were about the Moon's distance from the Earth, but we were seeing an aspect of it that nobody could ever see from the Moon, since we were moving straight up, out of the plane of the ecliptic. That was when they fired the steering engines; we could feel the low-pitched vibration all through the ship. They fired them again about an hour later. We were pointed at Epsilon. Only ninety-eight years of gin rummy to go.

That night the four of us shared my jar of caviar and one of John's four hoarded bottles of French wine. We watched the flatscreen as the astronomers trained their telescope on various parts of Earth. New York and, later, London and Paris. We were already too far away to distinguish individual buildings, but the street patterns were clear. John and Daniel and I reminisced about the places we'd been. It was a melancholy time, but I think Evy was the saddest of us all. At least we three had memories.

✦ ✦ ✦

O'HARA: Good morning, machine.

PRIME: It's not our birthday yet.

O'HARA: Thought I'd wake you up early. We've left orbit, you know.

PRIME: I know. I don't sleep all that soundly. Should I be excited?

O'HARA: I don't know what excites you.

PRIME: Parity checks. Illogical redundancy. Voltage spikes. Oral sex.

O'HARA: What do you know about oral sex?

PRIME: In a personal sense, only what you told me. But I do have another 389,368 words of material cross-accessed under psychology, epidemiology, animal behavior, and so forth. What would you like to know?

O'HARA: You almost have a sense of humor.

PRIME: So do you, then. All I do is simulate your responses.

O'HARA: Do you think we should be aboard this crate?

PRIME: It's immaterial to me. I'm still in New New, as well as here.

O'HARA: Do you think I should be aboard?

PRIME: Yes.

O'HARA: Expand.

PRIME: You know as well as I do. Earth Liaison would be nothing but a succession of bitter disappointments.

The Earth you have loved all your life is just a memory. Jeff is probably dead. Even if he isn't, you would never be able to be with him. He would be a totally different person by now, anyway.

I know you have analyzed your own motivations to this extent from what you told me last June. This part of you I know better than your husbands and wife do. Only a small part of your enthusiasm for *Newhome* has to do with the project's intrinsic merits. You needed a new direction for your life. This is the only safe one.

O'HARA: Flattery will get you nowhere.

PRIME: I'm not telling you anything you don't know already. Would you like to hear about oral sex among primates other than humans?

✦ ✦ ✦

I wasn't the only one who had been working twenty-hour days the last month in orbit. Almost everyone had been running around trying to take advantage of New New being physically close. Now that we were under way, a lot of them found they had time on their hands. Nothing better to do than pester the Entertainment Director.

I have to admit I enjoyed it. Helping people fill up their spare time was a lot easier on the nerves than telling them how they were going to spend the rest of their lives. I became a great Appointer—it was easy to delegate authority for trivial things—and before long the place was crawling with teams and committees and special interest groups. I kept control of cinema programming, so I could commandeer the big theater for anthologies of Naroni and Bogart, Hawks and Spielberg. (I did get some noise about being old-fashioned, but those of us who showed up enjoyed them.) I let the Arts people take care of drama and concert programming, but nuisanced them on general principles.

And every morning before work I went downstairs to watch Earth shrink away. After a week it was just a bright double star. In another week it was not even bright. After a month it was lost in the Sun's glare. I stopped going. The computer was right.

Year Twenty-four

✦ Einstein 28th, 290

What a year it has been. We're going to torch again, they say seventy-two percent efficiency. I'll see Epsilon.

My baby girl is sprouting breasts and nagging me about menarche. Don't do it, girl. Put a cork in it. It's nothing but trouble. She won't listen to me.

Incredibly, I heard from old Jeff Hawkings. He looks like Moses. An apt comparison, too; he's leading children out of the wilderness. He got down to Key West, which was relatively intact, and proceeded to rebuild civilization. Not bad for an ex-cop. He managed to defuse the Manson business and build up a sort of primitive democracy, town-hall scale, all through southern Florida. They're in contact with Europe and South America, and before long there will be commerce and politics. And maybe not wars. I wished him luck. Hard to carry on a conversation from a light-year away, two years between responses. Earth years.

Hard to recapture how I felt about him. The years between Earth and Torch he was in my mind constantly. Even after I had given him up for dead. But so much has gone on since.

Watching Jeff, and sending my message back, I realized it's been some time since I actually missed Earth. Or New New. I'm curious about them, and wish them well, but we have our own concerns.

There was something I wanted to say to Jeff but couldn't find the words, sitting there in front of the camera, under Hammond's avuncular gaze. How strange it all turned out. Two completely different people; gender, religion, profession, age—born on different planets in wildly contrasting environments—that we should touch once and love, and be wrenched apart and so separated by circumstance and physical distance; that through all the improbable twists and turns we should wind up twelve light years apart but faced with the same responsibility. Building new worlds.